MYSTIC

JASON DENZEL
MYSTIC

A TOM DOHERTY ASSOCIATES BOOK

NEW YORK

This is a work of fiction. All of the characters, organizations, and events portrayed in this novel are either products of the author's imagination or are used fictitiously.

MYSTIC

Maps by Rhys Davies

A Tor Book
Published by Tom Doherty Associates, LLC
175 Fifth Avenue
New York, NY 10010

www.tor-forge.com

Tor® is a registered trademark of Tom Doherty Associates, LLC.

Library of Congress Cataloging-in-Publication Data

Denzel, Jason.
  Mystic / Jason Denzel.
    pages cm
  ISBN 978-0-7653-8197-2 (hardcover)
  ISBN 978-1-4668-8568-4 (e-book)
  1. Imaginary wars and battles—Fiction.   I. Title.
PS3604.E64M97 2015
813'.6—dc23

                                    2015023069

Our books may be purchased in bulk for promotional, educational, or business use. Please contact your local bookseller or the Macmillan Corporate and Premium Sales Department at (800) 221-7945, extension 5442, or by e-mail at MacmillanSpecialMarkets@macmillan.com.

First Edition: November 2015

Printed in the United States of America

0 9 8 7 6 5 4 3 2 1

To you, Jennifer,
Because this journey began
When we shared haikus

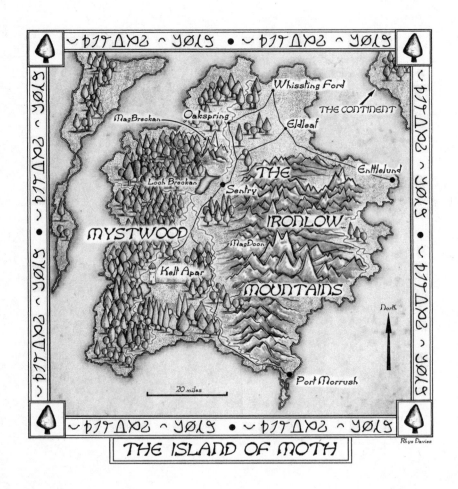

THE ISLAND OF MOTH

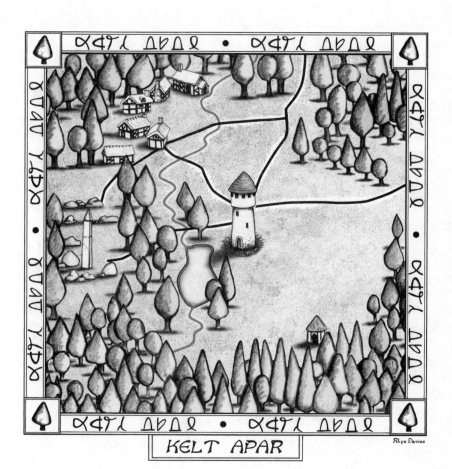

KELT APAR

Rhys Davies

On the wind, my breath

By the light between

My eyes to far-lost Fayün

So shall I hold dear

All that lives in harmony

Within the Myst and

Carry it into the Deep

MYSTIC

ONE

SPRINGRISE

On the island of Moth, under a swollen moon, Pomella AnDone stormed out of her house, slamming the door behind her. She hurried, expecting Fathir's yell to sound behind her. It was like waiting for thunder after a flash of lightning.

"You're not a jagged noble!" he finally screamed from behind the door. "Cut your hair and know your place!"

Pomella knocked aside a half-made barrel and strode away from the house, not looking back. She snatched up a wicker basket and carried it under one arm past her flourishing garden. The hateful man could choke on gunkroot for all she cared. She'd grow her hair whatever length she wanted.

All around her, the villagers of Oakspring prepared for tonight's Springrise festival. A cluster of men fed a young bonfire to push back the darkening night. A swarm of children chased one another, leaving behind frazzled mhathirs trying to bundle them up. Pomella ignored everyone, and headed toward the forest.

The bustle of village activity faded as she hiked to a nearby hill on the edge of the Mystwood. Comforting silence greeted her as she passed the tree line. The rushing flow of the Creekwaters sang to her from the far side of the hill, down in the thicket.

Pomella relaxed her heaving breaths. Tucking back a strand of her dark hair, she inhaled deeply. This place, the forest, was her solace. She'd never traveled outside the barony, but she couldn't imagine a more peaceful place on Moth. Out here, nobody would holler at her, saying it was improper for a commoner to have long hair. Nobody would—

The night erupted with howling wolves.

Pomella froze, hugging the basket tight to her body. The howls faded, replaced by the trickle of the Creekwaters and the Springrise revelry coming from her village.

Biting her lip, Pomella wondered whether she should tell the Watcherman about the wolves. Maybe he'd believe her this time. Maybe, but probably not. She looked down the hill toward the distant village. Women and men laughed around the bonfire, and somebody pummeled the drums.

With everyone here for the festival, wolves could bring a bundle of trouble for the outlying homesteads.

Assuming, of course, they were *normal* wolves.

Setting her jaw, she hurried farther up the hill to a cluster of boulders. She climbed them with long-practiced ease until she stood at their summit, overlooking the shallow valley on the far side. Moonlight blanketed the Mystwood like a lingering winter frost. She listened for more wolves, but no further howls came. Pomella inhaled deeply, savoring the night, letting the fresh air calm her.

A rush of light flashed across the treetops. Her heart raced. It came again, revealing a glowing, silvery owl, trailing wispy light that quickly vanished behind it.

A familiar tingle of fear rose within Pomella. It'd been the life of the stars since anyone believed her about seeing strange, misty animals in her garden or the Mystwood. Each time she'd told somebody, they'd looked at her like she was a dunder. It was the same reason she'd learned long ago not to talk about her books or how she sometimes tried to feel and use the Myst. If her fathir found out about either, especially the Myst, he'd ensure with a firm hand that she didn't blather about it again. Commoners were forbidden from meddling in such things.

Still, sometimes, on cool nights like this, she felt something different in the air, like a song in her chest, demanding to be sung.

She shook her head. The owl was gone, and the wolves weren't likely to be a concern tonight. Or maybe she *was* a dunder and had imagined the whole thing.

Jumping down the rocks, Pomella found her nearby drying line and snatched up the clothes hanging there. She quickly folded each garment, tucking them inside the basket. She hummed as she worked, trying to raise her spirits for tonight's Springrise festival.

Stepping barefoot across the cool hillside grass, Pomella returned to her village. But instead of heading toward the bonfire, she skirted around Goodman AnClure's smithy, its furnace banked and quiet for the night. She found a dark corner behind the thatch-roofed building and dropped the basket. Quick as a luck'n so as not to be seen, she pulled her work dress over her head and let it drop to the ground. The night air pebbled her dark, almond-colored skin and she prayed to all the Saints that spring would bring warmer weather.

This would have been easier if she'd just gone home to change, but she was afraid Fathir might still be there. That, and her brother Gabor might be lurking, and the last thing she wanted was the little twerper running off with her dress as a prank like he did last Summeryarn.

Pomella fumbled through the basket, and pulled out her Springrise dress. She'd sewn it herself in autumn, having saved her nugs and even a clip in order to afford the fabric before winter came. She hoped to Brigid the dress fit. Pomella had grown more than usual over the past year, both in height and in the chest. Blessed Saints, how she hoped she was done growing! She was sixteen and it was time to be quit of it.

When she wiggled the dress over her hips, it settled nicely, if a bit snug, over her curves. She checked the length of the long sleeves. Embroidered ivy and sunflowers wove themselves around the cuffs and hem. It would have to do. Grandmhathir had always said Pomella's best talents lay elsewhere.

"*There* you are!" called a familiar voice.

Pomella looked up as Bethy AnClure, red haired and crowned with a golden wreath of winter leaves and pine needles in the likeness of Saint Brigid, hurried over. A heavy, shamrock-green cloak hung across Bethy's shoulders, clasped in front with a pin shaped liked a Mothic knot.

"Were you off talking to birds in the woods again?" Pomella's friend said. "The *Toweren* is about to begin, and you promised me you wouldn't miss it."

"I know, sorry, Bethy. I had to get out for a bit. My fathir was being a culk again. Do you like my—"

"Oh!" Bethy gasped, her blue eyes widening. "Your dress! Look at it! These ocean waves are so beautiful."

"They're ivy," Pomella said, frowning.

"Oh, shite, sorry," Bethy snipped, brushing off her mistake. "It looks wonderful."

"Thank you. Your Brigid costume looks nice, too. The cloak is beautiful. With that and your hair, you were born to play her."

Looking at Bethy, Pomella was reminded of how she'd always wanted hair like her friend's. Her own shoulder-length dark-brown hair was nice enough, but it just wasn't as pretty. Pomella wondered again, as she often had, if red hair would look good against her own darker skin. If she couldn't change her hair's color, she could at least grow it longer, like the merchant-scholars and nobles did.

And the Mystics.

Bethy's eyes shone above her smile in the moonlight. "Danny AnStipe was looking at more than my hair just a little while ago. After the play, I'm taking him to the underworld." She grinned knowingly.

Pomella humored her with a smile. Danny AnStipe was probably the handsomest boy their age in Oakspring. But despite this, Pomella had never been as drawn to him as she had to a certain other.

Bethy stepped back and pulled open the cloak so Pomella could see the full dress. She leaned in with a cunning smile on her face. "Mhathir made the cloak and helped me with the dress. But I lowered the neckline."

Pomella gaped at her. "Bethy!"

She waved Pomella off. "Yah, yah, I know. She'll buzz like a honeyhive when she sees it. Oh, and Fathir forged a real iron sword for the play! But I'm not allowed to touch it until the play begins. I listened to him about that because I didn't want to kick my luck too much. I saw Sim eyeing it hungrily, though."

"I wish I had your confidence," Pomella grumbled.

"Come on," Bethy said, tugging Pomella's sleeve. "We shouldn't dawdle like ganders. I need to—"

"Bethilla!" called a man's voice. They turned just as Bethy's older brother, Simkon, stepped out of the light, peering into the shadows where the girls stood. Pomella thanked the Saints that she'd managed to get her dress on before all these people showed up.

Not that she would mind if Sim managed to glimpse her wearing slightly fewer garments than normal.

Seeing the girls, the older boy strode over. Bethy snickered when she saw her brother. He wore a makeshift laghart costume crafted from a pair of green-dyed pants, along with a shirt with scales stitched into it. A ridiculous, vaguely lizard-shaped leather mask covered most of his face. Pomella grinned. He was meant to be the leader of the forty lagharts from the Brigid legend, and it *was* funny looking.

"Hi, Pomella," Sim said, only briefly meeting her eye. "I was looking for Bethy."

"I'm right here," Bethy said, crossing her arms.

Sim stared at his sister. "What did you do to your dress? You can't go onto the green like that!" He reached over to tug her cloak closed.

Bethy slapped his hand away. "Don't order me around, lizard-boy!"

Pomella rolled her eyes and eased between them. "Your fathir will give both of you lip if you don't hurry. I'll catch up as soon as I put this laundry away. I don't want it to gather biterbugs."

Bethy glared at her older brother. "Fine. Hurry, though, Pom. The baron's daughter is here. Let's go, *scale face*."

Pomella's face blossomed into a smile. She'd forgotten that Lady Elona was coming today. The girl had a fascination with the Myst, and for the Springrise festival. For the past two years she'd insisted that her fathir, Baron AnBroke, allow her to celebrate with the commoners. The rumor around Oakspring was that Elona planned to become a Mystic's apprentice. Pomella suppressed a pang of jealousy. Maybe Elona would show them the Myst tonight.

Sim lingered and removed his mask with one hand, revealing a head of tousled, straw-colored hair. Pomella bit her lip upon seeing his strong jaw and piercing eyes.

He looked down at the ground and cleared his throat. "I like your dress. It's pretty."

"Thank you," Pomella replied, cautiously waiting to see where this led. She'd known for years that Sim returned her affections for him. Recently it'd become more obvious, which Pomella didn't mind. But things had become awkward after he'd found her trying to read noble runes by the Creekwaters last week. She prayed to the Saints that he wouldn't bring it up.

He took a deep breath and gazed down at her. "I was wondering if we could walk tonight, after midnight when Springrise arrives. Walk and, um . . . talk."

Excitement and anxiety swirled inside Pomella. She forced herself to meet his gaze. Most girls her age in Oakspring found Sim handsome, but she was drawn to his humble blue eyes and gentle manner. They had been through so much together. In a strange way, Sim probably knew her better than anybody, including Bethy. Normally, Pomella would gladly accept any time alone with Sim. But right now, she was just too confused to know what was supposed to happen next.

She opened her mouth to tell him so, but his pleading eyes made her hesitate. "Perhaps I will, yes," she said. He'd only asked her to go for a walk. She could handle that. Walk. And talk.

It was the talking that worried her.

Sim frowned. "So . . . did you just answer 'yes' or 'perhaps'?"

"Yes," she replied.

"Yes, you answered, or is 'yes' your answer?"

She pushed him gently, her fingers sinking into the scaled wool. "Go to the play, Sim," she said, forcing a smile. She couldn't help but notice his chest felt very strong beneath the costume. He'd grown a lot in the last year, especially in the shoulders. That was certainly a clip in his favor. "Go slither around your sister like the laghart you're supposed to be. I need to put these clothes away. We'll walk after."

His lips parted into a charming smile. "I'll see you then.

Oh, and the embroidery on your dress looks very nice." He ducked around his fathir's smithy toward the bonfire and celebration.

Pomella sighed. She picked at her ivy embroidery. Grandmhathir was right. Pomella would just have to focus on her other talents.

Lifting the basket, she hurried toward the house. She'd just have to hope that Fathir was at the bonfire by now.

As she neared home, her garden came into view. A bursting array of flower bushes, vegetable patches, and even a few fig trees surrounded the house, seemingly trying to encroach on the little wooden home. Barrels in various stages of construction or repair stood along the side of the house, waiting for her fathir to complete them. They huddled together as if seeking protection from the overwhelming onslaught of Pomella's garden.

She passed the towering plants, enjoying the wild aroma of her spring flowers. Beets and carrots, yams and potatoes, all flourished under the soil in carefully plotted rows of dirt, already showing their first shoots, way ahead of anybody else's efforts. The garden had been Grandmhathir's once, starting as just a tiny patch by the front door. Pomella's heart ached every time she thought about how her grandmhathir would never see what the garden had become under her care, nor would she ever hear about all the villagers that came from Eldleaf and Whissting Ford who had come to see it with their own eyes.

Stepping across the tiny porch, Pomella ducked through the front door and set the basket atop the carved table Fathir had made. A quick peek around the house told her Gabor wasn't hiding. She found her brush and tidied her hair. It fell nearly to her shoulders now. She grudgingly admitted that maybe her fathir was right, that maybe she'd have to trim it soon if she didn't want the Watcherman lecturing her on commoner appearance laws.

Outside, she heard the villagers settle as the *Toweren* began. The Watcherman always began the saga, setting the stage on the village green with his charming voice. She barely heard his words at this distance, but mouthed the lines from memory anyway.

> *Come follow me*
> *On memory free*
> *Of Brigid old*
> *And tales long told*
> *Of abandoned hearth*
> *And tiresome trails*
> *In soaring Tower*
> *Her child pales*
> *Caught by death's dark power*

Pomella set the brush down and hurried out the door, toward the green. Her grandmhathir had always said the *Toweren* was written to be sung. Pomella wished she could hear it performed that way. Strolling to the green, she sang the next stanza, trying to find a tune of her own for it.

> *"Come search with me*
> *Across the sea*
> *With Brigid sold*
> *Her sad tale told*
> *Of a master's demand*

From Tower steep
'A branch of banes
Or I will ever keep
Your son in chains'"

She scowled to herself. Her tune wasn't quite what she wanted. She loved coming up with little melodies and singing. When she did it well, it drew people's attention. She'd developed a reputation for it in Oakspring, until her fathir strictly forbade her singing around others.

She arrived at the green just as Bethy slipped into the grassy clearing, standing alone in a wide circle of torches. Pomella's friend slinked around the grass barefoot, pretending to swim in darkness, playing out Brigid's search for the entrance to the underworld. Pomella edged her way along the back of the crowd, hoping to get a clear glimpse of Lady Elona.

She caught sight of her brother, Gabor, up ahead. He and some of his twerper friends crouched behind the crowd, huddled over what she suspected was a gaggle of pranks. On the green, Bethy asked the Nameless Saint where she could find the the entrance to the underworld.

"Gabor!" Pomella hissed, trying to catch his attention. If Fathir couldn't keep Gabor out of trouble like Grandmhathir had, then Pomella would have to do it herself.

Lady Elona, small and delicate, not much older than Gabor, played the Nameless Saint and wore a stunning silk and gossamer gown with faerie wings and face paint. Dark, shimmering hair with delicate emeralds woven within cascaded down her back nearly to her hips. She answered Bethy with a musical voice that sounded like tinkling bells. "Beyond the veil, by my eyes, to fa-erie skies, seek and find!"

Gabor looked up at Pomella and grinned like a luck'n. Pomella hesitated, torn between discovering what mischief he was up to and watching the play.

A soft glow emanated from the stage, drawing murmurs from the crowd.

Elona lifted her hand. Thin strands of light spun above her palm, weaving a flower shaped like a Mothic knot. Its shimmer gleamed on her pale skin.

Pomella forgot Gabor and stared in wonder as the little girl summoned the Myst. At least, Pomella assumed it was the Myst. What else could it be? The flower spun and lifted, drawing all eyes upward. Voices flew from the flower, filling the village with soft singing. The music resonated with something inside Pomella, coaxing her to join with its melody. A desire arose within her, steady and burning, to know how the girl did that.

By the Saints, if only Pomella weren't a commoner. She didn't *really* mind keeping her hair so short, but it seemed silly that she couldn't keep it longer like a noblewoman. Pomella had never known the feel of silk, either, but how could she miss what she'd never known? She wished she didn't have to try to teach herself to read noble runes in secret, and that people would believe her about seeing silver animals in her garden and in the forest. But most of all, she wished, desperately, that she was allowed to learn of the Myst.

A low rumble filled the village.

The shaking wasn't gentle, like the Mystic flower, but was a heavy, deep tremor that quickly escalated into a chaotic quake. Somebody screamed. Panic raced up Pomella's spine.

Villagers bumped her as they ran past, but Pomella could only look toward Elona, the girl's face paling with fear. The flower vanished, like a flame snuffed by wind. Beside the noblewoman, Bethy fell backward, tripping on her cloak.

Grass churned and surged upward, shaping itself into a massive form. The smell of freshly turned dirt wafted over the green. Soil and stone rolled together, forming broad arms and shoulders. A head, tilted down, gathered dirt and grass. Pomella felt a chill of terrified fascination as a long beard of leaves wove itself around a face.

Several people dove to safety or fled entirely. Watcherman AnGent moved quickly despite his bulk, yanking Elona out of the way. Sim rushed to help Bethy scramble away from the rising figure. It towered over them, twice the height of any person.

A rounded crater now existed where the green had been, its soil forming the creature before them. On the far side of the decimated stage, Pomella saw her fathir staring with wide eyes. Despite the chaos, an irrational worry came to her mind that he'd punish her for wasting money on her festival dress.

A gray-haired old man, Goodman AnMere, pointed at the creature. "The Green Man! I sees the Green Man!"

The creature's head lifted, revealing eyes of polished stone, seemingly pulled from deep within the ground. His mouth opened and a voice thundered across the remains of the green.

"Who is the Watcherman?" he boomed.

Pomella had heard stories of the Green Man, and nobody

except a skeptic or dunder denied he was real. But she never, in her whole life, expected to actually see him.

Goodman AnGent stepped forward, his bushy brown beard jutting out. "I am Watcherman Argeleff AnGent. I represent this village."

"By Saints, th' Green Man has returned!" Goodman AnMere shouted, clapping his hands.

The creature's face softened into a smile, the dirt shifting like skin and muscle. "So I have."

Somehow, his smile and easy manner calmed Pomella's nerves. It must've had a similar effect on the other villagers, too, because all around her people eased back toward the place where the stage had stood. Some dusted themselves off, while others rounded up the children.

"Your timing is poor, Green Man," said the Watcherman, crossing his arms. "Fifty years absent and you choose to arrive during our Springrise feast. You interrupted Lady Elona, and the *Toweren*."

The Green Man bowed, loose grass fluttering off him. "Oh, so I did. Forgive me, Lady and Watcherman, but I bring a timely message."

Elona's face lit up. "Is it from the High Mystic?"

Watcherman AnGent held up a steadying hand toward the baron's daughter, clearly trying to keep her back but not wanting to overstep his position. She was a noble, after all.

"Yes, I bring news from the Mystwood," the Green Man said, sweeping his gaze across everyone gathered.

The villagers hushed. Somewhere in the crowd, a mhathir scolded her child in a whisper to keep quiet.

"A new High Mystic has been anointed. By the grace of the Myst, Mistress Yarina Sineese now occupies Kelt Apar. It is she who sent me here to summon one of you."

More murmuring. Pomella's heart twisted as she saw the joyous expression on Elona's face. The noblewoman's time had come. Her entire young life had been focused on this moment, waiting for the opportunity to rise above even the nobility and become something greater.

Elona wrung her hands. The Green Man waited until only drifting sounds from the forest and the crackle of the bonfire could be heard. Even the wee tykes held their breath.

"The High Mystic summons Pomella AnDone."

TWO

THE BOOK OF SONGS

Silence gripped the village green.

Pomella gaped. Her mind wobbled as she tried to understand what had just been said. The Green Man had spoken her name, as clear as spring rain.

Pomella AnDone.

Across the green, the blood drained from her fathir's face. The villagers looked around, whispering, trying to find her in the crowd. She picked a fingernail to steady her hands from shaking.

Lady Elona's mouth moved as if she were trying in vain to find words.

The Watcherman drew himself up and dusted off his sleeve. "What does the High Mystic need from Goodmiss AnDone?"

A hand settled on Pomella's arm, startling her. Gabor stood there, his normally mischievous eyes rounded with concern.

Pomella had no idea what the message for her could be, but she hated the scared look on her brother's face. Maybe the Green Man spoke the wrong name. Surely he meant to call Elona's. Why would the High Mystic summon a lowborn commoner?

"Mistress Yarina seeks an apprentice," the Green Man intoned. "Goodmiss AnDone has been invited to attend the Trials as a candidate."

Pomella's skin pebbled. The High Mystic lived deep within the Mystwood to the south. Grandmhathir had frequently spoken of the previous High Mystic, although nobody from the village had seen him in living memory.

Pomella's heart thundered. She didn't understand. Didn't dare hope. Her earliest memories were of Grandmhathir speaking of the Myst, whispering to Pomella at night how it was the source of all life and energy. They sang songs about it, played simple games about it, and years later, even recently, Pomella tried, while alone in the Mystwood, to sense and control the Myst as Grandmhathir said was possible. Pomella never succeeded, but she daydreamed of one day meeting a Mystic who would teach her.

Elona, who looked as stunned as Pomella felt, finally found her courage. "Green Man! You surely announced the wrong name. She invited *me*, did she not?"

The Green Man bowed to the young noblewoman. "I'm sorry, Lady AnBroke, but it is Goodmiss AnDone whom I was instructed to summon. Will you call her forth?"

Pomella reassured Gabor with a pat on the hand, although she didn't know if it was for herself or him. Pulling away from her brother, she stepped out of the crowd to stand beside the Watcherman. She curtsied to Lady Elona as was proper, and hoped the young noblewoman didn't become angry. Pomella dared not meet Elona's gaze, and instead turned to the Green Man. She also ignored her fathir, who was surely frowning at her.

She steadied her voice. "I am Pomella."

The whole village seemed to lean in.

The Green Man turned his massive body to face her. He towered over her like an ancient oak. "Pomella AnDone. You are hereby invited by the High Mystic of Moth to call upon her at Kelt Apar within the Mystwood and apply for the position of her apprentice."

Pomella's hands shook. Bethy stared wide-eyed. Sim twisted his mask in his hands.

Questions roared through Pomella's mind, mixing fear and doubt. She opened her mouth to ask why she'd been chosen, or to insist that there'd been some mistake. But the song in her heart that she heard when she tiptoed through the forest, or looked across the land from nearby hills, refused to be silent. Hardly believing what was happening, she found her voice.

"I accept."

The crowd rumbled with chatter.

The Green Man nodded. "That is well. I will leave you to your celebrations." He held out his hand, and a small, marbled stone emerged from the center of his palm. It lifted into the air like a butterfly fluttering off a branch and drifted toward Pomella.

"When you set out, toss the stone onto the road before you," said the Green Man. "It will lead you through the Mystwood to the meeting place. A ranger will meet you in two days at the northwest border of Sentry. From there he will take you out of your barony to Kelt Apar. Do not be late."

The Green Man dipped his head in farewell, then collapsed into the ground. Dirt and stone tumbled into place, rolling and churning back to where it had been, with the grass becoming a gentle blanket over it all once again. For a hushed moment, nothing stirred except a gentle wind over the now-perfect green.

Pomella inhaled the fresh scent of the soil. A tenuous smile lifted her lips.

"Yer not a noble!" old Goodman AnMere hollered from the crowd. Angry stares from some of the villagers pelted him, while others nodded in agreement. Pomella's smile vanished.

"Aye, a commoner's place is in her barony, not skivering up 'n' down the countryside," said Goodness Ilise AnCutler, her round face wrinkling in the torchlight. She'd recently inherited her fathir's farms, which were accounted as the oldest in the barony.

"But the High Mystic personally invited her!" said Lathwin AnClure, Bethy and Sim's fathir. His wife, Cana, pulled at his arm, her eyes pleading with him to shush.

"Only the nobility can become Mystics," Goodman AnMere argued. "Yeh can't just become something yer not! Even this Mistress Yarina can't change tradition like that. Mean'n' no disrespect, but she's only been High Mystic a few months!"

"'Tain't disrespect to say it like that," said Goodness AnCutler, her gray hair shaking with her fist. "The barons and highborns are bred for that Myst-learn'n'. Our place is here, working the land. You ain't a special butterfly, girl. Lady Elona should go. As the baron's daughter, she represents our village."

Elona beamed and nodded.

Goodman AnMere nodded furiously. "There's an order to things, and we wouldn't want to insult the baron. Wouldn't yeh say, Watcherman?"

The round Watcherman stepped forward. Behind him, Bethy barely held tears back. Sim stared blankly at Pomella, his face pale.

Before Watcherman AnGent could respond, a familiar voice cut in with a hard tone. "This is a family matter. My daughter and I will speak." Firelight danced across the dark features of her fathir's bearded face. He seemed to avoid looking at Pomella.

A sickening feeling swirled in Pomella's stomach. Why did Fathir always have to decide things for her? She opened her mouth to protest, but seeing the chiseled expression on his face, she snapped it shut.

"No." Elona's soft voice cut like a shearing knife. She slipped off her faerie wings. "You are all mistaken if you think this is a matter for a commoner family. It is a matter for *mine*. The girl is not allowed to leave my fathir's barony."

Nobody in the village seemed to breathe. The Watcherman cleared his throat. "Lady AnBroke, you understand the High Mystic directly summoned Pomella and—"

"I understand perfectly, AnGent," Elona said, picking a piece of dirt off her lacy sleeve. "If the High Mystic feels wronged, she can petition my fathir at a later time. But she should know better than to pilfer commoners from him."

Pomella looked to the Watcherman for help and then back to Elona. The young noblewoman most likely realized that the High Mystic's summons would supersede the baron's, or any other noble's. But a sickening fear wormed through Pomella as she realized Lady AnBroke could still make her life miserable if she wanted to.

Elona stared at Pomella, anger storming behind her eyes. "I do not give the girl permission to put a single grubby toe outside the barony. Let it be known that if she leaves the barony and returns without becoming a Mystic, my fathir will declare her Unclaimed."

Somebody in the crowd gasped. Anxiety roared in Pomella's chest. Unclaimed! She might as well be dead!

Watcherman AnGent flexed his hands and steadied his voice. "Lady AnBroke, I don't think it's fair to punish Pomella for—"

"You are incapable of determining what is fair, *commoner*. That is why you are cared for by your betters. Ready my horse and escort. I must report this atrocity to my fathir at once."

Watcherman AnGent bowed his head. Nothing else could be said. Pomella and the rest of the village curtsied or bowed, as was appropriate. Elona turned her back and stormed off the stage, dropping her faerie wings onto the grass.

Trying to salvage something of the festival, the Watcherman urged Bethy back onto the green to try to continue the *Toweren*. But one by one the villagers shook their heads, slipping back to their homes, where they locked their doors for the first time in memory. At least one voice mumbled, "Spoiled child," from the darkness.

Hoping to disappear unseen, Pomella slipped away and leaned against the hidden side of a nearby home. Her eyes burned as she struggled to find her breath.

Unclaimed.

By the Saints, what would she do now?

As she began to walk home, she caught sight of Sim coming over to her. It was too much. She couldn't deal with him, too, right now. She broke into a run, and fled.

Fathir scratched his beard. "You can't go."

Pomella slouched in her chair, mindlessly picking the embroidery on her dress. Her clothes basket still sat on top of the table. Her fathir paced their small living space while one of his calloused carpenter hands rubbed his temple.

Maybe he was right. Maybe it was foolish to leave the barony. But by the Saints, she wanted to go! She wished again for Bethy's confidence.

"Fathir, I already—"

"No, Pomella!" he snapped. "I won't even consider it. You could become Unclaimed!"

"But—"

"The baron's soldiers will look for you on the road. If you're outside Oakspring tomorrow, they'll cut you down."

Pomella shook her head. "N-no. The baron wouldn't do that. I have the little stone from the Green Man."

Fathir pushed off from the mantel and loomed over her. She shrank back. "You're blind, girl. You think a rock will protect you from those soldiers? You're in danger. And even if you made it to Kelt Apar, you'll be Unclaimed when you return home. You cannot fathom what it's like to be Unclaimed! Living without even a name on broken roads, eating insects, gathering disease. Nobody will touch you or even hand you a scrap of moldy bread. Animals live better than the Unclaimed!"

Pomella clutched her fingers. "But I'm of age now. I'm old enough to make this decision for myself."

"What decision is there to make? Whatever shred of a life you have will be ruined."

Pomella tried to find the words that would make him understand. She could feel, down to her bones, that the Myst called to her.

"But I won't be Unclaimed if I become the High Mystic's apprentice," she said.

"You'll never become a Mystic!" her fathir roared. She started, her heart pounding. "You're a blathering dunder if you think otherwise! I don't know what schemes this, this . . . Yarina has, but by all the Saints, you'll just be a pawn in some game. Becoming a Mystic is best left to the nobility, who have nothing better to do with their lives. Why would you risk your life for something like that?"

She trembled beneath his anger. Despite the fear, she forced herself forward, reckless. "What's so terrible about the Myst? Grandmhathir said it's something we all can feel and learn to use!"

"And it chaps me that she did!" he flared.

Silence drifted in the air like the motes of dust.

"Your grandmhathir did more than just talk about it, Pomella," he said at last. "She dabbled in it. I don't know how she got exposed to it. She never explained. But I know she meddled without supervision, and it . . . it killed your grandfathir."

Pomella's nails bit into her skin. "What do you mean? I thought Grandfathir died from—"

"No!" he snapped. "She killed him."

Pomella shook her head. "No. No, you're lying!"

"Don't call me a liar under my roof, girl!" he snarled. "You don't know a clip's worth about your grandmhathir like you think you do. It was an accident. I'm not calling her a murderer. But by my unsainted life, I saw my fathir die because of her meddling. The Myst is for those better than us, Pomella. You and me? We're barely good enough for this shite village. We don't own this land. We live here at the whim of the baron. I know you don't like to hear it, but, like you said, you're old enough to know how it is in the world."

Pomella narrowed her eyes. Her nails dug deeper as she tried to balance the pain inside with something she could control. "Then why did the High Mystic invite me? Did it have something to do with Grandmhathir? Was she a Mystic?"

Fathir scoffed. "No, she was definitely *not* a Mystic. She fancied herself something like one, but it was just blather in her mind. She was a foreigner, as obvious as her black skin. She brought foreign ideas to Moth along with fanciful dreams." He looked into the cold fireplace. "I once believed all her stories. I even went to find a Mystic once. I left home, just like you're thinking of doing. I traveled all through the barony, following the rumor of a wandering Mystic. I found him. I groveled at the hem of his torn robes and begged him to take me as his apprentice."

She blinked, not believing what she heard. Could he be lying? She'd learned long ago to weigh his words carefully. But these had a note of honesty about them. "Wh-what did he say?"

"He kicked me as I knelt in the dirt. He spit snot on me and told me to lick the ground. Said that if I ever spoke to him again, he would strip me of my name and brand me Unclaimed."

Pomella's breath froze in her chest.

Fathir turned to her and held her gaze. "*That* is how Mystics think, Pomella. That is their world. The happy love and Mystical power your grandmhathir spoke of is a dream. It's time to wake up."

He left her and she sat in silence until midnight passed, bringing Springrise at last.

Hours later, in the deep silence of the night when even shadows sleep, Pomella sat awake on the floor of her small room, staring at the wall. A trail of old tears stained her cheeks. They'd come at first when she barred herself in her room, but she refused to let them dominate her tonight, or any night.

A thick tome rested in her lap. It had belonged to Grandmhathir, who quietly passed it to Pomella in her final days. *The Book of Songs,* she'd called it.

A symbol of a tree, woven like a Mothic knot, decorated its leather cover. Running her fingers over it, Pomella traced the embossed shape. Unfamiliar letter-runes were stamped into the leather. The shapes were from the script reserved only for the merchant-scholar caste and above.

She opened the book to a random page in the middle. The leather spine creaked, and her grandmhathir's scent danced around the room. The first time she'd opened it, Pomella had been surprised to see the book wasn't a collection of songs. She didn't know *what* it was. Grandmhathir had only managed to indicate it related to the Myst and therefore Pomella had to keep it hidden.

Pomella flipped through the pages, trying again to understand their contents. A hundred illustrations accompanied the book's hand-printed text, creating a mesmerizing collection of pages. Colorful star diagrams, cross sections of plants, strange letter charts, a trail map of an unknown mountain, and depictions of hand gestures fought for room against the hand-printed letter-runes.

In the center of the book an elaborate drawing sprawled across two facing pages. The runes above it read, in the common script, *The Mystical Hierarchy*, and showed stylized rankings of water, flesh, stone, iron, blood, fire, and other essences Pomella did not recognize.

Most wondrous of all, though, was her grandmhathir's familiar thin handwriting, scrawled throughout every page in rose-colored ink. Most of Grandmhathir's notes related to music. Bars and musical notation, along with lyrics and poems, filled the open spaces of each page. Pomella didn't understand what the original text was meant for, but could plainly see her grandmhathir was leaving behind songs.

"I wish you were here," Pomella said aloud.

She studied page after page as the night deepened. The notes bewildered her, but she recognized many of the songs scribbled inside, including "A Sail to Pull the Moon" and "Into Mystic Skies." She hummed some of them aloud, tasting their familiar sounds. Clearing her throat, she tried again, this time with her whispered voice rather than a hum.

> *"Turn my heart to rain*
> *And I will illuminate*
> *I will illuminate*
> *The sky"*

As far back as she could remember, Grandmhathir had always encouraged Pomella to sing. She recalled games they'd played together, where Grandmhathir taught her how to run scales and find melody. In recent years, singing had become her safe place. Nobody could take that from her, not even her fathir.

A gentle tap sounded at her window, startling her. She froze, wondering if she'd imagined it.

The tapping came again.

"Pomella?" came the barest hint of a whisper.

Pomella closed the book and stashed it under her mattress. She cracked open the window and peered out. "Bethy? What are you doing?"

"Let me in! It's freezing out here!"

Pomella opened the window all the way and stood back as Bethy climbed through, her green Brigid cloak covering her nightdress. Bethy landed on her feet as Pomella closed the window behind her. "Were you asleep?" Bethy asked.

"Yah," Pomella lied.

"You've been crying."

"It's been a long night."

Bethy frowned and moved to hug her, but Pomella shied away.

"What did he say?" Bethy asked.

Pomella's face hardened. She sank down to her knees, and stared back into the darkness.

Bethy settled beside her and draped her cloak over Pomella's shoulders. Pomella wished Bethy would just go away, but she found herself unable to say that. They remained on the floor for what felt like the life of the stars.

"Tell me, Pom. What did he say?"

Anger and despair flooded Pomella's veins. "That I would be foolish to go. That the Mystics don't care about me. That *nobody* cares about me. That I'll be Unclaimed, and—"

Bethy reached out tentatively to find Pomella's hand. "Pom. Hush. Your fathir doesn't know anything. The Green Man came for you! Pomella! The *Green Man* came for *you!*"

Pomella snatched her hand back. "He should've come for Elona. At least she already knows how to use the Myst. I can't go. I'll just fail. There'll be others who want to be the apprentice. They're all noble and better than me."

"Shite and blather on them," Bethy said. "I don't care if every firstborn from Moth and the Continent show up. The High Mystic invited you, and she sits above anyone. You have a chance to rise beyond our caste, Pom! You're special; I just know it. And look, so do others."

She unwound a long, emerald string from her wrist and handed it to Pomella. Pomella recognized it immediately. It was a Common Cord, filled with intricate knots. At least twenty families had woven their unique style of knot into the rope in a show of solidarity.

Pomella accepted the Cord. She imagined each Goodness lovingly tying her family's knot into it and passing it to the next woman.

"Don't you see?" Bethy said. "You represent something to us. You're not just a commoner. You're a commoner *with a chance.*"

"I wish I hadn't been invited. I should just stay home."

Bethy sighed. "And what would happen if you did?"

Pomella fingered each family's knot in the Common Cord. Not everyone from Oakspring had tied one, but many had. She traced the AnClure knot from Bethy's family. The AnKellys'. AnGents'. Others. None of these families had bad lives. Pomella's own might be a blathering mess, but what would really happen if she declined the invitation?

"Nothing," she said, and realized what that meant. If she stayed, she would not only be rejecting the High Mystic; she'd also be dismissing an opportunity the families of Oakspring would never have. She'd be letting down her village and her grandmhathir. And Pomella would be denying herself the one deep desire she'd always had.

To learn to use the Myst.

If she turned away from this opportunity, the thin strand holding her otherwise dull life together would break, and so would she. She would wilt as surely as a flower without rain.

"I know nothing of the Myst," she said.

"Yah, neither do I, but I suspect it is far more than waving hands and glowing flowers. They say Mystics are always surrounded by light and music, and there's music in your heart like I've never seen. Think about how you lift people up with your singing! If you hold on to that, then the Myst will flow on its own."

Pomella thought of her garden. She tended to it each day, and made smart choices when it came to planting, pruning, and harvesting. But in her heart, she knew it thrived from more than her careful attention. She'd never told anybody else, but she sang to the plants. And when she did, she sometimes saw silvery fog wafting through the leaves, or across the ground. It was always in the corner of her vision, and when she turned to face it, it vanished like mist on a sunny day. Just last week she saw a silvery bumblebee floating between flowers before vanishing after a few heartbeats.

"I want to go," Pomella said, "but I'm afraid, Bethy. I'm afraid of going and being made into a fool. And I'm also afraid of staying and being a bigger one."

Bethy smiled, as gentle as a mhathir with a wee tyke. "I'll support whatever you decide. But I know you'll regret it if you don't try. You're strong and brave, Pom."

Pomella scoffed a laugh at that, but quickly silenced herself. "I'm none of those things, and you know it."

"Buggerish!" said Bethy. "You've always been strong! We were, what, four years old when your mhathir passed away? Just knee-high tykes! Sim and I also lost Dane to the Coughing Plague at the same time. I cried every day for a year. But not you. You helped your grandmhathir, who I think should be a Saint by the way, and helped with wee Gabor. Not a day goes by where I don't admire your strength! I'd wager everything I have against the luckiest gambler on Moth that the High Mystic recognizes those traits in you somehow."

"How would she know?"

Bethy smiled. "Go ask her yourself."

Pomella's heart swelled with emotion. *Thank you*, she mouthed, unable to make sound come out.

Bethy hugged her, and this time Pomella let her.

As Pomella wiped her cheeks with her sleeve, Bethy opened a rough canvas sack Pomella hadn't noticed. "I packed some rations and a waterskin for you," Bethy said. "The Green Man said it would take two days to get to Sentry, so watch how much you gobble."

"You . . . *packed* for me?"

"You're on your way to become a Mystic," Bethy said with a wink. "I'm just a lowly commoner. I suppose it's my duty."

"I don't know what to say."

"'Thank you' is sufficient. Oh, and, keep the cloak. That's my real parting gift. You're going on a real adventure, just like Saint Brigid. You might not have her red hair, but I think the cloak looks beautiful on you regardless."

With a mischievous smile, Bethy opened the window and began to climb out. Pomella stopped her. "Thank you," Pomella said, as sincerely as she could manage.

Bethy smiled. "Make us proud. You'll find the Myst. I just know it!"

"Will you take care of Gabor? Ask your mhathir and fathir to give him . . . affection?" Pomella choked on the last word.

Bethy nodded and squeezed Pomella's hand before slipping out the window and ducking her way through the night toward her house. Pomella closed the window, her hands shaking. She took a deep breath. Dark fears of becoming Unclaimed threatened to invade once more.

"No," she said aloud to them. "Leave me be. I'm doing this."

Quick as a skivering luck'n, she emptied her drawers of clothing. She hastened out of her nightdress, and threw on her best work dress. She packed two others into the canvas bag holding her food. After only a moment of consideration, she packed her Springrise dress, too.

She counted out her meager nugs and clips, tossing the small pouch she had into the larger canvas one. She fetched *The Book of Songs,* and tucked it away, too. With nothing else of value, she slipped out of her bedroom.

She considered waiting until morning, but sunrise was surely only a few hours away at this point, and she didn't want to deal with her fathir. She peeked into Gabor's room. He lay sprawled across his bed, mouth open and hand stuffed in his too-short pants. A lump formed in her throat. "Good-bye, twerper."

She tiptoed into the main room of the house and slipped toward the door. She paused at the threshold and glanced across the room, fearful that her fathir lurked there, ready to trap her. But the room was empty and she breathed a sigh of relief.

Outside, she whispered a farewell to her garden, silently hoping somebody would harvest the vegetables and water the rest. Not looking back, she found the road leading south, and set out. Grandmhathir always said a traveler needed a tune, so Pomella recalled the one she'd come up with earlier and sang the final stanza of the *Toweren.* It wasn't a very good melody yet, but it would suit the road well enough.

> *"Come fall with me*
> *My Brigid free*
> *Her heart now cold*

And all foretold
Of accomplished quest
And purpose begotten
A scorned master crossed
Mother and child forgotten
In death's dark Tower, lost"

Pomella strode away from Oakspring, and her old life. She stretched her legs and let the wind catch Bethy's cloak. The road rose before Pomella, and she met it with an eagerness as fresh as the promise of the new day. It wasn't until the sun's first rays touched the eastern horizon that she recalled with sudden guilt that she'd forgotten to meet with Sim.

THREE

THE MYSTWOOD

The first day on the southern road proved to be more challenging than Pomella had expected. Her feet ached after the first sprinkling of miles. The waterskin dangling from her belt and the canvas pack across her chest became bulky annoyances.

The sun hung high above the eastern horizon by the time her nerves finally settled from the night's urgent rush. Pomella found herself frequently glancing back, worrying that her fathir would catch up and drag her home. She wondered how he had reacted when he'd discovered she'd left. A part of her knew she shouldn't care what he thought, but she couldn't help it.

But despite her worries and sore feet, the gentle spring morning soothed her. She breathed in the beautiful green countryside. Fir and oak lined both sides of the road, slowly growing in density as she approached the edge of the Mystwood. She spied the Ironlow Mountains to the south, with MagBreckan rising at their westernmost edge, its peak covered in cloud and snow.

By highsun she passed the AnGrey farm where Goodman Danni and Goodness Jhanni were bringing the sheep in for shearing. A pang of apprehension chilled through Pomella. This was the farthest she'd ever been from home, and she worried they might try to stop her from leaving the baron's land. She detoured on a wide path around them, hoping to remain out of sight.

Past the AnGrey farm, she fished in her pocket for the smooth stone that the Green Man had given her. She examined it up close. It looked like a simple rock that could be found on the village green. Feeling a bit foolish, Pomella tossed it in front of her.

The little stone tumbled to the ground.

But just as it was about to land on the road, an echoing sound like a twirling bird popped from the stone. Pomella jumped in surprise as it rolled upward, lifted through the air, and hovered before her. A soft, green light emanated from it, pulsing as if breathing.

This had to be the Myst!

She reached out a trembling hand. The stone skittered away, just out of reach.

She swallowed. "I-I need to find the ranger who's waiting for me north of Sentry, please."

The stone spun like a toy top and zoomed away, heading

toward the Mystwood. A grin spread across her face, and she hurried after it.

Her happiness didn't last. In the late afternoon, heavy clouds pushed up from the south. Rain began to fall, and quick as a luck'n, a heavy torrent turned the road to mud. The wind drove the rain straight at her like a hail of arrows. She thanked the Saints for Bethy's hooded cloak, and trudged on.

A heavy jangling sounded on the road behind Pomella. She glanced back, and pulled her hood aside to give her a clear view. A handful of mounted soldiers rode toward her. Cold terror gripped Pomella. Each man wore the Baron AnBroke's gold and green atop his mail armor. The lead soldier carried a spear topped with the baron's standard, depicting a laurel-crowned harp over emerald treetops.

Without thinking, Pomella sprinted off the road for the cover of the trees. The little guiding stone remained where it was, hovering in place above the road, waiting for her to return. As Pomella crossed the tree line, she looked back at the soldiers. They marched forward, gritting their teeth through the rain. None of them called out or chased after her. Perhaps she'd hidden before they saw her.

Pomella spied a broad oak tree nearby, its leaves fully in bloom, tucked away from the road. Its thick branches reached out like arms offering embrace. She scrambled over and pressed her back to the trunk.

"Lookit this," said one of the soldiers. "Jagged floating rock."

"Aye, looks like the Myst to me," said a second.

Pomella stifled a curse.

"She's got to be around here. Spread out. Eban, you stay here."

One of the soldier's horses whinnied and another clomped its hoof. Heavy boots thumped onto the muddy road. Pomella's breath came in heavy gasps. Her fathir had been right; they were going to kill her. She was going to be murdered and left to rot in the forest.

Footsteps padded behind her, getting closer. Pomella squeezed her eyes shut. He was going to find her. She prayed silently to Saint Brigid that he'd pass her by. She considered running, but the man was too close now. He'd see her for sure. She wished she didn't feel so powerless.

She took a trembling step forward, ready to sprint.

"Hey! The rock just dropped!" called the soldier still on the road.

Pomella stiffened back up against the tree again, her heart storming in her chest. The soldier who had been approaching her turned around.

"She can't be far," said one of the others.

"Sure she can. She abandoned the spiking rock! She's probably long gone. C'mon."

Pomella stood like a statue for several minutes after the soldiers rode away and into the rain. Breathing a sigh of relief, she slipped to the ground and huddled into her cloak, teeth chattering. She drank from her waterskin and ate some vegetables and dried meat before slumping against the oak. She picked at the cloak, trying to think what to do. She didn't dare go back to the road, even to see if she could find the guiding stone.

She took out Grandmhathir's *Book of Songs*, hoping it would soothe her. Her *Book of Songs* now, she supposed. She opened it to the first page, looking for nothing in particular.

On the inside of the cover was a stylized sketch of a fox, partially concealed by tall grass. Its eyes were rendered so cleanly on the page that Pomella felt they were staring at her. When her gaze slipped away, she thought she glimpsed its tail swish.

Thunder shook the forest. The wind whipped the pages of the book. "Ah, buggerish!" she snapped, closing the book.

Glancing around, she became aware that it wasn't just raining; it was *storming* like a shaken honeyhive. The oak tree had sheltered her well, but now the rain slanted in, soaking her.

Something splashed behind her.

Panic gripped her. She stood, spinning around so fast she lost her balance and collapsed. Her heart thundered as she scrambled to her feet again. Her dark hair whipped in front of her eyes, obscuring her vision. She brushed it away.

"Who's there?" she called.

"Pomella? Relax. It's me."

The person in front of her blinked into view.

"*Sim*? What are you doing here?"

"I followed you," said the tall boy. "To make sure you were safe." His soaking blond hair dripped onto a plain traveling cloak, the same one he'd had for years. He gripped an iron sword in his right hand.

"*Clearly* you followed me! Sweet Brigid, you scared the buzzards out of me!" Her face warmed. "But as you can see, I'm perfectly safe."

"Yah, I suppose you are," he said, looking at her book. "What were you doing?"

"I was just . . . reading."

"You shouldn't be reading about—" He stopped when he saw Pomella's eyes narrow. "Isn't it a little . . . wet to read?" he said instead.

With a frustrated grunt, Pomella snatched *The Book of Songs* from the soggy grass and brushed it off before the pages could be ruined.

"All right, I'm sorry," Sim said. "I know reading is important to you. I just don't understand why you feel you need to read noble runes when you could get in trouble for it. But I'm willing to try."

Pomella puffed out a strand of wet hair that had fallen across her face. Sim's presence complicated matters. In a way, she was glad to have him here. She hadn't expected the road to be so lonely. Or dangerous. And she had to admit there was something comforting about his scruffy face and hair dripping rain. But he was part of her old life. *Needed* to be. She wasn't sure if she could begin her time as a Mystic with him around.

"I don't think you should be here," Pomella said. "There are soldiers on the road."

"You left without saying good-bye," he said, ignoring her warning. "We never got that chance to talk. I have a lot things to say, and—"

Lightning and thunder tore through the sky, right on top of each other. Pomella nearly jumped out of her dress, and even Sim seemed skivered.

Sim scratched his head. "Besides, it's not right for anybody to travel alone."

"Then why are *you* traveling alone?"

He grinned that winning smile of his. "I knew I'd catch up to you soon enough."

Pomella bit her lip. "I'm not going home. You'll become Unclaimed if you leave the barony, so don't try to—"

"I'm not trying anything," he said, stepping forward. "And I won't leave the barony. I'll only escort you to Sentry."

"I *had* an escort. Can you put that sword away?" Pomella asked, uneasy with it pointing in her general direction. "Where'd you get it, anyway?"

"Fathir forged it for Bethilla. For the play last night. It's supposed to be Dauntless, Saint Brigid's sword. I think it was going to be a gift for the baron."

Pomella raised an eyebrow. "But?"

"But I . . . borrowed it."

"Do they know you 'borrowed' it?"

Sim replied, but Pomella didn't hear it. Twenty feet away, just over Sim's shoulder, a silver fox sat in the underbrush. It appeared semi-translucent, with fine silver dust smoking off of it. It swished its tail and yawned.

"Sim, look."

"Look at what?" he asked, looking over his shoulder.

"I'm going to follow it."

"Follow *what*?"

She brushed past him. The fox looked exactly like the one she'd seen on the inside cover of her book.

Seeing her, the animal quirked its head and stood, then scampered into the forest. She ran after it, not waiting for Sim to snatch up the rest of her gear and follow.

"What are we doing?" he asked when he caught up to her, out of breath.

"Don't you see it? The silver fox?"

"I don't see anything."

The fox burst from a bush and darted away. Pomella ran after it.

"Wait, Pomella! Come back!" Sim cried, hurrying after her.

She raced through the trees. Sim followed somewhere behind her. "Is this a Mystic thing?" he called.

The fox scurried around a tree just as another silver animal jumped from a nearby bush. A rabbit tore across the water, leaving wispy smoking light in its path. The surface of the puddle didn't ripple.

Sim caught up to her, panting. "What's the matter with you?"

"I saw a silver rabbit! It was wispy and like vapor. It just . . . *ugh*!"

He looked at her like she was saying it rained cows. "Are these animals like the ones you used to see?"

"Yes. I mean, maybe. Shite! I don't know. I lost the jagged fox and—"

The forest spun as a force of green and gold crashed into Pomella. She thought she heard Sim scream, but if he had, it was drowned out by the pounding in her ears. A heavy figure with sharp metal bits of armor pinned her to the ground.

"Get the other one!" the man on top of her screamed.

The baron's soldiers.

Pomella flailed as panic took her. The man who'd knocked her down held her hard by the wrists. She snarled at him, and heaved her whole body, trying to throw him off. But the soldier just glared at her behind a long, red mustache.

"Pomella!" Sim called.

Pomella whipped her head in his direction and saw him staggering to his feet, sword in hand. Another soldier knelt beside Sim on the ground, screaming and clutching his face with two hands. Blood oozed out from between his fingers. By the Saints, had Sim stabbed the man?

"Jagged Eban!" the soldier holding Pomella said. Screaming, Sim threw a punch at the man with his free hand. The soldier lifted himself off Pomella and dove for Sim's legs before the blow could land.

They landed in a tumbling pile of limbs. Pomella scrambled away from them and found her feet.

"Don't hurt him!" Pomella screamed, but wasn't sure which man she meant it for. Maybe both. Her mind raced. The soldier might be within his legal right to strike Sim down. But if Sim hurt the soldier—or, worse, killed him—his life would be forfeit as well.

The two men clawed for control of the sword. Pomella's eyes spied a thick branch on the ground. She snatched it up and hoisted it above her head. Maybe she could get a clean shot at the soldier.

Lightning and thunder roared around them. Pomella jumped, dropping the stick. Jagged shite! She bent to pick it up, and a low growl froze Pomella's heart. She tracked the sound to a spot behind her and felt her remaining sliver of courage drain.

Three wolves, each glowing with the same misty smoke as the

fox and rabbit, stepped toward them, hackles raised and bodies tense. They stood as tall as her chest, covered with angry scars and missing tufts of fur. She could almost see through them, as if they were shadowy dreams made of silver light. The rain fell right through them, leaving their scarred bodies dry.

"Sim!" she called, forgetting for a moment that he was struggling for his life. "Tell me you see those!"

One of the wolves jumped forward and snarled, ripping the air with its teeth.

She must've diverted Sim's attention, because she heard him cry out. She dared to dart her gaze at him. The soldier had Sim pinned to the ground, belly down, with his knees driven into his back. He held the sword up high, tip pointed down, aimed for Sim's back.

Torn between the misty wolves and murderous soldier, Pomella screamed, "No, please! Don't hurt him!"

"It's you the baron wants, girl. This boy bloodied my friend."

The panic in Pomella overwhelmed her. She screamed and threw the tree branch at the soldier.

In that same moment, the wolves charged.

Pomella ducked and covered her head. She felt a cold presence rush by her, and heard the soldier scream.

Ripping her gaze in that direction, she saw the wolves tearing at the man's face. He screamed and swung his arms wildly, as the strange, translucent creatures somehow bore him to the ground.

Sim scrambled away, his eyes wide with surprise.

Pomella snatched up her *Book of Songs*, ran to Sim, and pulled him into a run.

Behind her, two of the wolves growled and gave chase. "Run, Sim!"

Pomella sprinted as fast as her panicked legs could carry her. She clutched *The Book of Songs* to her chest. She imagined the creatures tearing her apart, and prayed she didn't trip.

The ground sloped upward. She heard the rush of water coming from beyond a ridgeline ahead. She looked back over her shoulder just as the wolves charged past Sim, staying wide of him, perhaps because of his sword. The creatures bore down on her. A river came into view, its water flooded nearly to the top of the bank.

With the lead wolf just breaths behind her, she closed her eyes and leaped. As she flew through the air, arms and legs flailing, she heard Sim scream her name.

The bone-cold water rushed around her, filling her nose and mouth. Her cloak pulled at her, tangling her feet as she kicked to the surface. Somehow she managed to fling *The Book of Songs* as far as she could onto the bank and watched it crash into a bush.

Her arms free, she balanced herself in the water and swam with the current. Sim ran after her, following her along the ridge. The wolves were nowhere to be seen.

She stroked her way as best she could toward the shore, actually grateful to her fathir for something. Living near the flood-prone Creekwaters, he'd insisted that she and Gabor become strong swimmers.

Grabbing hold of a heavy tree branch dangling into the water, she held tight until Sim rushed up and pulled her to safety. He threw his arms around her.

"What in the name of the jagged Saints were you thinking?

You nearly drowned!" He yanked her soaking cloak off and wiped her hair from her face.

Pomella looked around to be sure there weren't any wolves nearby. Perhaps they'd given up when she leaped into the water.

"Did you see them?" she gasped. "The wolves?"

Sim's eyes widened and he looked around, suddenly tense again.

Pomella's heart sank. "There were three giant wolves jawing at us. One of them almost got me. Didn't you see them attack the soldier?"

She could see them plainly in her memory, though they'd seemed only half-present, as if they were made from the light of a thousand lantern bugs. The rain had fallen right through them. . . .

Sim shook his head and sighed. "It all happened so fast," he said, handing her the canvas sack containing her food and clothing. "I didn't see them, but I believe you. What do you want to do now?"

"I-I don't know," she confessed. "I lost my book. We should go back to find it."

Sim held up a hand. "No. If you said those things were real, and you want me to take it seriously, then I'm going to treat them that way. We're not going back to where they were. Besides, those soldiers could still be looking for us."

Somehow, Pomella doubted the soldiers would be looking for them anytime soon. "That book is important to me, Sim. I'm going to find it."

"You can't have it both ways, Pomella!" Sim said. "We're in the middle of a jagged storm and standing beside a rapidly rising river. We need shelter. If those wolves really are a danger, I don't know how we can defend ourselves."

Pomella bit her lip and picked a fingernail.

He sighed again and scratched his hair. "I'm sorry. It's just that you're asking me to trust you. I'm trying. Now do this for me. Please? We can look for your book later."

She twisted her fingers, not knowing what to do. Swallowing, she finally nodded and followed his lead, hardly noticing where they went. Fleeing from the silver wolves had obliterated all sense of direction for her, and storm clouds concealed the sun's position. She distracted herself from the sadness of losing the book by shaking out her soaking cloak before draping it back on.

Darkness crept across the forest. They walked in silence through the woods, Sim leading the way. Pomella watched him, still not really believing that he'd followed her. It comforted her to have somebody else with her in case she ran into more trouble, but Sim brought a bundle of confusion with him. He cared about her, and tried so hard to show his affections.

Sim gestured. "There," he said, pointing to a structure up ahead. They approached a small gazebo set on the high point of the ridge looking far down onto the river below. A decrepit curved roof sat atop crumbling walls made of stone. Sim drew his sword as they approached.

Overgrown ivy clawed its way through the ruined structure. Gaping holes yawned where the roof had tumbled away. A twisted oak pushed against the foundation, shoving it aside with the bulk of its many years. Pomella peered inside.

An old shrine rested against one of the inner gazebo walls.

A moss-covered statue of Saint Brigid stood above offerings that had rotted long ago.

A damp emptiness filled the old shrine. The quiet patter of rain lulled Pomella's senses. Sim slipped beside her and peered in. "Looks dry enough for our purposes," he said. "Come on."

Moving around to the entrance, he gestured for her to go first. She brushed past him, across the threshold.

With a thunderous rush of wings, a cluster of flapping birds startled her from above. Pomella ducked as she stepped farther into the shrine.

The rotten floor shattered. She cried out as she fell. Sim dove for her, but he tumbled down, too. She bounced once against a stone wall, then hit muddy ground, losing her wind. For a panicked moment, the world spun around her. Her ribs ached, and she prayed they weren't cracked. Pushing herself to her knees, she found her breath and stood up. High above them, perhaps twenty feet, loomed a gaping hole. Three robins circled the inside of the roof before settling back into their nest. Soft feathers floated down.

Sim groaned and pushed himself up. His sword lay in the mud a short distance away. Pomella thanked the Saints neither of them had landed on it.

"Are you all right?" she asked. She fingered her filthy cloak, which had once been green and beautiful.

Sim nodded, and they wiped themselves off. They stood at the bottom of what appeared to be a ruined stairwell. Broken steps had once spiraled the outer walls, but most were cracked now and unusable.

"I'm going to try and climb out," Sim said. "Here, hold this." He scooped up his sword and shook the dirt off before handing it to her. He found a foothold and began climbing. He'd only managed to get maybe four or five feet up when he slipped and fell.

He cursed. "It's too steep."

Pomella pulled her cloak tighter. Gazing up, she looked for anything that could help. Only rain fell through the gaping hole in the roof.

As Sim tried to climb again, Pomella searched around the pit but found nothing other than mud, stones, and a muddy mouse hole. "It's going to be dark soon. We should try and set some kind of camp for the night."

They found a small area in the pit partially covered by the meager roof overhead. Their cloaks kept them from freezing, yet Pomella's teeth began to chatter as night set in. The rain slowed, and increased again, cycling back and forth as the evening wore on. She adjusted her cloak, trying to prevent the rain from soaking her skin.

Sim leaned against the wall next to her.

Pomella rolled her head toward him and managed a grin. "Those soldiers were a bunch of buzzard bastards."

Sim grinned and rubbed his chest. "That one rammed me pretty hard." His eyes flicked to Pomella, then looked away. "I'm sorry for any trouble I caused by coming."

"No, Sim, don't. I would have been arrested if you—"

Sim held up a hand. "We helped each other. But even before that attack happened, you were right. Sometimes I push too hard. It's just that . . . that I care for you. A lot. This whole invitation from the High Mystic just doesn't make any sense. I feel like . . . like . . ." He wilted.

The heavy rain had stopped, replaced by a gentle misting. "Like what?" Pomella asked.

"Like I've only just begun to get to know you, and now you're leaving."

Pomella stared at the mud between her feet. "I don't see why you like me. I just get into one disaster after another."

"Don't be so harsh on yourself," Sim said. "You're great at a lot of things."

"I don't feel like I am."

"The High Mystic seems to think you are."

Pomella kept her silence, not wanting to get into why she thought she was doomed to fail at the Trials. She stirred the mud with her fingers.

"Why do you want to do this?" Sim said.

"Do what?"

"Become a Mystic?"

A swarm of reasons buzzed into Pomella's mind. She wanted to become a Mystic because she loved nature. Because her grand-mhathir's stories of the Myst resonated with her. Because she wanted to understand why she saw silver animals in her garden and in the forest. Because she didn't want to let down all the people who'd tied their knots into her Common Cord. And because, sometimes, *something* called to her heart, challenging her to look at the world in a different way.

But mostly, she wanted to become a Mystic because if she didn't, she'd be denying herself. Somehow, she just knew that was true.

"I just do," she mumbled.

The rain eased up, and a few stars managed to poke their way through the thick clouds. Pomella pulled her cloak tighter and began to hum, glad to have some outlet for her emotions. She thought of the song she'd sung the previous night, one of the familiar ones she'd found in *The Book of Songs*. Lifting her voice, Pomella sang it, filling the cold pit with lingering words and feeling.

"Hope drowns
Amid no sound
Fear claims
What faith can't reach
But I carry strength from you
Now gone
Don't let me give in. . . .

"I will never leave you
We'll share
The mountains and fate
Turn my heart to rain
And I will illuminate
I will illuminate
The sky"

As she sang, lantern bugs blossomed in front of her, little tiny pricks of golden light that faded in and out like soft breath. More and more appeared as if they danced to her song.

She sensed Sim watching her through the tiny lights as she began the final stanza.

"Parting will never leave us alone
Crush fate once set in stone
Turn my heart to rain
And I will illuminate
I will illuminate
Tonight"

When the song finally faded, she found her face floating near Sim's. She hadn't realized that she'd been leaning closer and closer to him. Her heart thundered, but her hands were surprisingly steady.

Pomella thought she could hear Sim's heart beating, too. She had so much to say to him, so much feeling inside that needed to be let out. She wanted to tell him that she cared for him, too. That she *was* glad he was here with her. That, if she had to be chased by soldiers and silver wolves, and trapped in a mud pit, he'd be the one person whose company she wouldn't mind.

Sim leaned in to cross the final inch between them, but she turned her head. How did she tell him? He was part of her old life. He was *home*. And right now, it was time to leave home. If she was going to commit to the possibility of becoming a Mystic, there would be no place for him.

"I don't want to hurt you," she whispered.

The lantern bugs vanished, the clouds obscured the stars, and the rain began anew. Sim's hand found hers, and she gripped it back, hard.

FOUR

THE LOST CHAMBER

The morning came, but the storm continued. The pit became a soaking chamber of mud.

Pomella and Sim spent hours trying to scramble and claw their way up the sheer wall with no success. They called for help, but nobody answered. Pomella's food ran out, and Sim shared what little he had. They had plenty of water, at least. And if the soldiers survived the wolves, they weren't likely to find Pomella and Sim here.

Into the afternoon, dark thoughts swirled around a shivering and hungry Pomella. There was no way she could make it to Sentry in time now. The ranger waiting for her would probably assume she wasn't coming and return to Kelt Apar alone.

She stared at the opposite wall, thinking about last night and how Sim had tried to kiss her. Her stomach tumbled as she wondered what he thought of her and whether she'd made the right choice.

Rainwater drained into a little hole in the opposite wall. She focused on it, and noticed it was the same one she'd investigated yesterday. Having little else to try, she went over and looked again. The little hole was no wider than her wrist. The faint, echoing sound of trickling water came from within.

Echoing.

Lying on her belly, Pomella crammed her arm in. Surprise blossomed on her face. She felt nothing but open space on the other side.

"Sim, give me your sword."

She heard him trudge through the mud and lean over to peer in.

"It's a hole," he said.

Pomella rolled her eyes. "Just give it to me."

He obliged and handed the sword to her. Stretching her arm, Pomella stuck the sword into the hole to try to loosen or widen the opening. The blade struck something hard. Curious, she removed the sword and reached her arm in again. She couldn't reach whatever she'd found.

"Buzzards," she said. She yanked her arm out and kicked the hole, trying to make it bigger. A muddy chunk came free, enlarging the opening. She squeezed down on her belly and crawled in.

"I don't know if that's a wise idea," said Sim.

Pomella ignored him. Trying not to gag as mud filled her

mouth, she crawled deeper until she was submerged to her hips. Her groping fingers found the hard object the sword had struck. She yanked, and it came loose.

She emerged triumphant, holding up her prize like a Summer-yarn fishing champion. She spit mud out of her mouth and wiped her filthy forehead with an even dirtier hand.

Sim cracked a smile. "Now *you* look like something out of the *Toweren*."

She smiled back. It felt good, despite knowing that mud caked her face, hair, and everything to her hips. "Mud is good for the skin," she chimed.

Sim laughed, and helped her stand. Their fingers lingered together.

They looked at the object she'd pulled out. It was a simple flat stone, about as wide as her shoulders. "Look at that," Sim said, tracing the stone's perfectly rectangular shape. "Somebody cut this."

"But what is it?" Pomella asked.

"It sort of looks like a stepping-stone."

"But what would a stepping-stone be doing down here?"

Sim looked up. "Maybe there used to be more and they led up here?"

"Too bad we can't open the wall any wide—"

She stopped. Shoving the stone into Sim's arms, she faced the wall and shook her hands to loosen them.

"I saw a passage in *The Book of Songs* about opening a door. I remember the song my grandmhathir wrote on that page. If I sing it, maybe I can . . ." She trailed off, realizing how silly she must sound.

"I don't know, Pomella. The last time you meddled with that book you got chased by invisible ghost-wolves. Maybe you should wait until you're an apprentice before trying things with the Myst again."

"I didn't summon them!" she snapped. "And I won't even get a *chance* to be an apprentice if I don't get out of here." Closing her eyes, she relaxed her mind and hummed a few bars. Sim stepped out of the way.

Nothing happened. She cleared her throat and tried again, with the same results.

Sim raised his eyebrow. Pomella tried again but cut herself off with a frustrated growl. "I need a jagged master to teach me this stuff!"

Sim laughed, a sarcastic snorting sound.

She cocked her head at him. "Are you mocking me?"

"No, no," Sim said, holding up his hands. "Please continue. Singing to it seems to be working great."

Pomella felt her face heat. "Well, fine!" she snapped. She slammed her foot into the wall, right above the hole. She kicked again, and again.

Finally, panting and dragging a loose strand of hair away from her face, she stopped. They looked at each other, and burst out laughing.

The wall above the hole collapsed.

Sim screamed and leaped back.

They stared at each other in amazement. Stepping over the debris, they looked down a newly revealed tunnel, which stood taller than Sim. Stone steps like the one Pomella pulled out led down a sloping natural corridor of mud and exposed tree roots.

"I think your foot might make a better Mystic than the rest of you," Sim said with a smirk.

Pomella smacked his chest. "Those stepping-stones lead *some-where*."

Deep inside the tunnel, a sudden flicker of silvery light caught her attention. She peered forward. A silver mouse scuttled farther down the tunnel. It glowed with a soft light, brightening a small area around it.

Pomella grabbed Sim's arm.

The mouse dashed out of view. Pomella followed, pulling Sim after her while he grumbled about being attacked by wolves. The slick ground sloped downward. She steadied herself on the wall to keep from falling. The stepping-stones kept her steady, although they steepened until they were almost like a ladder. The distant opening Sim and Pomella had come from became lost to sight.

Darkness settled around them like a cold blanket.

Sim grabbed her shoulder. She opened her mouth to berate him, but he pointed ahead. "Look!" he whispered. "Do you see it?"

Pomella peered ahead, wondering how Sim could see anything at all. She expected to see the mouse or another silvery animal, but was instead surprised to see the outline of an archway. She gasped. "What is it? We're so far underground."

"I don't like it," Sim said, but led the way anyway, sword drawn. She rolled her eyes.

They stepped through the stone archway. Beyond lay darkness. Sim stumbled on some pieces of rotting wood lying at the entrance. The air felt different here, as if they'd entered a large room.

He lifted a thin piece of wood. "Hold this," he said, handing it to her. He fumbled through his pockets and pulled out his flint, some tinder, and an edged piece of iron. He struck it across the flint, trying to ignite a spark on the tinder. It caught after a third try.

He worked the sparks until the board lit into a makeshift torch, illuminating the chamber. Looking around, Pomella's eyes widened.

"Sweet Saints," Sim breathed.

He held up the torch, revealing the massive interior. Stone walls created a circular room filled with wooden wreckage and thick spiderwebs. A smashed table lay in the center, next to which ruined chairs and other unidentifiable objects lay strewn about. Shattered picture frames lay in pieces below thick nails driven into the wall that had once held them. The stone extended up to form a flat roof fifteen feet above. The farthest corners of the chamber were lost in shadow. Pomella wondered how far below-ground they were.

Pomella exchanged a glance with Sim and followed him deeper into the room. Brushing aside dusty webs, she tried to count chairs. The amount of wreckage suggested about eight seats.

Four thick candles slept in sconces mounted on the walls, their dry wax hanging like the gnarled roots of ancient oaks. Pomella took the torch from Sim and lit the one closest to them, brushing away thick webs to find the old wick buried in the depths of the candle.

"What do you think this place was?" she asked.

"I don't know. But look at this."

Sim lifted the shredded remains of a tapestry. He brushed it to clear the dust. Squinting in the dim candlelight, Pomella examined a circle of robed figures, each holding a tall staff, standing in a circle around a great oak tree. Some of the figures wore hoods that concealed their faces. Some had their hoods down, revealing lizardlike faces. One figure, crowned in gold, held a staff made of fire. The red threads outlining the flame were the same color as the figure's long hair. Saint Brigid. Three swirling circles, woven like a Mothic knot and arranged in a triangle pattern, hung in the sky above them.

"Who were they?" Sim asked.

"Mystics," Pomella whispered. "I've seen similar images in my *Book of Songs*. And look."

She pointed to the faded images of small animals traced in silver on the tapestry. A deer, a turtle, an eagle, and even a wolf. Silver threads rippled off each animal. Pomella's heart beat faster. She hadn't imagined them!

"You were right," Sim said to her. "Maybe you can see things like a Mystic does. Maybe that's why you were invited to Kelt Apar."

"What's this?" Pomella said, pointing to another scene depicted next to the first. This one was rendered as a fully detailed image, showing a human man and woman bowing before the feet of a lizardlike laghart. The laghart sat atop a great stone that had swirling shapes carved into it. The laghart was unclothed, but shone with power that wove across its body and up to the tip of a staff it held. A silver halo encircled the laghart's head.

"Looks like a laghart Mystic," Sim said. "Ever heard of something like that?"

Pomella shook her head. "There's another one over on that wall."

Sim set the first tapestry down gently as if afraid of ruining it further. They carefully stepped around the room's wreckage to face the torn tapestry that somehow still clung to the wall. This one showed five men standing atop one another.

The man at the top wore robes and carried a staff. Below him stood a man with a crown, and below again was a man holding bulging bags and a merchant's scale. Next down the column was a farmer with a hoe, and finally, at the very bottom, was a ruined pauper. Pomella noticed that the pauper was separated from the other four, as if he was not quite part of the world that the other four occupied.

"Well, this one's pretty obvious," Sim said. "If you're a Mystic, it would make sense that you would want a tapestry to remind yourself that you were in the highest caste."

"Perhaps," she mused. "I wonder what this place was."

"Maybe this is where they met," he murmured. "Either way, I don't think it ended well." He pointed.

A sudden noise startled Pomella. She whirled to face the deepest part of the chamber. Sim spun at the sound, too, his sword flashing in the firelight. He stepped forward.

"There's another door," Sim said.

They approached the door slowly, walking heel to toe. Pomella let Sim walk in front, but only, she told herself, because he was holding a sword.

Definite sounds—whispers, Pomella could hear—leaked from behind the door. Sim reached out and pulled the door open with his free hand.

Pomella gasped.

Rotten shelves hung on the wall of a small alcove, propped up in odd ways with smaller boards as if somebody had tried to hastily repair them. Inside, a cluster of ragged men and women huddled closely together, clutching one another. They wore torn shirts and filthy pants. Each man wore a long, scraggly beard that clearly hadn't seen a razor in many years. Pomella's hands shook. All of their heads were shaved.

Unclaimed.

"Oh, shite," Sim whispered.

Not speaking a word, each man and woman dropped to their knees and placed their forehead on the cavern floor. Pomella fought the urge to flee. She found herself taking half a step backward. She'd never actually seen one of the Unclaimed before. Her mind boggled as she imagined the terrible crimes each of these people must've committed. You couldn't be born Unclaimed. Even the rare child born to an Unclaimed woman was taken away and given to commoners to raise.

"Mercy, Lord," one of the women said. "Mercy, Lady." To the Unclaimed, everyone was a lord or lady, even commoners like Pomella and Sim.

Sim backed away from them, keeping his sword raised. "I think we should leave," he said.

Pomella agreed, but a new thought stopped her. Maybe these men and women hadn't committed a crime. Or perhaps their crime had been something as simple as leaving their barony without their baron's permission. She stared at the dirty figures with a new, horrifying revelation.

This was what she could soon become.

"Why are you here?" she found herself saying. She hadn't expected to speak the thought out loud.

One of the men spoke without lifting his head. "Shelter. Not fit to be looked at."

Sim took Pomella by the arm and pulled her away. "Come on. We can't do anything for them."

Pomella let him lead her away, but she couldn't take her eyes off the disheveled men and women prostrated before her. Each lacked a name, and a place in the world.

Sim moved ahead to shuffle through the chamber's wreckage. Pomella continued to stare at the Unclaimed. Her foot caught on something, and she jumped back.

A dull gray shaft protruded from beneath the chamber's smashed table. At first Pomella thought it might be some kind of thin, dead tree branch, but then she realized what it was. A bone. Piled atop more bones.

Pomella swallowed. "Sim?"

She turned to see Sim gathering long planks of wood from the table.

"We can use this as a ladder," he said. "Let's go."

Pomella leaped to help, silently thanking Sim for having the presence of mind to figure out a solution. She helped him lift the wood, and together they exited the chamber from the way they'd come in. Pomella gave one last glance at the Unclaimed, who still remained prostrated.

Working around the old bones, she and Sim stacked as many planks of wood as they could and struggled back up the tunnel. Managing the uphill slope proved to be a challenge, as the runoff from the rain slickened the terrain. Both of them fell at different times, and Pomella cut her ankle on the side of one of the stone steps.

At last they made it back to the open pit. The rain pounded harder than before, filling the hole with deep puddles. Water cascaded over the edges above. Pomella inhaled deeply, relishing the fresh air. It cleared her mind, washing it free of the dark thoughts the Unclaimed had brought forth. Still, despite the clean air, she was beginning to really dislike the constant rain.

"You should climb out," Sim said, wiping water from his brow. "You're lighter than me, and I can help steady the boards."

Pomella tilted her head back, feeling unsure about the slippery twenty-foot climb.

"I don't know, Sim. I'm not very good at—"

"Pomella," Sim said, his voice sincere. "'*Don't let me give in*,' right?"

The rain splattered on her face. Her teeth chattered. He was right. She nodded.

Sim leaned the longest, thickest board against the pit wall and wiggled it to ensure it was stable. "I'll give you a boost," he said, and nodded upward.

Pomella grasped the board and climbed using Sim's cupped hands. She scrambled up the angled plank as quickly as she could, and found a handhold in the wall. For a moment she balanced there, but then Sim's strong arms pushed her feet up higher. Stretching out, she stepped onto the top edge of the board she'd just scrambled up, and reached high for another jutting stone hanging above her. Looking down, she saw she was about halfway up the wall.

"You can do this," she told herself.

She suddenly wondered if Mystics could learn to fly. It would certainly be useful here. But if that were true, wouldn't that mean she'd have already seen them flying across the skies over Moth?

Another stone jutted out above her. Clenching her jaw, she found a foothold in the rocky wall and eased toward it. Another step, another pull, arm over arm. She fingered the jutting rock, and finally managed to grab it. She prayed to the Saints that it held her weight. She pulled herself up, grunting at the exertion. The top of the pit loomed above her, just a foot or two. She reached for it, and found the edge.

Sim laughed in delight from twenty feet below. "Well done!"

Relief washed over her like rain. Her fingers sought a firmer hold to pull herself up. She thought she might be able to—

Her foot slipped. She lost her hold on the edge and screamed.

Pain shot through her shoulder and elbow as a clawed hand grabbed hers. She wrenched her gaze upward. A scaled face with wide, protruding eyes and jagged teeth stared down at her. He seemed humanoid, and lay belly down at the edge of the pit, gripping her wrist.

Panicked, she tried to shake her hand loose, giving no thought to the drop below.

"Pomella!" Sim screamed. She vaguely heard him draw his sword and try to scramble up the wooden board.

The lizardlike creature pulled her up, and within moments she found herself gasping on the grass at the outside edge of the shrine. She scrambled to her feet and backed away.

"Don'tttt run, chhhild," the creature rasped as he stood. He wore strange dark-green armor consisting of layers of leather and padded wool. A strange pattern of swirling scales covered the visible parts of his body, circling around one another, creating mesmerizing vortexes. A line of short white spikes ran from his forehead, down his spine, and out the tip of his long tail.

The creature lifted a sheathed sword and an unstrung bow from the wet ground. A quiver hung at his waist, wrapped in canvas to keep the arrows dry.

Her mind raced to identify the creature. The name bubbled to her mind, and without thinking, she blurted it out.

"Laghart!"

A strange sound came from the creature, his chest heaving. "You don'ttt sssee many offf my kinnd in Oakssspring, do yyyou?"

The voice sounded male. "What do you want?" Pomella demanded, sounding far braver than she felt.

"Fffor you to telll your ffffriend to relaxx while I hhhelp him outtt," the laghart said.

"Pomella! Where are you?" Sim called.

Watching the laghart as closely as possible, Pomella leaned over the edge. "I'm safe, Sim. There's a . . . a laghart . . . up here. I think he wants to—"

The laghart uncoiled a rope and tossed it down the pit. He braced himself against a heavy stone and waited for Sim to begin climbing. A minute later, Sim crawled up out of the hole. He scrambled toward Pomella and pointed his sword at the laghart.

"Who are you?" Sim demanded.

Pomella found herself surprisingly comforted by Sim's presence. "Sim, it's all right," she said. "He helped us."

The laghart sheathed his sword. "I am Vlenar, and you're latttte."

"Late? What do you mean?" Sim said.

Pomella stepped around Sim, putting her hand on his shoulder to ease him. "He's the ranger who was sent to meet me. Aren't you?"

Vlenar nodded, his strange slitted eyes watching them. "Yessss, Goodmisss AnDone."

"You were supposed to meet us at Sentry," Sim said.

"Usss?" Vlenar's tone sounded unamused.

"I-I meant, her, obviously," Sim stammered.

"We knew ssshe would be lattte, becaussse of the storm, ssso I tracked herr herre."

"But how could you know that?" Sim demanded.

"Rangersss and Myssstics know evvverything about the Great Forressst. Where it growsss, we sssee."

Pomella bit her lip. She believed Vlenar was telling the truth. Besides, she and Sim were lost, and if Vlenar was a true ranger, he could guide them through the woods to Kelt Apar. She turned to Sim.

"I'm going with him," she whispered, putting her hand on Sim's arm.

His eyes wavered just a little. "I'll come with you."

"You know you can't. If you're caught outside the barony, you'll become Unclaimed."

Sim shook his head. "I'm not leaving you with him."

"This is already hard, Sim," Pomella said, trying not to let those blue eyes upset her. "Thank you for coming for me. I needed it more than I knew. But I need to go alone, now. I— Good-bye."

She danced on the edge of hesitation and, without thinking, tiptoed up to kiss him.

As her lips reached his, he turned his head just enough so the kiss landed on his cheek.

"Good-bye, Pomella," he said.

She watched him walk away, sheathing his sword. He paused beside Vlenar to murmur some questions. Without speaking, the ranger pulled some provisions from a bag and handed them to Sim. Vlenar pointed in the direction she and Sim had come from. With a final glance back at her, Sim headed off in the indicated direction. Soon he was lost to the rain and shadows of the forest.

"Come," said Vlenar. "Kelt Apaarr awaittsss."

Pomella lingered, then followed the ranger.

Sim trudged through the Myst-wood, heading back the way he and Pomella had come. Late-afternoon shadows dimmed everything around him. He tried to retrace their footprints, but the deluge had wiped them away. He settled for finding the river and followed it back.

He hated himself for leaving Pomella. He hated the laghart for taking her away. And, by the Saints, he hated himself for turning away her kiss. He cursed himself six times for being a dunder. He'd pushed too hard last night in the pit. Now, today, he didn't feel right kissing her when she was so muddled. Jagged Saints, *he* was all muddled! What would he do now?

At least the rain had stopped.

As he walked, he imagined himself returning home. He saw himself handing the iron sword back to his fathir, apologizing, and putting his work clothes on for another day in the forge or fields. He could see Bethy smirking at him as he hammered away at yet another horseshoe. He sighed as he imagined himself having to court and marry somebody else before taking over the family trade. With his older brother, Dane, gone, the expectation fell on Sim now.

Over and over, he imagined the limited possibilities his life might take. He was the iron, never having a say in how he could be forged. But that was life for a commoner.

Lightning flashed, bringing him back to the present. He'd come to a place he hadn't realized he'd been walking toward. Stopping just below the ridge where Pomella had jumped into the river, he hopped across some dry stones, trying to avoid falling in. He made his way upstream along the bank until he found Pomella's book sprawled open inside a blackberry bush.

He reached in and lifted the leather book out of the overgrown branches. The rain had ruined the pages exposed to the sky, and soaked a few beneath them as well, but overall the book seemed in good condition. He flipped through it, admiring the interesting artwork within, but not understanding the noble runes. Commoners couldn't read those.

Most commoners, anyway.

Closing the cover, Sim placed the book in his shoulder sack. As he was near the Creekwaters, his thoughts lingered on Dane. Even though he'd been the eldest, Dane would never've stuck around in Oakspring, Sim knew. No matter the risk, the moment he'd saved enough clips Dane would've broken the law and headed for a city, or maybe even the Continent. It sometimes seemed like Dane was a bird who'd just settled on Moth long enough to hatch and fly on.

You can come with me if you want, he'd told Sim years ago. *I'll go travel for a while and see what's out there. Then I'll come back and get ya. When you're old enough, you can come to the jungles of Gunna with me.*

"Yah," whispered Sim to himself now, trying hard to picture Dane's face. Strange, what you remembered about a person after he was gone.

What would Sim remember about Pomella?

He knew he didn't want to remember her as being sad. It seemed to him like all she'd known since the Coughing Plague swept through Oakspring and took Dane and her mhathir was sadness. And it didn't help that Goodman AnDone, her fathir, wasn't exactly the kindest man to live with.

Sim wondered about her fathir. The man was sour and prone to bursts of red-hot anger. What would cause a man to become so cruel? Losing his wife, maybe? Perhaps he wanted more for his life, but never attained it? Commoners from Moth could rise above their caste, though it didn't happen very often.

The thought brought Sim back to his previous thoughts and his own destiny. His fathir had been a blacksmith, and a farmer before that. His grandfathir had been a farmer, and his great-grandfathir before him, too. Since as far back as his family's history went, the AnClures had tilled the soil on Moth. They bothered no one, and asked only for a chance to lead a peaceful life.

So why was that not enough for Sim? Did Dane's spirit whisper to Sim from the Creekwaters? Why did he feel that returning home now would forever close the door on a once in a lifetime opportunity?

He gazed north toward Oakspring, and realized he couldn't go back. With or without Pomella, something had awoken in him. He rested his hand on the sword at his side. He wouldn't let life hammer him down. He would not become what Pomella's fathir had.

Turning to the south, Sim gazed in the direction Pomella likely had gone. She might not want him around, but that didn't mean he couldn't at least make sure she got to Kelt Apar safely. Yah, he would do that.

He bit his lip. And then what? If he followed this course, he would be declared Unclaimed for leaving the barony of his birth. He had to risk it. Pomella was making the same choice, just in a different way. After he got her safely to Kelt Apar, he could continue south. The road supposedly led all the way to Port Morrush on the southern tip of Moth. He could find work there, or even a ship to the Continent. He'd take Dane's memories with him.

He turned and walked three steps into a new life. Then he ran, noting that full dark was still a few hours away. He rushed faster, hoping to at least make it back to the shrine before night fell.

He ran for longer than he thought possible. Finally, he stopped to catch his breath. Water droplets fell from trees whose spring greenery was in full display. He drank from his water-skin, and pulled out some dried rabbit meat the laghart had given him. He'd have to hurry if he wanted to make it to Sentry before—

He stopped. A familiar sound came from the west, repeating in a steady rhythm. It was a sharp, piercing sound that reminded him of home. He crept toward it, and quickly recognized it as the sound of a blacksmith's hammer slamming onto metal. He wondered who would be smithing in the middle of the forest.

Stepping carefully, he brushed past the long vinelike branches of a willow tree and spied a small camp beside a thin creek. The camp consisted of two tents, a wagon, and three hobbled horses, each grazing hungrily. Sim couldn't see anybody, but could hear the blacksmith working on the far side of the wagon near the creek. No banner waved above the tents.

A chill swept over Sim. He shivered. His instinct screamed that it was time to go. Turning to leave, he stepped forward and nearly skewered himself on the tip of a spear aimed at his chest.

"Don't move, scrit," said a greasy voice.

FIVE

KELT APAR

Pomella's feet hurt. After a day of walking with Vlenar through the Mystwood, she was ready to burn her shoes. The laghart spoke very little, except to tell her to keep moving when she tried to stop and rest her aching feet.

He led her through the dense forest, always remaining beneath the thick canopy of trees. Despite the more difficult terrain, Pomella was glad they avoided the road. The only sounds she heard during the full day of walking were the chirping and fluttering of birds mixed with the fall of needles and leaves. She noted with annoyance that flies and biterbugs apparently bred large in this part of the island. Overall, she enjoyed the solitude, but found herself often humming just to break the monotony.

She missed her *Book of Songs*. Looking back, she wished she'd been more insistent to Sim that they go back to find it. If they had, maybe they wouldn't have fallen into that blathering pit. Shortly after setting out with Vlenar, she'd mustered the courage to ask him if they could go back to find her book. The ranger's hard, slitted gaze had been enough to tell her to forget it. Her heart ached knowing that the book was probably lost and ruined.

During that first day of travel, she worried that they would encounter more of the silver wolves. But she didn't see or hear any sign of the terrifying creatures or any other ghostlike animals. She refrained from mentioning them to Vlenar. He'd probably not take her seriously. That, and he terrified her in his own way. Although he stood on hind legs, he walked hunched over, so that his spine was almost parallel to the ground. She tried not to stare too much.

At night, around their campfire, she watched his tail swish back and forth across the ground, idly tracing patterns in the dirt.

They bypassed the town of Sentry on the second day of travel, skirting around it by taking a westerly route that put them within sight of Loch Bracken, the largest body of water in the forest. They followed no path that Pomella could see. Vlenar pushed forward with confidence, leading her south and west. Glancing upward, she had difficulty gauging the sun's position. The tall, moss-coated oaks spread their limbs high above her, intermixing their branches as if holding hands.

Pomella adjusted the pack slung across her back. When she'd first carried it out of Oakspring, she'd thought it had been light. Now, it felt like carrying boulders.

As they set camp for the second night, Pomella caught sight of a great snowcapped mountain peak, rising in the distance above the treetops.

"MagDoon," the ranger said, handing her a flat loaf of bread for her supper.

Pomella smiled as a thrill of excitement raced through her. Everyone on Moth knew of the great mountain, and the legends associated with it. She'd never so much as glimpsed it before, despite living less than a week's travel away. Saint Brigid herself was said to have walked those slopes.

Late on the morning of the third day, just as Pomella worked up the courage to ask Vlenar when they could eat again, he stopped. "We are hhhere," he said.

Pomella's head popped up. She'd been staring at the ground as they walked. "What? Where?"

The laghart pushed aside a branch to reveal an enormous circular clearing. Pomella gasped.

A wide, manicured lawn, bigger than she'd ever seen, shone under the highsun light. Scattered trees provided pools of shade, including a massive willow tree trailing its leaves in a gentle pond. Shaggy goats grazed lazily. The sounds of a nearby river drifted toward her and the laghart. A cluster of simple buildings rested on the far side of the clearing near the source of the sound. Pomella glanced down and saw a path of pebbled stones that began near her feet and ran toward the clearing's most dominant feature—a rounded stone tower, perhaps seventy or eighty feet tall and half as wide, rising from the center of the clearing. Ivy crawled up its sides, the tendrils spreading across the white rock beneath it. A series of small windows climbed the tower in a slow spiral, unevenly spread apart, their panes twinkling in the sun. Capping the tower was a conical green slate roof. Wildflowers surrounded the tower in a wide ring, rippling like the waves of a colorful moat.

A hawk soared overhead as they stepped out from the cover of trees onto the grass. A wide smile burst onto Pomella's face. She yanked off her shoes. Her toes found the soft grass and she wiggled them, feeling the comforting relief offered by the lawn.

Vlenar led her along the pebbled path toward the great tower. He walked in his hunched manner, his tail swishing in a steady rhythm. Pomella craned her neck, trying to take it all in.

The ground rumbled, and the soil ahead of them erupted into a massive humanoid shape. Pomella jumped back and yelped. Vlenar gave no reaction as the figure loomed over them. Steadying her tumbling nerves, she forced herself to calm. She recognized this creature.

"Welcome, Goodmiss AnDone," the Green Man said, his voice rumbling like shifting tree trunks. "I'm glad you made it safely. You are a bit early, in fact."

Relief flooded Pomella. She'd made it! She flashed the Green Man her best smile.

As before, his eyes were made from stones and his body was formed from the nearby soil. But instead of branches and leaves like she remembered him having in Oakspring, well-manicured grass now built his body. The shape of his face and his mannerisms remained the same, however.

She stared at him in wide-eyed wonder. Vlenar bowed, the tip of his face touching the grass. Pomella dropped to curtsy, suddenly aware of her absolutely filthy appearance. She'd washed most of the grime from the pit away in a creek the day the ranger found her, but her clothes and hair were still knotted and stiff. Her cloak still hadn't dried from the rain and falling in the river.

"Thank you, good Green Man," she said, not knowing the proper way to address him.

"Behold Kelt Apar," he said, sweeping a heavy arm across the clearing. "For over a thousand years the lineage of High Mystics has held presence here, tending to and protecting the Mystwood and its inhabitants. Perhaps someday that duty will become yours, so look upon it this one time with fresh, new eyes."

A warm wind blew across Pomella's face, catching her hair. On the far side of the tower a white spire peeked above the treetops. Off in the distance, an old gardener pulled weeds. A brown dog stood halfway between them and barked. Nearby, a wooden bridge spanned the river that she'd heard earlier.

The Green Man turned to Vlenar. "Mistress Yarina thanks you for delivering Goodmiss AnDone in a timely manner. The other candidates will arrive soon. Please escort them to the grounds."

Vlenar inclined his head and left. His slitted, golden eyes briefly met Pomella's as he walked past.

"He doesn't like to talk much, does he?" Pomella said before she could stop herself.

The Green Man shook with deep laughter. "Vlenar, like most rangers, finds his place in solitude. It is their job to listen, and observe, not to comment. Come, I will escort you to your dwelling. While you are here for the Trials, you may call me by my given name, Oxillian."

He walked away on long, powerful legs. Behind him, dirt and grass pushed up to fill the gaping hole he'd risen from. Pomella stared at the ground before running to catch up. "Can I call you Ox?"

Again the strange chuckling sound. "You may."

She crossed the wooden bridge, which spanned a steadily flowing river about eight feet wide. Ox walked beside the bridge, his long legs needing only two strides to cross the stream. The smell of fresh soil filled Pomella's lungs, reminding her of home, and working in the garden with Grandmhathir. Pomella gawked at everything from the Green Man to the nearby tower. Several times she dug her nails into her palm just to prove she was really here, walking with a figure of legend.

They arrived at a small cluster of low buildings with shingled roofs and glass windows. A ring of river rocks circled the modest dwellings, each of which had a tiny garden planted beside it. Seasonal vegetables were just beginning to sprout. Wooden wind chimes sounded somewhere nearby.

"Who lives here?" Pomella asked.

"As of today, you do," Ox said. "You will be joined by the other candidates. Beyond that, only Mistress Yarina and a few others occupy Kelt Apar. She has been very busy since becoming High Mystic. Once an apprentice is chosen, more will come to dwell at Kelt Apar. Ah, here we are."

Pomella stared at the cabin he stopped in front of. "Who will I share it with?"

"This one is just for you," Ox replied.

"But this is almost as big as my home in Oakspring!"

"We hope you will find it to your liking. I will let you settle in and rest from your journey. A highsun meal is ready for you within. Your first obligation will be to come to the main lawn at sunrise tomorrow, where you will present yourself to Mistress Yarina."

Pomella's stomach tumbled over itself. A hundred worries came to mind, ranging from whether she was truly ready for this experience to where she could find a bath. She took a calming breath to ease her anxiety.

"If you need anything, ring any of these bells." Ox indicated a palm-sized silver bell mounted beside the entryway to her cottage. He bowed to her, and her cheeks burned. The Green Man just *bowed* to her! Then, turning, he took three steps away from her and rumbled back into the ground, leaving no trace that he'd ever existed.

"First the Green Man, then a laghart, and now my own cabin," she mumbled under her breath. "Next, I suppose Saint Brigid will join me for dinner."

The cottage proved to be much smaller than she'd first assumed. Not that she minded. The long, rectangular room hosted a table with stone utensils and unused candles set atop it, and a thick-cushioned chair pushed in beneath. A wooden tray of mixed fruits, nuts, and vegetables sat beside a matching goblet of water on top of the table. At the far end of the room, the cottage angled to the left, revealing a narrow nook containing a wooden bed, a dresser, and a night pot.

She dumped her travel sack onto the floor, and fell back against the bed, arms wide. She sighed in contentment. A shelf laden with books caught her eye. It sat beneath one of the square glass windows. Pomella sat up; snatching a strawberry off the wooden tray, she slid onto her knees to examine the books. She grabbed one at random, a thick book of children's tales from the Continent.

Just as she opened to the first page, a knock sounded at the door, startling her. She hopped to her feet and opened the door, ready to see what else Ox needed.

She blinked.

A tall, dark-skinned boy, maybe a few years older than herself, waited outside with his hands clasped behind his back. Dark, braided hair hung past a set of broad shoulders. A crisp white shirt with loose collar strings gave her a glimpse of his broad chest, where a gold necklace—gold!—glimmered against his skin.

She stared at him, mouth open, taking in his handsome face. The boy smiled, which only made him prettier.

"You must be Pomella," he said in a thick, fluid accent. "My name is Quentin, of House Bartone. I'm from Keffra."

Pomella collected herself as best she could. The moment he'd spoken, she'd recognized the accent. He spoke with the quick, clipped sounds she associated with her grandmhathir and, to a lesser extent, her fathir. Each word part sounded musical to her, as if they were trying to somehow find a way to rhyme.

When she failed to reply, his smile slipped a little. "You *are* Pomella, right?"

"Yes," Pomella hurried. "She's me. I mean, I'm her. Bethy calls me Pom. And Ox, too. No, wait. She doesn't call me Ox. Ox calls me Pom. I think."

Her hand went to her hair as she realized it was still caked in mud. "Oh, shite, I'm making a fool of myself, aren't I?"

Quentin grinned, and a roguish gleam twinkled in his eye. "Hardly, Lady Pomella. In fact, I believe I may already adore you."

It was a miracle of the Saints her heart did not explode out of her chest. "You . . . you do?"

He shrugged. "You made me smile. That's a good way to begin a friendship, don't you think?"

"I suppose it is." Pomella took a deep breath. "Do you want to come in?"

He stepped into the cabin, looking around. "It's just like mine. So small."

Pomella quickly shoved the book of children's tales back onto the shelf. "So, um, are you one of the other . . ."

"Candidates? Yes, I am. I arrived yesterday, and my entourage left this morning. I've been bored ridiculous and've been waiting for the rest of you to arrive. You're the first besides me. I didn't see you arrive with anybody besides Oxillian, though. Where are your servants?"

"I traveled with a single escort. He left two days ago," she said. "One of the rangers, Vlenar, escorted me from Sentry."

It stretched the truth, but didn't *strictly* lie. She knew the other candidates wouldn't expect her to be a commoner, so it would be better to learn more about them before giving up that nug of information about herself. She'd find a way to explain the whole story at a more appropriate time, hopefully when she wasn't covered in mud. Besides, she didn't know if Mistress Yarina wanted her to reveal her humble upbringing.

"I see," he said. "Oxillian said you were from here on Moth?"

"Yes." She hoped he didn't press her for more.

"Your island's reputation is well known, even in Keffra. Many powerful Mystics came from here. You must be very proud to be of their nobility."

Pomella managed a weak smile. She hated being deceitful. Perhaps she should reveal the full truth.

She opened her mouth to explain, but at that moment the sound of ringing bells filled the air. They peered out the door and across the lawn, past the great stone tower. An elaborate caravan with a palanquin at its center emerged from the eastern edge of the clearing.

"Another candidate," Quentin said. "Coming from the eastern road, which means they came through Port Morrush. This must be the candidate from Djain."

Pomella watched as the palanquin entered the clearing, carried by six strong, bare-backed men. A mounted escort preceded them, the foremost of whom held a flag bearing the symbol of a golden key set against a field of red.

Ox rose up out of the ground and greeted them, although Pomella could not distinguish his words at this distance. The carriers set the palanquin down and opened the carriage door. Out stepped the most beautiful girl Pomella had ever seen. Long tresses of dark hair spilled down her back like shimmering silk. Her green embroidered dress rested off her shoulders, displaying a wealth of pale skin. Pomella sighed and fingered her muddy dress. Were all the nobility so beautiful?

Another round of bells rang, this time from the northern end of the lawn. "Another one?" she asked.

Quentin nodded. "It appears so. Oh, by the Graces, look at that. That can only be House Hanjalus."

Pomella watched as a line of at least fifty horses trotted into the clearing, each carrying an armored rider. In the center, surrounded by bannermen, rode an unhelmeted young man with perfectly styled blond hair. He held his head high, surveying the grounds and tower like a general. Moments later, his horse reared as Ox rose from the ground to greet him. The man deftly settled the animal.

"I bet they traveled overland together from Port Morrush and planned this dramatic entrance," Quentin said with a thoughtful look.

"How many candidates are there?" Pomella asked.

"I only know of four, counting you," he replied. "Decent odds, wouldn't you say?"

She laughed. "I don't think my odds are very good regardless of how many candidates show up."

His dark eyes caught hers. "You have a beautiful laugh."

Her heart hammered. It took every scrap of her will to keep her voice from trembling. "I'm . . . um, going to go bathe. I'm filthy."

The corner of his lip curled up in a small smile.

Pomella bit her lip. "Do you know where the baths are?"

He shrugged. "Just ring for Oxillian and he will draw one for you."

Before she could object, he reached out and rang the silver bell by her entrance. In the distance Ox looked toward them, and sank into the ground. A moment later, he rose up in front of the cabin.

"Yes, Quentin?" the Green Man said.

"Oxillian. Lady Pomella is feeling fatigued and road weary from her journey. Draw her a bath and bring soap. I imagine she would appreciate several draws."

"Oh, Ox, please don't trouble yourself. I can fetch my own. . . ." She trailed off as she realized that a noblewoman would never offer to haul her own water.

Ox bowed. "It will be no trouble. I will ready it immediately, Goodmiss AnDone." He stepped back into the soil, and vanished.

"Thank you," she murmured to Quentin. She noticed him staring at the place where Ox had vanished, a slight frown on his face. "What is it?"

Quentin shook his head. "It's just that he called me by my first name. I've never had a servant do that before. But I suppose that by becoming a Mystic, my old ways will have to change, right?"

Pomella nodded, but realized with alarm that the Green Man called her Goodmiss, and not Lady. "Yah, I mean, yes. But maybe he's not a servant?"

"He certainly looks like one to me."

Pomella rolled her eyes. "Let's just call him an assistant, then."

Quentin grinned. "Yes, I suppose that's fine. Enjoy your bath, Pomella-my. Maybe we can meet afterward and greet the other candidates?"

"I'd like that," she said, wondering what he meant when he

said "Pomella-my." She thought she'd seen another twinkle in his eye when he'd said it.

He bowed and left, striding over to one of the other cottages. Pomella watched him for a long moment, then closed the door and leaned her back against it, head thumping against the wood.

That boy was going to be a distraction.

SIX

THE CANDIDATES

Later that afternoon, after a luxurious bath in a tree-concealed wooden tub, Pomella toweled off her hair and put on a clean work dress. She returned to her cottage and unpacked her meager possessions, suppressing another dose of sadness as she remembered her lost *Book of Songs*.

Quentin came by, greeting her again as "Pomella-my." She decided not to question it. She liked hearing him call her that.

They walked together toward the northernmost cottages as the sun dipped below the western treetops. Two sets of guards stood outside one of the cottages. They wore heavy bronze armor and swords of the same metal at their sides.

"I don't see why they need guards," Quentin said. "Kelt Apar is protected by the High Mystic and the ceon'hur."

Pomella felt anxiety build within her as she wondered what the ceon'hur was. Once again, the worry that she wasn't ready for these Trials washed over her. She dared not ask Quentin to explain.

They approached the cottage entrance. The guards watched them, but said nothing. Pomella tried not to show her nervousness as their piercing gazes swept over her.

Quentin knocked on the door. A moment later an older, balding man opened it. He wore a black robe belted with gold silk. "Ah, my lord and lady. Lord Hanjalus and Lady Vinnay are expecting you." He opened the door wide and bowed as they entered.

The other candidates—the handsome blond-haired boy and the beautiful girl—sat on plain wooden chairs, sipping wine from crystal goblets.

The boy stood, a fine black coat covering his lanky frame. He was several years older than Pomella, with light-brown eyes and a narrow chin. A pin depicting a silver hawk clutching leaves in one talon and a knife in the other gleamed on his chest. He sipped his drink and studied them. Maybe it was his pin, but Pomella suddenly felt like a mouse being weighed by a hungry raptor.

The boy extended a hand to Quentin. "Lord Bartone," he said. "I am Saijar Hanjalus, from the Baronies of Rardaria. This is Lady Vivianna Vinnay, of Djain. I had the honor of meeting her for the first time this afternoon."

After Quentin introduced himself, Lady Vinnay rose. She had

changed out of the emerald dress she'd been wearing when she arrived, and was now wearing a low-cut maroon one. The noble-woman's long neck of pale skin led down to an ample bosom, which the dress barely concealed. "Oh, please," she said, shaking Quentin's hand, "call me Vivianna. We're all equal here."

"Until the High Mystic decides that we are not!" Saijar joked.

The noble candidates all turned to Pomella. She picked her fingernail, wondering what to say. A part of her wanted to flee from these mighty nobles, but another, growing portion was ready to stand its ground and proudly declare her common upbring-ing. But somehow, the timing didn't seem right. She needed to understand these other candidates first.

The black-robed servant appeared just then to offer her a cup of wine from a tray. She gladly took it and sipped, hoping for a surge of courage.

Quentin spoke before she did. "Lord Hanjalus and Lady Vinnay, may I present Lady Pomella . . ." He trailed off, and Pomella realized she'd never given him her surname.

"AnDone," she managed, barely preventing a dribble of wine from staining her dress. "Pomella AnDone."

"Lady AnDone is from here on Moth," Quentin said. "She walked overland with one of the laghart rangers and arrived just before you did."

"I'd always heard the Mothic commoners were hearty," Saijar said, swirling his wine. Pomella's heart raced. "But I didn't real-ize their nobility matched their ruggedness."

The bald steward bowed and slipped out the door, leaving them to their privacy. Nobody else seemed to notice him leave.

Vivianna lifted Pomella's hand, startling her. "You have lovely features. Your skin tone is simply beautiful. I've never heard of anyone from Moth having such color."

"My grandmhathir was from Keffra, Lady," Pomella replied. "I mean, Vivianna." Vivianna's smooth hands felt like silk against Pomella's calloused ones. She pulled her hand away.

"A product of mixed nobility?" Saijar sneered, disdain thick in his voice. He covered it quickly with a rigid smile. "Your homeland has such progressive . . . ideas."

"I-I suppose," Pomella said, wondering if she'd just been insulted.

"Have any of you seen the High Mystic yet?" Vivianna asked. "I'm surprised she hasn't greeted us."

Pomella shook her head. "No. But Ox, I mean, Oxillian, said she would receive us in the morning."

"That's not very considerate," Saijar said. "Tradition dictates that noble guests should be greeted as soon as they arrive."

"The Green Man greeted you," Vivianna chimed behind a cool smile as she sipped wine.

Saijar snorted. "That grassy construct? We should have been greeted by the High Mystic herself."

Quentin shrugged. "I heard she's young, and holds radical ideas."

"She'll learn quickly enough how things work," Saijar said.

Pomella couldn't believe what she was hearing. None of them had even met the High Mystic, and here they were criticizing her while each hoping to become her apprentice.

"What have you heard, Pomella?" Vivianna asked. "Surely, being from Moth, you have heard more about her?"

"Yes, tell us what you know, Pomella," Saijar pressed, taking another sip of wine.

"I-I know very little, actually," she said. "I know the previous High Mystic, Master Faywong, retired. Soon after, Mistress Yarina spent a month in contemplation. When she returned, she was anointed as our High Mystic."

"I wonder why he retired," Quentin mused. "Mystics don't do that very often."

"The High Mystic of Djain disappeared fifteen years ago," Vivianna said. "When he did, his replacement, Master Willwhite, declared him a Grandmaster who'd taken retirement."

"But nobody knew where he went?" Saijar asked.

"Indeed. He hasn't been seen since."

"Then he's probably dead. The Grandmaster title is just a formality."

"Do you think Grandmaster Faywong is dead?" Quentin asked Pomella.

They all stared at her, as if she would somehow know the answer to such an impossible question. "I never considered it," she admitted.

"He was exceptional, I can say that," Quentin added. "The Keffrican Mystics frequently sought him out for wisdom and guidance. I've heard rumors that he ranked First among all the High Mystics."

"I doubt that," Saijar said. "He was from Qin, wasn't he? Everyone knows the most powerful Mystics come from one of the larger nations."

Pomella wished she understood more of the politics and histories of the Continent. She hadn't even known that the other nations had High Mystics, let alone that there was a "First" among them. It made sense now that she knew about it, but she'd never considered it before. The High Mystic was just the person who protected the Mystwood on Moth, and that was all.

Vivianna set her glass down and stretched, arching her back and raising her arms above her head. A minor surge of jealousy washed over Pomella as Quentin and Saijar stared at Vivianna's lithe body.

"Whatever the reason," Vivianna said, completing her stretch, "I am glad Faywong retired and opened a vacancy for me to fill." She smiled sweetly.

Quentin bowed. "You will make a most excellent apprentice, and an even finer Mystic, I am sure."

"Well, it's been delightful, but I am going to retire for the evening," Vivianna said.

She slipped past Pomella but paused at the door. Turning back, Vivianna lifted the tips of Pomella's hair. "Do all noblewomen from Moth keep their hair short, like commoners?"

Cold fear gripped Pomella. "N-no."

"I knew it," Vivianna said, and blood drained from Pomella's face. "Your parents insisted you embrace this ridiculous 'humble lifestyle' that Mystics live in order to make a good impression. My mother hinted at the idea, but knew better than to actually suggest it to me."

She shook her head and let Pomella's hair drop. "I'm sorry you had to cut it."

Vivianna tapped on the door. A heartbeat later, the bald steward opened it from the outside. Vivianna leaned toward Pomella, and whispered in a tone that reminded her of Bethy, "I think they went too far in forcing you to wear that dress, though. Would you like to borrow one of mine?"

Pomella gaped, but forced herself to maintain her composure. "No. Thank you, though. I'll use what my family sent me with."

Vivianna offered the barest hint of a smile. "Very well. Good night, then."

The noblemen bowed low as Vivianna exited, and Pomella curtsied, figuring that was a safe enough gesture. Two guards bearing Vivianna's House colors escorted her into the evening.

"Well, I suppose that means this is your cottage, then," Quentin said to Saijar.

"Cottage!" Saijar scoffed. "A wooden shack at best! Had I known these would be our accommodations, I would have brought one of my family's large field tents. I might have my steward send some soldiers back to fetch it."

Pomella only had a vague idea of where the nations were in relation to one another, but she didn't think Rardaria was very close. In fact, it was probably a journey of several weeks away.

"How long are the Trials supposed to last?" she asked, risking showing some ignorance.

Saijar slumped onto the couch. "It varies," he said. "Some High Mystics like to take their time in deciding. I've heard of one who took over a year to make their decision."

"A year!" Pomella blurted.

"Saijar is speaking only of the most extreme cases," Quentin said. "Most take considerably less time. A week, or maybe two."

"I hope you're not calling me a liar," Saijar said with a smile. Despite the friendly gesture, he didn't seem amused.

"Of course not," said Quentin. "I'd never even consider it. But

I will leave you to enjoy the comforts of your *shack*." He clapped Saijar on the back. "Lady AnDone, may I escort you back to your humble dwelling?"

Pomella smiled. "Yes, please, Lord Bartone." The sun would rise in the west before she would refuse that offer.

Saijar nodded slightly, and the steward held the door. A light chill drifted in the evening air as she and Quentin strolled among the scattered cottages. High above, bright stars shone down on them, their light drowned out only by the fat gibbous moon. "Would you like to walk a bit?" he asked.

"I'd be delighted to."

He held his elbow out, and she took it, conscious of the fact that nobody had ever done this for her before. By all the Saints, she still couldn't believe she was here, walking on the arm of such a handsome nobleman.

"I think Saijar is a pile of shite," Quentin said.

Pomella gaped at him.

"What?" he said, smiling. "He's a culk. Do you disagree?"

"No. He is a culk bastard. I'm not sure he really gets the point of becoming a Mystic."

"Oh?"

"Well," fumbled Pomella, "it's just that I always thought being a Mystic was about connecting to nature and the world. Their job is to be caretakers, and to, I don't know . . . *care* about things. He only seems to care about his ability to get what he wants."

"You're probably right, Pomella-my, but all we can do is compete to the best of our ability and let Mistress Yarina decide."

Pomella nodded in agreement. They walked arm in arm past the last of the cottages, into a cluster of trees jutting out from the western edge of the forest. The path meandered through tall pines standing in soft moonlight.

"What is it?" he asked, evidently sensing her thoughts.

"Why are you so nice to me? I'm your competition for something you very much want."

He didn't immediately answer as they continued strolling. Finally, he said, "I think there's a good chance that what each of us wants will be different. Each of us came here because of tradition, or opportunity, or something else."

"So why did you come?" she asked.

"Because my family sent me."

"Tradition, then," she said.

He nodded, his gaze far away. "Yes, tradition."

"Do you *want* to be here?" she asked.

He shrugged. "It's a great honor. But if it were up to me, there're other things I'd rather do."

"Like what?"

"I'd rather not say right now."

"Oh," said Pomella, feeling awkward. A strange silence fell between them. She bit her lip. "You still didn't say why you're being so nice to me."

The corner of his mouth curled into a smile. "Do you really need me to say it aloud? I feel very connected to you. And, if I may be so bold, I find you beautiful."

Pomella's heart hammered against her chest until she was certain it would erupt. She fingered the tips of her short hair, then steadied herself, remembering she was a grown woman. "You . . . you flatter me," she managed.

"It's not flattery, Pomella-my, but the truth."

"Vivianna is beautiful, too," she said, but instantly regretted it.

"No, she's not," Quentin said without hesitation. "She may have a certain kind of beauty some men admire, but I've always been drawn to more genuine people."

Before she could think of a reply, the path opened onto a small clearing encircled by tall white stones. In the center of the clearing stood a towering obelisk, colored like bone, with letter-runes engraved in straight vertical lines along each side. In the distance to the east, MagDoon's snowcapped peak could be seen.

Pomella approached the obelisk and ran her fingers over it. Dirt and moss covered much of the obelisk, while time and weather had worn away other parts.

"There're names written here," Pomella said. "What do you think it is?"

Quentin shook his head. "I don't know."

"It feels old. Maybe even ancient."

A soft wind gusted through the clearing, chilling them.

"Maybe it's a grave," Quentin said.

"Whatever it is, it could use a shake or two of happiness around it," Pomella said.

"You could sing for it," Quentin said. "I heard you doing it earlier. While you bathed."

She snapped her gaze to him. "You . . . what?"

"Don't worry." He grinned. "It wasn't like that. I was wandering near the river and heard your voice. I admit I came a little closer, but only to hear you better."

"That's still creepy," she said, but a note of amusement betrayed her.

"Will you sing for me?"

"Here? *Now?*"

Quentin spread his arms. "You're the one who said this place 'could use a shake or two of happiness.'"

She sighed. "All right. But only because you've been so nice."

"And I called you beautiful."

Pomella grinned. "Yah, yah. Now what do you want to hear?"

He raised an eyebrow. "Surely you know something upbeat?"

Pomella bit her lip and shook her head. "Not really."

"Not even 'Boom-bung Dog-ding'?"

She burst out laughing. "Sweet Brigid! What is 'Boom-dung Dog-ding'?"

"'Boom-*bung*,'" he corrected.

She giggled so hard her side ached. "N-no, I've never heard of it."

"OK, maybe 'Boom-bung' is too silly. The warrums enjoy it."

Pomella smiled. "Warrums" was a term Grandmhathir had often used to refer to little children. Hearing Quentin say the word with his accent brought Pomella back to another time.

"It sounds wonderful," she said. "Teach it to me, please?"

Now he laughed. "Oh, no, I have no voice for singing."

"You suggested it. If you want me to sing, you have to teach me 'Boom-bung Dog-ding.' How does it start?"

"I have no idea how to find the rhythm," he said.

"Ah blather, come on," she said. "Clap the beat until you feel it. Sway your hips and clap, one at a time, until it comes to you."

She demonstrated, rocking back and forth, clapping her hands once, twice, three times.

"Boom-bung dog-ding," she sang, picking a tune at random.

He rolled his eyes and shook his head. Then, reluctantly, he clapped his hands a few times, repeating a pattern that Pomella picked up and mimicked. His shy voice sang:

> *"I woke one morn*
> *And heard him sing,*
> *'Give me a dance*
> *Or feel my sting!'*
> *Boom-bung dog-ding!*
> *Boom-bung dog-ding!"*

Pomella thought she might die of laughter.

He shook his head and waved her laughter away. "See? I told you it wasn't very good."

"Sweet Brigid, it's wonderful!" Pomella said, keeping the beat going with her claps. "Let me try." Her voice lifted, smooth like silk, repeating the lyrics.

> *"I woke one morn*
> *And heard him sing,*
> *'Give me a dance*
> *Or feel my sting!'*
> *Boom-bung dog-ding!*
> *Boom-bung dog-ding!"*

"You're much better than I," Quentin said.

"Give me the next verse," she said.

He shook his head. "I honestly can't remember it. It has something to do with the sky."

"OK, then we'll make it up as we go," she said, and sang. They clapped the beat together.

> *"I walked one noon*
> *And heard her cry,*
> *'Give me a toy*
> *Or flee the sky!'*
> *Boom-bung dog-bye!*
> *Boom-bung dog-bye!"*

Quentin's smile set her heart racing again. She spread her arms and twirled. Quentin kept the beat. As she sang, the clearing seemed to grow brighter.

> *"I ran one night*
> *And heard them wail,*
> *'Give me a kiss*
> *Or hang the scale!'*
> *Boom-bung dog-ale!*
> *Boom-bung dog-ale!"*

For the first time in a long time, Pomella felt her worries melt away. She was just about to start a new stanza when she caught sight of a pair of glowing eyes behind the obelisk. She stopped dancing. The song died on her lips.

"What's wrong?" Quentin asked.

The eyes slid closed and vanished.

"I saw a pair of eyes over there," she replied.

Quentin looked from her to the obelisk. He approached, and looked behind it. "I don't see anything. An animal perhaps?"

Pomella knew it wasn't an animal. At least, not a normal one. Those eyes had belonged to some kind of silver animal, and they'd been looking at her hungrily.

Seeing Quentin's confused expression, she smiled to dismiss his worry. "Let's walk back to the cabins," she said.

She took his arm and walked to her cottage. She didn't dare look back over her shoulder. Instead, she tried to focus on other things. Like Quentin. Pomella snuck little glances at him that she hoped he wouldn't notice. His rugged looks, exotic eyes, and heartwarming accent all mixed together beautifully.

When they arrived at her cabin, Quentin dipped a small bow to her. "Good night, Pomella-my. I will see you tomorrow." He kissed her trembling fingertips, and Pomella vowed silently to all the Saints she would never pick them again. She wanted him to kiss a lot more than her fingertips, however.

A small smile lingered on his lips, then he strode away without looking back before she could invite him to stay longer. She watched him until he was out of sight. She went into her cottage and flopped onto the bed. Exhaustion rolled over her, but too many thoughts filled her mind for sleep, most of them related to Quentin, and not all of them chaste.

But memories of Sim crept in as well. Quentin had called her beautiful, but Sim had followed her into the Mystwood. Sim knew her better than anyone, and that counted for something. If Quentin was a fine noble feast, Sim was comforting stew beside a warm fire.

Thinking of food made her stomach rumble. She poked her chin up and saw a covered plate sat on the table. She went over and found a meal consisting of more vegetables and warm bread. Twin-sized slabs of cheese and butter sat beside it, along with some stone utensils.

She dug in, and found herself wondering if Quentin suspected she was a commoner. She prayed to the Saints he didn't. She thought of her Springrise dress, which she'd carefully packed and intended to wear when she met Mistress Yarina. Then she remembered Vivianna's dress, and its brightly colored silk.

She gulped the rest of her food. Throwing her cloak over her shoulders, she hurried to the cluster of other cabins. She didn't know which one Vivianna was in, but didn't have to look long because she recognized the guards outside one of the doors.

"I need to speak to Lady Vivianna," she said.

The guard bowed. "She is asleep, Lady. We should not wake her."

Pomella took a breath. She might just be a commoner, but this guard didn't know it. She mustered her most commanding voice. "I understand your concern. Please rouse her."

The guard bowed, then turned and knocked before slipping inside. Pomella momentarily felt bad for the man. She hoped Vivianna wouldn't get upset with him. Or her.

The guard returned a moment later, standing at strict attention. Vivianna stood in the entrance with a thick fur blanket over her shoulders. Circles stood out beneath her eyes.

"What is it?" Vivianna asked.

Pomella took a deep breath. She was committed now.

"Actually, I *will* borrow a dress."

SEVEN

THE FIRST TRIAL

A thin mist hovered over Kelt Apar in the pre-dawn light. Standing on the damp lawn near the stone tower, Pomella wrapped her arms around herself and shivered. She wore the dress she and Vivianna had chosen for her a mere few hours before. The red silk brushed her skin in a pleasant way, so much that she constantly found herself feeling its smooth edges with her fingertips. She'd never before been allowed to wear anything like this. Two of Vivianna's attendants had worked to loosen it slightly to account for Pomella's wider hips, but the rest fit well enough.

She adjusted her bosom, where it *especially* fit. Bethy would've been proud.

Her teeth chattered from the chilly air as she waited alone on the lawn. At least, she assumed it was the cold, and not her increasing nervousness. She wished she had her cloak for its warmth and familiarity.

The stone tower loomed above her, its roughly hewn walls rising through the drifting fog. Lights shone in some of the windows, building her anticipation.

Perhaps she'd come too early? She looked toward the cottages and saw Saijar and Vivianna approaching, but no sign of Quentin. Saijar carried some kind of a stringed instrument partially wrapped with a blanket. She wondered what it could be. Oakspring didn't have many musical instruments like that.

Vivianna wore one of the dresses Pomella had wanted to try on, a sturdy blue one with beautiful cream-colored accents. It was nowhere near as low cut as the one Vivianna had worn the night before, nor as accentuating as the one Pomella wore now.

She tensed as the other candidates joined her. They formed a line, standing shoulder to shoulder. Saijar wore a black suit with brightly polished silver buttons running down the front. His matching pin shone on his chest, right above his heart. He openly started at her, measuring her within the dress. A tiny smile crossed Vivianna's face, but she said nothing.

They waited in silence until Pomella's curiosity got the better of her. "Do you know where Quentin is?"

"No. But he will be here," Saijar said, not looking at her. "He would be a fool to be late."

As if on cue, Quentin dashed out from the cottages, still fastening a wide leather belt. He settled beside Saijar, on the opposite end of the line from Pomella. He leaned forward and looked across the other two candidates toward her. He grinned. She smiled back.

They waited in silence. The air brightened as the sun rose. Pomella picked at her dress sleeve. Saijar frowned as he shifted from foot to foot. A bark broke the silence and Pomella saw a large brown dog lope over to them. He barked again, playfully, his tongue hanging out.

"Go away, mutt," Saijar grumbled, but not loudly, as if he was afraid the dog might bite him. The dog barked again, crouching on his front paws, clearly wanting to play.

A shrill whistle called from across the lawn. The dog sprinted toward a large willow tree standing a short distance away. A figure with a wide-brimmed hat stood beneath the tendril-like branches of the tree, holding a rake. As the dog joined him, he bent over to ruffle the animal's fur. The dog leaped up affectionately and bumped the man's hat off. From this distance, Pomella could see the man was older, and had a shaved head.

Saijar craned his neck in the direction of the willow. "Who's that?"

"Probably the gardener," Vivianna said, also glancing in that direction. "I saw him raking when we arrived yesterday. He looks Unclaimed. I've heard some Mystics will actually take them in."

Pomella's stomach lurched. The memory of the Unclaimed beneath the old shrine made her uneasy. Generally, people only became Unclaimed as the result of punishment, doled out at a whim by the nobility or Mystics. It didn't help knowing that she could soon become one.

The ground shook, tearing her thoughts and attention away

from the gardener and the willow tree. Oxillian erupted out of the soil, pulling up the grass to form a cloak, hood, and beard. "Arise and lift your hearts," he said. "Mistress Yarina, High Mystic of Moth, comes!"

In the distance, the door at the base of the stone tower opened just as the sun lifted above the treetops. Warm light spread across the lawn, and Pomella wondered if it came from the sun or the open door.

A tall, graceful silhouette emerged and glided toward them. A tingle rippled across Pomella's skin. The High Mystic walked completely at ease, moving as slowly and surely as a drifting cloud. She carried her traditional wooden staff, gnarled and as tall as she could reach, and wore a long light-blue gown with a wide trailing hem. A wreath of tiny white flowers held her long black hair up in an elaborate weave above her head. Her slippered feet left no discernible footprints, as if she walked above the ground and not on it.

The High Mystic kept her eyes forward, never looking directly at Pomella or the other candidates. The ground rose as she approached, reacting to her presence, forming a gentle hill. She faced the candidates at last, and an ornate throne of grass, soil, and flowers blossomed beneath her. Without looking at it, she sat and crossed one leg over the other, her arms easing onto the soft armrests.

Excitement rippled through Pomella. Mistress Yarina was radiant beyond words. A subtle pattern of lotus flowers decorated her blue-and-cream-colored robes, which moved as smoothly as a flower in the the wind. Wide, voluminous sleeves cascaded down her arms. Her blue eyes scanned the candidates, and

Pomella felt the power in them as they drifted across her. She noticed the High Mystic's skin, which was a creamy brown, and not more than a few shades darker than her own.

Quentin fell to a knee, followed by Saijar. Vivianna curtsied, and Pomella copied her, keeping her eyes low.

Oxillian lumbered over to stand between Yarina and the candidates, but did not block her view of them. "Candidates!" he boomed. "Rise. You stand in the presence of the High Mystic of Moth."

They stood, and Pomella felt a lump rise in her throat. *Here* was a truly powerful and beautiful woman, beyond any of the nobles Pomella had ever seen.

"Welcome to Kelt Apar," the High Mystic said, and her voice filled the clearing like chimes on a crisp day. "I thank you for coming, and commend you for taking the long journey. After carefully considering applications from noble families as far away as the East Continent, I have selected you four to attend these Trials. This is an old tradition, dating back to the earliest High Mystics of Moth. I hope you understand the honor it is to be here. You stand on hallowed ground in the heart of the Mystwood, where the Myst flows free and deep."

"Step forth, one by one, and declare your intent!" Oxillian called.

Pomella's heart skipped. She didn't know the formalities. Were there certain words she was expected to say?

Quentin leaped forward and knelt, his right knee pressing into the ground. "Mistress Yarina, thank you for receiving me. I am Quentin Bartone, of your homeland of Keffra. I seek to become your apprentice."

Pomella's eyes widened. The High Mystic was also from Keffra! That was certainly a clip in Quentin's favor.

Yarina nodded to him. "The Bartone family has produced some of history's finest Mystics. I am delighted to see you here."

Quentin returned to his place in line. Vivianna stepped forth next, and curtsied. Pomella noticed the blue and cream shades of her dress perfectly matched Yarina's. Had Vivianna known what Yarina would wear? If so, how? Pomella suddenly felt even more disadvantaged than before.

"Mistress Yarina, your grace and power inspire me. I am Vivianna Vinnay, and I seek to become your apprentice."

"Welcome, Lady Vinnay," Yarina said. "Your family spoke very highly of your affinity for the Myst when they wrote me. I look forward to seeing you demonstrate it."

Sweat formed along Pomella's hairline. Vivianna slipped back to her place in line. Saijar strode forward with his instrument and bowed. "High Mystic Yarina," he said, puffing his chest out. "I am Saijar Hanjalus of the Baronies of Rardaria. I have come to your dwelling per the old agreement made by my ancestors to learn the ways of the Myst. I wish to become your apprentice, the sun and Myst willing."

He readied his instrument by removing the blanket and lifting it to his collarbone, then pulled a long wooden bow across the strings. A violin, Pomella recognized. She'd never seen one before, but was familiar with how they were supposedly played.

Saijar closed his eyes and deftly slid the rod across the strings, slowly at first and then with increased energy. The music added a pleasant warmth to the chill morning. Pomella found herself enjoying the tune. Just as her mind drifted and she began to wonder what lyrics she could sing to such a song, a thin weave of silver light formed above the violin, shaping itself into a vague bird shape. Saijar peeked his eye open and increased the pace of the song. He nudged the bird forward as he played, prompting it to flutter toward the High Mystic. Pomella's eyes popped. He'd just created something with the Myst! She felt her inadequacy double.

The bird drifted toward Yarina, but Oxillian reached out a hand and gently snuffed it out. Saijar ended his song and bowed again, violin and bow spread wide.

"I acknowledge your fulfillment of the old agreements and welcome you," Yarina said, nodding him back into line.

The absence of Saijar's music emphasized the silence across the lawn. Pomella squeezed her eyes shut and prayed to the Saints for bravery.

She stepped forward, stumbling into a curtsy. "I-I am Pomella AnDone," she said, her voice quavering. "And I—I am over-whelmed." She bit her lip, silently chastising herself for saying something so stupid. She rushed on, hoping to just finish it. "I would like to become your apprentice, should you find me worthy." She peeked up, and saw Yarina's blue eyes pound through her.

"Thank you for accepting my invitation on such short notice," Yarina said. "I am pleased to host a common candidate for the first time in our recorded history. The garden outside your home is spoken fondly of in several villages here on Moth."

The blood drained from Pomella's face. She couldn't help but look back at Quentin, whose eyes widened with surprise. Vivianna's jaw dropped. One of Saijar's fists clenched. Pomella swallowed her fear and stepped back into line. The urge to lower her head swept over her. She imagined each of them, especially Quentin, glaring at her. She'd lied to them. She knew it, no matter how much she rationalized to herself that she just had let them convince themselves of something they assumed. Here on this early morning, Mistress Yarina had revealed the truth Pomella had feared to say aloud. Perhaps that was a lesson in itself. She glanced up to meet Yarina's gaze. The High Mystic watched her carefully. Pomella hardened her expression. She would never deceive anyone again, especially in this woman's domain. Flexing her fingers, Pomella held her chin high. Let them look at her. She was here on fair terms.

Still, it was hard not to feel inadequate when all she had to compare to Quentin's legendary family legacy was an overgrown garden back home.

The Green Man squared his bulk to the candidates. "You have each declared your intent to become Mistress Yarina's apprentice. Your applications are accepted. By tradition, because there is more than one candidate, the High Mystic offers you an opportunity to prove your worth by competing in three Trials. Based on the outcome of those tasks, she will select one of you to become her apprentice, and give you your Mystic name. Her decision shall be final and exempt from appeal."

Pomella risked a quick glance at the other candidates. They all faced Yarina, backs straight. She noticed a tightening around Quentin's jaw. She hoped to Brigid he would listen to her explain the situation. She began to think of what she would say.

"Beginning immediately," the Green Man continued, "during the days in which you are involved with the Trials, you are to remain within the boundaries of Kelt Apar unless given permission to leave. You will live within the dwellings provided, and keep no outside assistants, advisors, or guardians. You are to complete these Trials alone, with the exception that you may help one another if you choose. You are cautioned to remember, however, that the High Mystic will only select *one* of you. Failure to abide by these terms will result in your dismissal. Do you all understand and agree to this?"

Pomella managed to reply "yes" along with the others. Oxillian looked to Yarina for confirmation, and she nodded, still quietly scanning each candidate. The Green Man turned back to them. "It is agreed. Your first Trial begins now."

He stepped back and Yarina raised her voice. "Since our arrival at Moth, in a time forgotten by most people, we Mystics have tended the Mystwood and its inhabitants. The threats challenging us over the centuries have been great and varied. Now we are faced with a new one."

Pomella shifted uncomfortably.

"There is poison in the Mystwood," Yarina continued, "and it clouds our perception of activity. Three days ago, one of the rangers found a black bear near the northern border. The poor creature had succumbed to severe iron poisoning. Yesterday, an entire family of deer were found. I examined the bodies and determined that they died the same way. Trees and other plant life, too, have drunk tainted water and rotted. But most disturbing of all is that this poison is somehow affecting the fay as well. It corrupts them, drawing them into this world, and drives them mad."

Pomella wondered what the fay were. She glanced at the other candidates to see if they looked as confused as she felt.

"I possess the means to treat all of these animals with a salve," Yarina said. "But my supplies have dwindled, and the key component is only found by those who possess the skills of Mystics."

A patch of ground near Pomella's feet churned. Startled, she took half a step back. A pillar of soil rose from the grass, twisting around itself, clutching a shimmering object at its peak. Similar pillars appeared in front of the other candidates.

"Fay blood," said the High Mystic. "Go into the Mystwood, no more than an hour's walk from the tower, and find one of the fay. Do not harm it, but demonstrate your affinity for the Myst to convince it to offer a few drops of its blood into these glass vials."

Praying her hand wouldn't shake, Pomella reached out and accepted the vial. As she took it, the pillar of soil rolled back into the ground, leaving no evidence of its existence.

Yarina went on. "Here on this island, more so than anywhere else in the world, the veil between worlds is thin. Legend has it that first humans noticed this phenomenon when they saw a silvery moth fluttering in on the shores near where they had arrived. The moth led them to the heart of the Mystwood, where it alighted upon a stone that eventually became the foundation of our tower."

Realization of what the fay were swept over Pomella. The translucent animals she sometimes saw in the forest. The strange wolves she and Sim had encountered. So they had a name, besides just "silver animals." Pomella gazed once more at the central tower, and found herself wondering what it would've been like to be the first person to arrive here, from a distant land, following a misty moth.

"Go now," said Yarina. "Know that the Myst is unveiled by each one of us through our natural talents. Let it shine forth, and it will lead you. Return before sunset to complete this first Trial."

Yarina stood and glided down the hill back toward the stone tower. Pomella and the others bowed or curtsied as she passed. The hill rumbled and sank back into the ground. They watched her re-enter the tower, and the green door closed behind her.

Oxillian spoke one last time. "Be careful in the forest. The Myst stirs of late." With that, the ground rumbled and he slid back into it, leaving Pomella alone with the other candidates.

Off in the distance, the brown dog barked.

Vivianna rounded on Pomella. "You're a *commoner*?"

"I should have known the moment I saw you," Saijar sneered, his lip curling in disgust. "How dare you?"

"Mistress Yarina *invited* me," Pomella said, sounding more confident than she felt.

"So you just accepted knowing it spit in the face of a thousand years of tradition?" Vivianna said, crossing her arms.

"Disgusting," said Saijar. "Not to mention that Yarina will make everything easier for you. It's an unfair advantage and I shall inform my father regardless of who is chosen."

"You think I have an *advantage*?" Pomella blurted.

"Let's just go find the blood," Saijar said, and pulled Vivianna's arm away.

Vivianna paused beside Pomella. "You lied to me. I thought—" She caught herself and adjusted a loose strand of hair, then followed Saijar.

Pomella watched them go, fuming. She looked at Quentin, daring him with a hard expression to say something negative about her caste. But for all her outward determination, she prayed to the Saints he wouldn't reject her. Without him, she would be utterly alone. Until this moment she hadn't realized how terrifying the idea was. Even when she'd set out from Oakspring, a part of her had been worried about taking the path by herself. It's why in her heart she'd wanted Sim there, and why Vlenar had been such a welcome companion, despite his silence. Now, faced with the first Trial, she needed someone. Not because she couldn't succeed by herself, but because the thought of being in this alone made her sick.

The cool morning breeze swept her hair, and she tucked it behind her ear. Quentin met her gaze, then sighed. "I don't see anything common about you."

Relief washed over her like rain. "Thank you." It was all she could do to keep from throwing her arms around him.

He stepped toward her. "But you didn't have to lie to me."

"I know, and I'm truly sorry. It's just that you're—"

"I understand," he said, cutting her off. "You're in a difficult position. Just promise me you won't do it again."

"I promise."

"Besides," he added with a smile, "I sort of suspected."

Pomella's stomach turned over. "You did? How? Was it because I was so nervous?"

He shrugged. "No, it wasn't that. All of us are nervous. I saw Vivianna dry heaving this morning before she came out."

Pomella had felt like vomiting herself this morning. She couldn't imagine Vivianna being that scared.

"It wasn't even your clothes. It was how you wore them, and how you cast your eyes downward whenever one of us spoke to you for the first time. I'm surprised the others didn't suspect, although now I'm sure they'll say they did."

"I don't feel like I should be here," Pomella said. She forced herself to not look away or lower her eyes. "Not just because of my caste, but because you're all so talented. That bird Saijar created . . . what was that? How did he do it? Can *you* do things like that?"

"People like Saijar have been trained in apprentice-level Mysticism since they were young. Some noble families even employ Mystics to train them in hopes that a High Mystic will one day seek an apprentice."

"Were you trained?" Pomella asked.

Quentin shrugged. "A little, but it's been a while since I had an actual Mystic for a teacher. But don't worry; I don't think Mistress Yarina expects any of us to actually be able to use the Myst."

"I hope not. If she does, then I definitely have no chance."

"Well, right now we just need to find a special, mystical animal or whatever and convince it to give us some blood. That might be a bit awkward," he said with a wry smile.

"We?"

Quentin smiled. "Of course. Oxillian said we could work together. Do you not want to?"

"No, no!" Pomella said. "I'd love to work with you. I just thought . . . I mean, we're sort of competing against each other now."

Despite his words, Pomella still feared that Quentin wouldn't want to be near her. Standing in Vivianna's dress made her feel like an impostor.

"Yes, we're competing, but there will be plenty of time to distinguish ourselves. For now, I'd like to enjoy your company."

She smiled at him. "So where do we find a silvery, uh, fay creature?"

He shrugged. "I have no idea. Pick a direction." He swept his arm wide, indicating the towering trees lining the grounds.

She laughed and covered her eyes, spinning and pointing at random.

"Northeast it is!" Quentin said, and strode in that direction.

Stilling her nerves, Pomella followed.

EIGHT

THE GARDEN

Pomella shivered as she stepped out of the early-morning sunlight into the shaded cover of the Mystwood. Tendrils of mist drifted around her, their movements disturbed only by her breath.

"Where do you think we should go now?" she asked.

Quentin scratched his jaw. Pomella couldn't help but admire his strong features. Back home, there were some attractive boys her age, Sim included, and a few older than her who were spoken for. In Oakspring, no one made it far into adulthood before marrying. She'd seen ruggedly handsome men pass through with the spring merchants, and even a dashing young nobleman in a carriage once. But all of them paled in comparison to Quentin's broad shoulders and smile.

"You're from this island," Quentin said. Pomella realized she was staring and snapped her attention away from him. "Do you know where we can find some of the fay?"

Pomella shook her head. She thought of the wolves she and Sim had encountered, and hoped she wouldn't run into another pack like that. "I've never been this far into the Mystwood. The few times I've seen them, they didn't exactly come when I called."

"Then along the river is as good a direction as any other."

They pressed into the forest, drifting toward the sound of the river. Birdsong and leaf fall filled the otherwise silent woods. Squirrels and other critters scampered about in the branches above.

"How exactly *did* Saijar make that bird appear in the air?" Pomella asked.

"He Unveiled the Myst," Quentin said.

"Unveiled?"

"It's a term Mystics use to mean creating phenomena with the Myst. Mistress Yarina used the term this morning. Like I said, Saijar's been trained, so he probably worked on that little illusion for a long time in preparation for today. I doubt he knows much else."

"But *how* did he make it?" Pomella asked, thinking of the wind flower Lady Elona had conjured at the Springrise festival.

Quentin shrugged. "Everyone is different. It has something to do with expressing yourself through an action. I was never good at it in my lessons. Some people play music, like Saijar did. Some people paint. Some people chant. You start off doing what feels natural to you and over time that becomes your way of Unveiling. From there, Mystics learn to internalize it until they can Unveil without needing to do those things externally."

Pomella nodded as though she understood. "What's yours?" she asked. "Your Unveiling, I mean."

Quentin eyed her. "It's considered impolite to ask."

"Oh, I'm sorry, I didn't know—"

"I'm just teasing you," he said, smiling.

She smacked his shoulder. "Tell me!"

He shrugged. "I don't like to talk about it. Like I told you, becoming a Mystic isn't exactly my first choice in life."

Pomella frowned. "Why don't you just quit? Tell Mistress Yarina you don't want to be her apprentice."

"It doesn't work that way," he said. "In Keffra, family comes above all else, even personal desires. To *not* strive to become the High Mystic's apprentice would be to insult my ancestors and living relatives."

"I see. I'm sorry," she murmured. "I shouldn't have questioned your dedication."

He shrugged and waved her off. "I may not be striving as hard as I possibly could at the moment, though."

"So do you have an Unveiling?" she asked.

He shrugged. "I think so."

"What is it?"

He looked around as if to ensure they were alone. Sighing, he began to unlace his shirt collar. "It's harder in this shirt."

Pomella stared in surprise as he lifted his long shirt up over his head. She blinked as he stuffed it into her arms. A series of tattoos stood out against the brown skin of his left shoulder, running down his well-muscled torso and onto his rib cage. Pomella had never seen anything like them before, and found herself wanting to see more.

He stepped away from her, hands at his sides. For a moment, nothing moved except the fog. Pomella wondered if she should look away. Not that anything could *make* her do so.

Quentin moved, leaning to the side and raising both arms above his head. He shifted again, swinging his arms in a graceful arc and bringing one leg up, toes pointed down. Then he began to fight. At least, that's what it looked like to Pomella. He moved like a fish in water, like a willow in the wind. Swaying, shifting, twisting in a hard, almost sensual way. His open palms struck the air with such ferocity that the air seemed to *snap*. He leaped, and both legs twisted like a whirlwind before landing in a solid stance. Pomella watched him, transfixed. Could this man do anything poorly? Her heart thundered to the unheard music of his motion.

Finally, he came to a stop with a final finishing stance, and bowed to her. She stared, dumbfounded, before remembering to breathe again. She quickly tucked his shirt under her arm and clapped. "That was . . . amazing," she said, trying not to be distracted by his muscular chest. Unbidden, she thought of Sim, with his toned blacksmith arms. Sim might be strong, too, but he'd never done what Quentin had just done.

Quentin wiped his brow as he approached her. A sheen of sweat covered his skin. "Thank you."

She mumbled something like a blathering dunder about thanking him, then handed him his shirt, but he didn't put it on right away. He nodded his head toward the nearby river to indicate they should continue.

Pomella forced herself to look at his face and not get lost in his tattooed body. "It was a wonderful dance, but, forgive me, I don't see what that has to do with the Myst."

He shrugged in his characteristic way. "Nothing, maybe. Mastering the movements of the *kenj* is an old tradition in my family. I began learning when I was four years old. It's what I do best, and therefore is how I Unveil the Myst. Or so my old teacher told me."

"Did you use the Myst then? Did it do anything?"

He looked at her. "It changed your hair red."

Without thinking, she put her hand to her hair and pulled a strand to look at it. Quentin burst out laughing.

She smacked him again, harder this time.

"I don't know if I Unveiled anything," Quentin said. "The Myst isn't always about making pretty birds like Saijar did. I simply performed the *kenj* and if the Myst wanted to do something with that, then it was free to. It is said that the island of Moth, and Kelt Apar specifically, is one of the strongest places in the world to Unveil the Myst."

The forest sloped downward until they approached the river flowing at the bottom of a shallow ravine. The tree line inched all the way to the water's edge, with a couple of trees dipping their roots directly into the current. The afternoon sun cast a radiant glow on everything.

"There's nothing here," Quentin said. "Let's follow the river north."

Movement caught Pomella's eye.

"Shush," she said, holding her hand up. She pointed behind him, using slow movement.

A huge, silver animal resembling a deer, glowing with wispy light, burst from the underbrush. It thrashed its antlered head, kicked its hind legs, and tumbled to the ground.

"Shite, Quentin, look at it! Can you see it?" Pomella asked, remembering that Sim hadn't been able.

The elk crashed around on the ground between bushes, but failed to disturb a single leaf. It was strange to see it thrashing without disturbing the normal forest around them.

Quentin's body tensed. He nodded. "Yes, it looks like an ancient kind of elk. My family used to hunt them before they vanished. I've never seen one so large alive."

An unexpected lump formed in Pomella's throat. The validation that somebody else could see fay creatures lifted her heart.

"What do you think is wrong with it?" Pomella asked.

"I don't know," Quentin said. "Maybe it has iron poisoning like Mistress Yarina talked about. Let's try and get its blood."

Before Pomella could protest, Quentin moved toward the deer. Uncertain, she followed. "How're you going to get its blood?" she said. "Do you have a knife? Will it even work on them?"

Pomella jumped as the deer lurched to its feet and seemed to look right through them. A second later, its smoky eyes focused on them, and it bolted away.

"Damn," Quentin said. "I think we scared it."

"I saw other animals like that when I was coming to Kelt Apar," Pomella said. "Some wolves actually chased me."

Quentin stared at her in surprise. "They chased you?"

She nodded and would have said more, but a harsh cry interrupted. Quentin heard it, too, and peered through the trees. Another silver animal, a crow this time, snapped its wings in the air near a berry bush. It screeched in anger, its smoky wings striking the air aggressively. A feather shook itself loose and vanished like mist under the sun.

Near the crow, a silver hummingbird dove again and again, trying to drive it off.

Pomella ventured a smile. Despite the odd behavior of the fay creatures she'd encountered so far, it delighted her that she was seeing so many of them in the Mystwood.

A sense of panic radiated from the bush. It washed over Pomella in a way she couldn't explain. Without thinking, she hurried to the bush and swatted her arms at the crow. "Go on! Get out of here!"

The crow flapped and cawed in defiance before flying away, cursing as it went.

The silver hummingbird buzzed past Pomella's head, trailing smoky mist and vibrating her ear. She ducked.

"Hey! I was only trying to help!"

"Look," Quentin said, pointing at the bush.

Pomella saw nothing special about it other than the hummingbird swooping frantically. Little pink berries dotted the bush, ripe and ready to be plucked. The hummingbird dove past her again.

"I'm just looking," she told the bird, feeling only a little silly for talking to an animal.

Deep in the bush, hidden behind leaves and berries, was what the crow had been seeking. A little nest, no wider than the cup of Pomella's hand, held two baby hummingbirds. They looked mature enough to possibly fly, with their feathers newly grown and shimmering a vibrant silver. They fought for space in the tiny nest, nudging each other and occasionally flapping their wings as if testing their capabilities.

"I see the wee ones," she said to Quentin. "They're all right." She wondered if they somehow had called to her. What else could that sense of panic from a moment ago have been?

Pomella stared as the mhathir bird landed on a branch next to the overcrowded nest. The mhathir stuck her beak into one baby's mouth, followed by the other. Pomella watched in fascination.

Quentin peered over her shoulder. "Should I get their blood or will you?"

Pomella gaped at him. "Don't you dare touch these birds!"

"But—"

"They're wee babies! You'll kill them if you try to get any of their blood!"

Quentin gave her a flat stare.

"You're not touching them, Quentin. We'll find another fay creature, one that won't die if we take some of its blood. We're supposed to be protecting them, not skewering them!"

Quentin shrugged. "As you wish. Hopefully we'll encounter more of the fay before it gets dark."

The larger of the young birds stretched his wings and buzzed them, but kept his feet on the edge of the nest. Not wanting to be outdone, the other bird hopped onto the edge of the nest and buzzed her wings as well. Jealous of his sibling, the first bird pushed the other with his beak. With a sudden leap that startled Pomella, the little hummingbird flew out of the bush, brushing her hair as it passed. The other baby followed, enraged that the other accomplished flight before him.

The two hummingbirds swirled around each other. Pomella stared in wonder. Their wings hummed in unison, speaking to her in a way that almost seemed familiar. Their trails of mist made it seem like a silver circle spun in the air. Her heart raced with excitement as if she were flying for the first time herself. She longed to spread her own arms and join them.

"Are you all right?" Quentin asked.

"Did you *see* that?" she marveled. "They just flew for the first time!"

"How do you know it was for the first time?"

She paused. "I don't know. It just seemed that way, I guess."

He walked away, heading west toward the river. "Well, that's all very nice. But we should get going."

The mhathir hummingbird raced over to Pomella and hovered in front of her face. The babies tumbled above them, wrestling in their own way. Before Pomella could react, the mhathir flew away, heading east. She paused in midair, waiting for her babies to follow. They did, but still the mhathir waited.

"I-I think we should follow them," Pomella said, feeling a bit silly.

Quentin stepped beside her and looked at the hummingbird, who waited patiently. "How do you know?"

Pomella shook her head. "I don't know. I'm probably being a dunder."

Quentin continued to eye the bird. "She *is* acting a bit unusual. I think we should follow your instinct."

"Really? Y-you believe me?"

"Of course. Besides, any direction is as good as another right now. Let's see where it leads."

Pomella smiled. It was refreshing to have somebody believe her, without her having to fight and plead for their understanding.

She and Quentin followed the ghostlike hummingbirds, who zoomed ahead. Occasionally the mhathir stopped at a tree, or patch of flowers, where she and the babies would sip on some unseen food. Pomella couldn't shake the fresh feeling of excitement coming from the babies, nor the sense of wide-eyed wonder she heard in their movements.

It made no sense. Yet here she was, following these strange silvery birds deeper into the forest, dragging Quentin with her.

She startled as Quentin gently touched her arm. He put his finger to his lips and gestured, *Quiet*. Pomella listened. She heard the hummingbirds swooping ahead and above them, but nothing else. Focusing more, she listened to the sounds of the forest. She was about to open her mouth to ask Quentin what he meant when she heard it. Running water. They must be near another stream.

The hummingbirds darted ahead once more, heading toward the sound of water. Pomella hurried after them, with Quentin following. A building sense of urgency filled her. The baby hummingbirds seemed less playful now, and more curious, following their mhathir.

They broke into a small clearing, in the center of which stood a quiet pond, fed by a small spring trickling steadily out of a boulder. Tall grass, foxtail weeds, and wild shamrock grew at the water's edge. A large tree, dripping with vines and dangling branches, shaded the pond.

Resting atop the gently rippling surface was a sprinkling of lotus flowers. Three silver swans drifted between them, mist wafting off of them, their bodies not rippling the water.

Pomella's face blossomed with a smile and she felt the hummingbirds echo her joy. The lotus flowers seemed to shine with a light all their own, as if each housed a wee sun within its petals. She took a step toward the pond, but Quentin grabbed her arm.

"Wait," he said, his eyes intent on the water and the tree above it.

Silvery mist hung above the water, with all three hummingbirds flying through it. The babies chased each other away from the pond toward distant trees. The mhathir hovered above one of the lily pads and dipped her beak to drink the nectar.

A flash of searing fire erupted across the pond.

Sheets of silvery fire tore outward, scorching Pomella. She screamed and dove to the ground. Quentin landed beside her, his arm trying to cover her. She gasped for breath, trying to find air that wasn't searing.

Pomella lifted her head and blinked to clear her vision. A heavy stillness fell across the clearing. A ringing filled Pomella's ears. Eyes watering, she peered around.

The pond lay undisturbed except for the silver swans and mhathir hummingbird, which were gone. Pomella stood on wobbling legs. Her dress—Vivianna's dress—dripped with mud. Pomella felt no physical pain, except for a dull ache in her hip. Quentin groaned and pushed himself up.

A massive silver snake, wider than Pomella's leg, lowered

itself from the tree, its forked tongue zipping out to taste the air. Misty flames danced atop it as if it were on fire, but the burning did not appear to cause it pain.

Pomella's eyes widened as two thin forelegs unfolded from the snake's body, each dipping into the pond to support its great weight. Whatever sort of creature this was, it was more than a mere snake. A glowing diamond shape stood out on its forehead. Slitted eyes fixed on Pomella.

"What's this?" it asked. The ringing in Pomella's ears slowly faded. Its mouth did not move, but the voice clearly emanated from the snakelike creature. "A new face walks these woods? Welcome, young Mystic."

The baby hummingbirds swooped down, whirling in desperate circles above the snake. It raised its head and gazed toward them, flicking its tongue hungrily.

"L-leave them alone," Pomella said, stepping forward.

The snake considered her. "What? These morsels?"

Quentin's hand touched Pomella's shoulder. "We should leave. We're in danger."

"You should listen to the young man," said the snake, amused. "I *am* dangerous."

Pomella pulled away from Quentin and addressed the snake. Her heart raced as she registered the fact that she was *talking* to an animal. "Why did you attack us?"

"This is my pond and tree," it said.

"You hurt my friend and me!" Pomella said. "And you killed their mhathir!" She jabbed her finger at the hummingbirds.

"Pomella . . . ," Quentin urged.

A strange sound rippled from the snake and Pomella realized it was laughing. "Are you sure you are a Mystic? You have much still to learn."

Pomella swallowed. "We came looking for something. Perhaps you can help us."

The snake lowered itself farther from the tree, and stepped lightly through the still water. Its head slid through the air, independently of the rest of its body. Pomella gaped at its massively long form, which wound throughout the branches of the tree.

"What do you offer in return?" it asked.

"I don't think I have anything you'd want," she said.

The snake tilted its head back and forth, peering at her. "All those who use the Myst have something to give."

Pomella exchanged looks with Quentin, who gave her a hint of a shrug.

"We're not Mystics," she said. "We're candidates to become the High Mystic's apprentice."

"Ah," said the snake. "I see. Then I forgive your ignorance. That you can even see me is special indeed."

"It is?"

"Only those who touch the Myst can see the inhabitants of Fayün."

"Fayün?"

The snake's face slithered to within her arm's reach, its body stretched across the whole pond. Fear pumped through Pomella's veins as it slinked toward her face.

Quentin put a protective hand on Pomella's arm, but she shrugged it off. This creature was just what they needed.

"The High Mystic is a powerful woman," the snake whispered. Its forked tongue flicked her ear. "But she is young, and does not know the secrets of Moth like I do. You can forgo her silly Trials and learn from me instead. I will teach you the truth of the Myst, and of the hidden things in this land."

"I don't like this, Pomella," Quentin said, his voice urgent.

"Mistress Yarina invited me," she told the snake. "It's an honor to have been invited. I have to finish the Trials."

"The Mystics of this island value different lessons than those I would teach," the snake said. "They force you to prance before them, burdening you with needless ceremony. In the Old Days, before politics intertwined with studies of the Myst, when a master and his apprentice lived in the wilds among the fay, there was no need to conduct tests of worthiness. A *true* master could instantly see beyond the fresh skin of youth and discover the potential they possessed. They could Unveil you with a glance."

Pomella straightened her back. "Are you such a master?"

The snake's silver, slitted eyes held hers. It flicked its tongue. "I freely offer to teach you how to discover and use the Myst. You shall be safe and comfortable under my care, and free to explore the forest as part of your training."

"Lies," Quentin snarled.

"It's all right, Quentin," Pomella said, keeping her attention on the snake. Pomella found herself wondering about the snake's offer. *Could* it teach her? How would she live near this pond and learn? "You would really do this for me? Why?"

"I hate to see such potential wasted. We could begin today, without needing to gather whatever she sent you to find. You would never again fear the consequences of failing the Trials."

Pomella flicked a glance at Quentin. Fear tumbled in her stomach, but not because of the snake. Strangely, she found herself considering its offer. Her mind raced, considering the possibility of being free from the fear of failure. She could cast off the stigma of being a commoner, and never worry about becoming Unclaimed. She licked her lips.

"You don't need this creature," Quentin said.

"Do you really think the High Mystic will choose you?" the snake said. "I promise you, in the end, she will choose one of her own. You aren't the first commoner to try, not that anybody but me remembers. The others all died, their bones crumbling and unclaimed."

The last word shivered through Pomella. She could feel her heart pounding. "I—"

"Come back with me, Pomella," Quentin said. "Please."

Pomella bit her lip. She had been about to say she'd accept. But Quentin's pleading eyes pulled her back. She remembered how lonely she'd been at the possibility of not having him around. Surely, if she accepted this snake's strange offer, she would live alone, away from other people.

"I must complete the Trials," she said to the snake, dropping her gaze. "I am certain."

"Very well," the snake said. "But remember my offer. When the High Mystic rejects you, and you find yourself cut off and alone, unable to drag yourself home, remember my words. Remember Mantepis."

It drew away, stepping back and folding its legs and body back into the tree. A pang of regret surged over Pomella. Maybe if she called the snake back . . .

Quentin's hand found hers and she felt him squeeze. Pomella looked at him and swallowed. Why did she feel like such a dunder? From a distant part of her mind, she remembered something else. She called to the snake, "Wait! May we take some of your blood? For the Trial, and to help other animals in need."

"I have sensed the iron poisoning parts of the forest," the snake, Mantepis, said. "But my blood is my own, and not for the Mystics of this land."

Pomella swallowed her fear and waded into the pond. She stepped lightly, careful not to disturb the drifting lotus flowers. She approached the snake and lifted the vials up to it. "Please."

The snake eased its head down above the vials and hovered above her. "You cannot take my blood. But you may have my venom. Perhaps it will eliminate . . . obstacles . . . in your way." It bared its fangs.

Venom. Poison. *Eliminate obstacles.* Did it intend her to poison the other candidates? Pomella couldn't help but peer into the creature's silvery throat, wondering if it could consume her whole. A drop of silver liquid pooled at the tip of one of its upper fangs. Pomella glanced back at Quentin, but could not read his expression. She returned her gaze and watched as the liquid swelled, grew heavy, and finally dripped.

The venom slid down the glass vial, pooling like honey. Pomella shivered.

The snake seemed to grin, and without another word, it withdrew completely into the tree, its silver eyes vanishing.

Beside her, Quentin relaxed, the tension draining from his body. "Let's go. We need to find our way back by dusk."

Pomella made her way back to the shore, but stopped near the edge as she caught another glimpse of the lotus flowers drifting in the water. Peering closer, she saw the flowers were smokey silver, like Mantepis and the other fay creatures. The only color they had were their golden sun-centers shining within. Pomella dipped her hand into the cool water and touched one of the flowers. Her fingers passed through it, yet she felt a soft breath of icy air as they did. She frowned. If the fay wolves could hurt the baron's soldiers, and if Mantepis' venom could drip into her glass vial, then somehow she should be able to touch those silver things back.

"What are you doing?" Quentin asked.

"Shush. Just a moment."

Closing her eyes, she tried to clear her mind, and focus on feeling the flower. She scooped her hand, and once again found nothing but chill air.

"Jagged flower," she mumbled, and followed Quentin.

But a short distance from the pond, the two little hummingbirds buzzed past her and hovered in front of her face. Dangling from each of their feet was a small flower stem, with a seed tangled in its roots.

"Sweet Saints," she breathed. The hummingbirds dropped the stems and seeds into her outstretched hand. As the seeds touched her skin, they solidified, but kept their shiny silver color. The stems wisped away in a silvery puff of smoke.

"Thank you," she told the strange birds. They flew away, but she could feel their content pleasure lingering behind.

Quentin looked impressed. "Come on, let's hurry," he said.

Pomella followed, but not before looking once more at the lotus seeds, and back toward the tree and the strange creature hidden within.

They emerged from the forest as the sun dipped below the western treetops. This was the second time in as many days that Pomella had trudged into Kelt Apar with mud and exhaustion splattered across her. She glanced at Quentin, and he grinned back. Perhaps some things had improved.

The little hummingbirds buzzed past her, eager to explore this new wide-open place. They'd followed her as soon as they'd left the pond. Somehow, she understood them. In a flash of a moment, these wee birds had lost everything in their lives. Nobody would be there to introduce them to the world. Like her, they were ready to face it, but had no guide to show them the way.

She and Quentin crossed the lawn and strode past the stone tower. On the far side, Oxillian and the other candidates had already gathered. Pomella imagined each of them with vials of fay blood. Mistress Yarina sat on a throne of stone and soil. Behind her, a small loch fed by the nearby river dazzled in the sunlight.

Everyone turned as Quentin and Pomella approached. The High Mystic's eyes gave nothing away. Saijar fumed at them. At Pomella. Vivianna stared at the hummingbirds, eyes wide. She turned to Pomella, surprise plain on her face.

"Sorry about the dress," Pomella mumbled as she stepped beside her. Mantepis' warning echoed in her mind, angering her. She might be a commoner among nobles, but she had still been legitimately invited to Kelt Apar. She thought of her grandmhathir, and the strength she'd shown in life. She thought of the mhathir hummingbird, who had died leading her to the pond. She straightened her back, and waited for the High Mystic to speak.

"You have each returned before sunset, as instructed," Yarina intoned. "It is well done. Vivianna was the first to arrive, followed shortly by Saijar. They each brought a vial, given freely by a badger and sloth, respectively."

Pomella stiffened. She'd hoped that the other two candidates had failed as well. She tightened her jaw, and squeezed her fist behind her back until she felt the harsh bite of her nails.

Oxillian spoke. "Quentin and Pomella, have you brought your vials of fay blood for the High Mystic?"

Pomella exchanged looks with Quentin. He stepped forward and bowed. "Mistress Yarina, I'm sorry to inform you that we did not bring any."

Pomella eyed the other candidates from the corner of her eye. Neither gave anything away other than their typical sour expressions.

Yarina's expression remain unchanged. "Very well. I'm sorry to hear that. We will move on. Tomorrow—"

"Wait, please, Mistress," Pomella interrupted. Everyone turned to face her. Her heart thundered in her chest. She just interrupted the High Mystic!

"We did not return with vials of blood, but Quentin and I brought lotus seeds. They seem Mystical in nature, so perhaps, with time, they could grow and we could use the flowers for a good purpose. With your permission, I would like to plant them here, on the edge of this loch, so that they will be nearby for future need."

Yarina drummed her fingers as she considered her. Pomella forced herself to stand tall, and not wilt under the terrible beauty of Yarina's gaze. Somewhere behind her, she heard the two hummingbirds fly by.

"A wise suggestion," Yarina said at last. "You may plant them now if you wish."

Pomella walked past Yarina's throne to the loch shore. From her pocket she pulled the two thumb-sized seeds. She bent and planted each seed in the mud beneath the water, patting them down. Standing, she stepped back from the water's edge and remained there. It wasn't much, just two seeds. Something more needed to happen in order for it to feel like an accomplishment. The hummingbirds swooped past her and she heard their song.

Following her instinct, she sang.

It began as a quiet note, lifting from her lips as her eyes remained shut. The words were ones she'd read in *The Book of Songs,* but the melody was her own.

> *"Like the wind she came*
> *Over the hills from far away*
> *Across the tides and*
> *Around the lane*

The lonely man called
And so she came"

The clear tone of Pomella's song rose like a high wind gusting across the loch. She felt strength in her singing like never before, and knew with a sudden clear certainty that this, *of course,* was her Unveiling. The realization doubled her confidence. To her ears, the sound of strings and wind instruments rose to accompany her.

"Like the light she danced
Amid the stars so far away
Across the sky and
Among the blue
A lonely man clapped
And so she knew"

Pomella understood hardly anything about Unveilings and how Mysticism worked. All she knew was that she was ready to stop worrying. She wanted to not only compete for this apprenticeship but also *earn* it. She thought of the poor elk suffering in the forest. The hummingbird who died. Her grandmhathir. She sang as loud as she could, caught up in the power of the song.

"Like the moon she sailed
Beyond the heavens from far away
Across my time and
Among our glade
A lonely man died . . ."

Pomella paused before the last line. She lifted her eyes to meet the High Mystic's.

"And so she stayed"

Behind Pomella, the water rippled. A familiar puff of light swished above the surface, leaving behind a silver lotus floating where she'd seeded it. A part of her registered that only one flower had emerged, and not two. But still, *a flower had sprung.* This was how her garden had flourished back home.

The High Mystic stood. A smile crossed her face. "Well done," she said. Then she lifted her staff toward the sky, where the late sun made it appear to be on fire.

Hundreds of silver lotus flowers bloomed, springing to life from the water where none had been before. Their collective light covered the loch like fog, churning and fading as the flowers bubbled from the water. Each lifted tight buds skyward before blossoming its miniature sun. Finally, the last of the silver light vanished. Pomella's hummingbirds swooped into the flowers, seeking nectar.

"Oxillian," said Yarina, "see that this new garden is kept and tended." She turned to face the candidates. "Two Trials remain. You may rest tomorrow, but do not leave Kelt Apar."

The candidates and the Green Man bowed as the High Mystic stepped down from the throne. She walked to the stone tower and melted into the light shining from beyond the doorway. Oxillian nodded to Pomella and the others, and sank into the ground like the throne.

Pomella faced the other candidates, slowly letting her breath out. Saijar clenched a fist and looked at his feet. Vivianna avoided looking at Pomella. Only Quentin beamed, an admiring smile spread across his face.

Pomella stilled her trembling hands. After all the challenges she'd faced in getting here, and the hostility Saijar and Vivianna had shown, maybe she still had a chance.

Maybe she was here to stay.

NINE

THE BLACK CLAWS

The spear pushed against Sim's chest. He lifted his hands and slowly eyed its wielder. A short man in dusty clothes with a ratlike face glared at him. Behind him, another man emerged from a bush holding a drawn bow. Even in the dim, early-evening light, Sim could see the sharp tip of the arrow pointed his way.

"You're snooping where you shouldn't," said the spear holder in an unfamiliar accent. Sim estimated the man was ten years older than he was. Greasy hair hung past his ears, and a patchy beard attempted to grow on his chin. "What ya doing here?"

Sim swallowed. "Going home."

"Oh, yeah? Where's that?"

Sim narrowed his eyes. He could tell from the man's expression that nothing he said would help him. This was trouble no matter how the metal cooled. "I escorted a friend to Sentry. Now I'm going back to Oakspring."

"Ya hear that, Hormin?" the spear holder said. "The scrit says he's from the same Oaktown as the girl."

Sim's guts clenched. "What do you mean?"

"Careful, Jank," said Hormin. "He might be a ranger." The bowman was maybe a year or two younger than Sim, barely old enough to shave. Hormin's sharp eyes pierced Sim from behind the ready bowstring.

"Don't be an idiot," Jank sneered, keeping his spear aimed at Sim. "Does he look like a blowing ranger to you? He's dressed like a commoner."

"With a sword," Hormin pointed out.

"Besides," Jank continued. "Look at him. He's all worked up on the girl. You know her, scrit?"

Sim forced himself to unclench his fist. "I'm just passing through," he said. They had to be talking about Pomella. What other girl from Oakspring could they possibly care about?

Jank shook his head. "Then why were ya spying on us, huh? Sorry, scrit, now that you've seen our camp, you can't go anywhere. You might go talking to the wrong people." His spear dropped as he turned to face Hormin. "Zicon wants—"

Sim knocked the spear aside and lunged at him. He easily overpowered the smaller man, slamming him to the ground. Somewhere in his mind, a voice told him this probably wasn't the wisest of ideas. He ignored the voice and plunged his fist into Jank's jaw.

The force of the punch and resulting pain in his hand knocked Sim off balance. He struggled to regain his position. By the Saints, did all punches hurt the attacker, too? The hilt of his sheathed sword jabbed into his ribs. The jagged thing was more of a hindrance than a benefit!

He pushed himself off Jank and ran. The back of Sim's head tingled as he imagined Hormin aiming an arrow at him. He ripped to his right, hoping his skittering movements would prevent an arrow from lodging in his back.

"Get him!" Jank roared.

Sim angled around an oak tree. He looked back to find Jank. In the dim evening light he couldn't see—

A thick club slammed into him, sending his feet skyward. He hit the ground hard, the last of his breath knocked away.

When the world resolved back into focus, a thick man stood over him. Sim blinked a few times before he managed to find his senses and some air. The large man looming above him was actually a woman with wispy blond hair pulled tight into a short braid. The club she'd hit him with had just been her arm.

Jank strode over to stand beside the large woman. He rubbed his jaw and glared at Sim. "If it weren't for our orders, your blood would be on the ground," he said. He kicked Sim in the stomach twice. Sim rolled in agony as Jank snatched his sword and canvas sack from him.

The rat-faced man rummaged through the sack and pulled out Pomella's book. His expression darkened as he examined the cover. "Bag him," the man said.

Sim's heart skipped a beat as the woman hauled him to his feet before throwing a sack over his head and tying his hands behind his back. They spun him around and shoved him toward the camp.

The sound of the blacksmith's hammering returned as the three bandits led him forward. Beneath the patchy sack, Sim managed to see only a few vague shadows.

"Get Zicon," Jank muttered to one of the others.

The large woman's thick hands shoved Sim, then ducked his head into one of the tents. He heard the clank of heavy iron, and moments later found himself bound at the wrists and ankles.

"Cause any trouble," Jank breathed beside Sim's head, "and I'll gut you."

Fear charged through Sim. But alongside that fear ran a surge of anger. He heard Jank leave the tent, and sensed he was alone. He took a steadying breath, and tried not to imagine what they were going to do with him. Tugging his wrists, he tested the manacles, but found no yield. They were solid iron, and nothing was going to break that.

Long minutes passed, and Sim realized all he could do was wait. Finally, he heard the tent flap open again, and several footsteps thumped in.

Somebody yanked the canvas sack off his head. Sim blinked. A large man with a black beard and blue eyes stood in front of him. He was taller than Sim, which was uncommon. Atop a black shirt he wore layered leather armor dotted with small studs. A braided cord hung around his neck, its end tucked beneath his shirt. Behind him, Jank and Sim's other captors—Hormin and the tall, meaty woman—stood glaring at him.

The bearded man stared at Sim, weighing him as he scratched his chin. Finally, he turned to Jank and spoke with the same cutting accent as Sim's other captors. "What's this scat you dragged in?"

Jank shifted his feet. "He was spying on us."

"This lumbering grunt? He's not old enough to have hair in his pits."

"I was walking home," Sim replied. "I heard the blacksmith. I came to see—"

"Nobody asked you, boy," snarled the large man.

Jank sneered. "He's lying. He had that book, Zicon. And he attacked me."

The large man, Zicon, grunted and studied Sim. "I don't really care what you were doing. But you're going to have to stay awhile. Can't have you running off and talking about us."

"I won't say anything to anybody. I'll just go home."

Zicon sneered a laugh. "It's not that easy." He nodded to Jank. "Keep him tied up. Make sure he gets food and water twice a day. Keep him quiet."

"You're just going to leave me tied?" Sim snarled. "You jagged culk!" He'd show this man some backbone. Sim's stomach churned in fear, but he'd be spiked if he let it show.

The bearded man loomed in Sim's face. His breath stank in Sim's nose. "What'd you just call me?"

"Culk," Sim repeated, holding his eye and saying it nice and slow. "A jagged *culk*."

"I'll cut him up for you, Zicon," Jank said, sounding eager.

Zicon fumed silently for a moment before leaning close. "You're with the Black Claws now. An' you know what I think? I think you're just a stupid, skivering brat. But I can't bleed ya, and I can't let ya go." He turned away, then twisted back and slammed a massive fist into Sim's stomach. It took a moment for Sim to realize he was on the ground, curled up and coughing. "But I *can* make your maggoty life miserable," Zicon said over him. "Don't *ever* call me a culk again or I'll set Jank loose on ya."

They filed out of the tent, Jank sneering as he passed. Trying not to vomit, Sim dragged himself to his feet, his chains clanking.

"Put me to work, Zicon," he said. His guts ached.

Zicon stopped. "What?"

"I can sit here and eat your food twice a day, or you can put me to work for the camp. I'm a blacksmith apprentice."

Zicon glared at him. "And why would you offer that?"

Sim wondered that himself. Maybe the punch had shaken the sense out of his bones, but the thought of remaining chained up terrified him. If they took the chains off, he might find an opportunity to escape. He'd also have a better chance of discovering what they planned to do with Pomella. Working in the camp would help him more than sitting in a dark tent.

Zicon burst out laughing. Jank and Hormin joined him. The woman remained silent and unmoving.

"You've got less smarts than the corn you grow in Oakville if you think I'll let you walk about free in my camp."

"Let him."

The voice stopped the laughter cold. A chill sense of dread ran up Sim's spine. Hearing that voice, Sim thought of a knife being sharpened. A thin man stepped through the tent doorway. He wore rust-colored robes, trimmed in black, with the hood pulled up. It obscured most of his face, but a long red and gray beard jutted out. The man clutched a tall iron staff.

Jank, Hormin, and the woman bowed immediately, while Zicon barely dipped his head.

A Mystic. Only one of them could carry such a staff and command such respect. It had been years since Sim had actually seen one. The natural urge to bow tugged at Sim, but he remained tall. It was a small defiance, but he held on to it. He did, however, lower his eyes. Some habits were just too hard to drop.

"Tell it again, boy," the Mystic said in an unmistakable Mothic accent. "Are you a 'prentice smith? Speak true. I will know if you lie."

Sim swallowed. "Yah, I am."

"He'll just run away," Zicon grumbled to the man.

"Then put a guard on him," said the Mystic, unfazed. "Surely you can spare one of your otherwise useless mercenaries for the job."

Zicon sneered. "You'll watch your tongue, Mystic, or—"

He stopped as the Mystic pulled back his hood, and turned his full gaze upon Zicon. The tent seemed to grow colder, more dim. Sim slunk back before he realized it.

The Mystic had familiar Mothic features: red hair laced with gray, green eyes, and light skin. Scars laced his face, and Sim could see blackened teeth as he spoke. But the strangest part of the man was the curved plate of iron fused into the dome of his head, like a cap stitched onto him. Raw edges of flesh, black with dry blood, lay exposed along the seams of metal. Now that he noticed it, Sim glimpsed bits of metal sewn into other parts of the man's body, along his hands and jaw.

"You will not threaten me," the Mystic whispered.

Zicon swallowed. "I'm not afraid of—"

Zicon's eyes widened, and Sim wondered why he stopped talking. A small trickle of blood oozed from Zicon's nose. He touched it and his hand began to tremble.

"And you will remember your place, commoner," said the Mystic. "This filthy band may follow you, but you are mine."

Zicon's eyes bulged as both nostrils began to bleed. His hands went to his throat.

"I've traveled too far," said the Mystic, stepping closer to Zicon, "and come too far for you to challenge me. I have plans for this island. Fall into line, like an obedient dog. Do you know what my name means?"

Zicon shook his head, frantic.

The Mystic peered into his face. Jank and the other mercenaries kept their eyes on the ground. "The language of the lagharts is nuanced, and beyond comprehension for your maggoty mind. They have a word that means 'pain.' But also 'love.' Passion for something so deep that you would accept any risk, or go to any length for it."

Zicon crashed to his knees, trembling, "Stop! Please!"

"Speak the word," the Mystic said. "My name."

"Ohzem!" Zicon managed. Sim shuddered at the harsh, almost hacking-like sound of the name.

The Mystic, Ohzem, replaced his hood. Zicon stopped his thrashing and steadied himself on a table before glaring hatred at the man.

A quiet shiver tingled over Sim's body as the Mystic stepped toward him. An icy resonance drifted off him. Ohzem reached into a large pocket within his robes and pulled out Pomella's book. He turned it over in the dim candlelight.

"I believe this is yours," Ohzem said, his voice barely above a whisper.

Sim swallowed. "Y-yah."

"It may be wiser to let it collect dust on your mhathir's book-shelf. Commoners cannot become Mystics, you see."

Holding Sim's gaze, he handed the book over. Sim took it with trembling hands. He hated that the Mystic put so much fear into him.

"I have need of this boy, Zicon," Ohzem said. "You will let him work the forge. You will not make him bleed. We are short on time and resources. His skilled labor is of use to our task. The Myst delivers in our time of need."

"As you wish," Zicon growled, standing up. "But if he ruins anything, he'll be back here in twice as many chains. Jank, you're in charge of watching him. Don't scowl at me; just do it."

He turned his angry blue eyes onto Sim. "And as for you, if you so much as look toward home without permission, I'll let Mags have her way with ya. Understand?"

Sim glanced past Zicon at the heavy woman. She crossed her

arms across her large bosom and stared at him with calm, muted hatred. He suppressed a shiver and nodded. "Yah. I got it."

"Get him some food and get him working in the morning, Jank. Tonight, he sleeps in the rain."

It did indeed rain. Sim woke a few hours before dawn, shivering. He'd slept beneath the smaller of the camp's two wagons under some thin blankets. At least, he'd tried to sleep. The freezing rain and miserable wind kept him awake, his teeth and bones chattering. Jank had chained the manacles to the wagon's axle, so Sim had no choice other than to wait until somebody came to rouse him.

"You might have Zicon and the Mystic fooled," Jank said after the sun rose, unlocking his wrist chains. "But I know you're more than just a village brat. You're up to something."

Sim stood and tested his ankle manacles. He noticed Jank wearing a familiar sword on his hip. *His* sword, the one Fathir had forged. Jank grinned, following Sim's gaze. Mags stood a short distance away, glaring silently at Sim. Sim wondered if she even had the ability to speak.

"Thanks for holding my sword, Jank," Sim said. "I always wanted my own squire."

Jank sneered up at him. "I'll skewer you someday, scrit. Just give me a reason."

He unlocked the ankle chains from the wagon and shoved Sim forward. With Mags following behind, he led Sim toward the other, larger wagon. Now that it was daylight and he wasn't blindfolded, Sim could clearly see the entirety of the small camp. Besides the wagons, two large tents, similar to the ones used in the Summeryarn field festivals, rested in the clearing. One of them, the smaller one, was where they'd dragged him after he was captured. The other, he suspected, was where Zicon slept.

Sim wondered where the Mystic slept. Or if he did at all.

Three brown geldings and a large black stallion stood tied to nearby trees. The stallion stomped his feet, restless. Hormin moved among them, brushing them down and feeding them.

They arrived at the larger wagon, whose extra wooden bulk was supplemented by thick metal bands. The wheels and axles were made of iron, and part of the bed as well. Sim recognized several familiar tools used for blacksmithing, including an actual anvil bolted directly to the center of the wagon. A man he hadn't seen before lifted a crate and slid it onto the wagon bed. He was heavyset and bald except for a shaggy, graying beard hanging from his chin.

"Hormin!" he barked, wiping a dirty hand on the blacksmithing apron he wore. "I need those horses ready!"

"Dox," Jank said.

The heavy man looked up. "Aye, what'd ya need?"

"Have a prisoner here for you. This scrit says he's a 'prentice smith. Zicon an' the Mystic says to put him to work."

Dox lumbered over to them. Sweat beaded across his forehead. "He's big enough to swing a hammer, at least. You any good, scrit?"

"Put me to work and find out," Sim replied. "And I'm not a scrit. My name's Sim."

Dox laughed, wiping his brow. "I like you. Grab an apron and let's see what you've got. One of those horses bent a shoe. Need it reshaped before we move out this morning. Make it match the other one over there. The forge should still be hot, but it'll need some pumping. Get going."

With a final glare, Jank left, Mags following behind. Sim found an apron and began working the bellows. Dox watched him without comment. Although smaller than what he used back home, the wagon cleverly contained everything that was necessary to run a portable forge.

As he worked, the others broke down the camp and prepared to travel. Zicon didn't talk to Sim, but the mercenary leader kept an eye on him while he ordered everyone else around. Ohzem was nowhere to be found.

Once the forge was glowing hot, Sim rummaged through the wagon, looking for tools. An unusually large, iron-wrought chest sat in a corner, strapped tightly to the wagon. He pulled at the lid and found it locked.

"Hands off that one," Dox said, checking the coals. "Get what you need over here."

"What's in there?" Sim asked.

"Not your concern. Let it be."

Sim frowned but left the chest alone.

"That shoe's for Zicon's stallion," Dox warned. "You mess it up and he'll be spitting."

Sim set to work as Dox left to handle other tasks. It felt good to lose himself in labor. He'd forged or fixed many shoes over the last few years, so this one came easily to him. The iron heated quickly, and the hammer dropped hard. By the time the sun lifted above the horizon, he'd worked up a good sweat, the familiar muscles burning.

Dox returned and climbed onto the wagon. He looked over Sim's shoulder and grunted in approval. "Not bad. Did you check it against that beast's hoof?"

Sim nodded. "Yah."

Dox grunted in approval. Then, pausing as if deciding whether he should continue, Dox murmured, "Why're you a prisoner?"

Sim shrugged and wiped his brow. "I heard you working the anvil yesterday and came to see what was happening. Jank assumed I was a spy, but I was just heading home. Zicon says I can't leave, so I offered to help."

"Yeah? Why's that?"

"Because going home isn't really an option, and it beats sitting in chains all day."

Dox grunted again as he peered at the shoe. "How'd you learn smithing?"

"My fathir."

The blacksmith nodded. "It's good enough. I'll give you more to do this evening when we stop again. Clean this wagon up and have it ready to travel in five minutes. The coals can remain where they are."

"Where are we going?" Sim asked.

Dox slid off the wagon. "Deeper into the forest. Just do your job and do what you're told." Dox had the same accent as Jank and the other Black Claws, but Sim couldn't place its origin.

When the camp was packed, and Dox had reshod Zicon's horse, they moved on. The company followed the road south through the forest, meeting nobody. Zicon rode at the head, while

Ohzem sat on the smaller wagon pulled by two of the geldings. The Mystic's hood covered his eyes, and Sim wondered if he was sleeping.

They found a suitable place to stop early in the evening, and set up camp. Dox put Sim back to work immediately, heating the coals and repairing a broken tent clasp. Sim didn't complain. It was a simple enough task for him. The villagers of Oakspring always had need for small metalwork, and Lathwin AnClure was more than glad to pass that work onto his son when he could. Sim paused only to wolf down a sizable bowl of hearty vegetable stew that Hormin brought. He noticed Zicon eyeing him on occasion, and once he even felt Ohzem's cold gaze linger on him.

When Dox finally told him to stop for the evening, Jank came and chained him back to the wagon axle. Not even the hard ground could keep him from sleeping off his exhaustion.

The next morning before they broke camp, as Sim worked on a broken buckle for Zicon's saddle, a commotion broke out on the far side of the camp.

Jank and Mags shoved a writhing prisoner along in front of them. It was a tall woman, dressed in padded armor bearing green and white markings that seemed to help her blend into her surroundings. Her hands were bound behind her back. The same canvas sack they'd used to blind Sim was pulled over her head. A leering smile filled Jank's pinched face.

Zicon and Ohzem emerged from the main tent and met the scouting party in the middle of the camp. Mags kicked the prisoner's knee out, and the woman fell to the ground. Sim tried to look busy, but positioned himself behind the horses so that he could be close enough to overhear.

"Caught this ranger!" Jank boasted, not bothering to keep his voice low. "Sneaking from tree to tree, trying to get closer to us."

Ohzem stepped forward, his face lost in his deep cowl. "Let me see her," he said in his rasping voice.

Mags ripped the hood off, and Sim nearly gasped. The woman had brown skin, darker than Pomella's, striped with thick lines of jet black that were outlined in white. She was probably in her late thirties. Her violet eyes rose to meet Ohzem's.

"A virga!" Zicon blurted. "Haven't seen many of you in my life. Meinrad's Menagerie back home will pay handsomely."

The striped woman held her head high. "Whoever you are, you are unauthorized to be here."

Jank and Zicon laughed. Sim had heard of the Striped People in stories, but had never actually seen one. Like the lagharts, they came from a far distant land, though the virgas were human. Only their eye color and unique skin patterns differentiated them in any way.

"How did you find us?" Ohzem asked her.

"We know everything that happens in the Mystwood," she said, her voice hard.

Ohzem scoffed. "Arrogant as always, ranger. I see your lies as plainly as your stripes. Yarina does not know of us. She *cannot* know anything besides that her precious forest is slowly being poisoned by my presence."

The virga woman held the Mystic's eye, not wavering. "Nothing can move through these lands without the High Mystic knowing it."

Ohzem stepped closer to the prisoner. He pulled back his hood. The iron plate doming his head did not reflect the morning light. Straining to listen, Sim heard him say, "You will answer my questions truthfully."

"You are demented. I will not—"

The prisoner screamed. She fell onto the dirt, writhing. Her eyes rolled back in her head as she convulsed, spittle flying from her mouth.

Sim found himself clutching the hammer hard, his knuckles white. This was wrong. He had to earn the Black Claws' trust until he could help Pomella somehow, but he couldn't stand still while they tortured prisoners. He stepped forward to help, but a meaty hand clasped his shoulder.

"Nothing you can do," murmured Dox. "The Mystic does whatever he wants. Zicon fears him, whatever he says, and we all know it."

Sim shrugged Dox's hand away, but remained where he was. The prisoner had stopped screaming, and had pushed herself up to her hands and knees. Ohzem spoke again, but too softly for Sim to hear.

"What are they—we—doing out here?" Sim asked the blacksmith.

Dox eyed him. "I don't know the details, and even if I did, I couldn't tell you. But Zicon is feverish about this job. He's paying the others triple. Which he damned well better. We're a long way from home."

"Paying the others? What about you?"

Dox grunted. "I got my own reasons for being here."

The prisoner lunged at the Mystic, but Ohzem stepped easily out of the way. He leaned against his iron staff almost casually, and she screamed again, writhing in the dirt.

Sim forced himself to take a calming breath. He couldn't watch anymore. He wished he could block out her screaming. Would they do this to Pomella if they caught her? "Now will you tell me where you're from?" he said to Dox.

Dox sighed. "The Baronies of Rardaria."

Sim clenched his jaw. The Baronies were from the Continent. It might as well have been a world away. He looked at Dox. The older man reminded Sim of his fathir, and not just because they were both blacksmiths. Maybe Dox would help him. Sim proceeded carefully. "You're a long way from home. Whatever your reasons are, I hope they're worth it."

Dox eyed him for a long moment. "Sometimes, we don't really have a choice, do we? Zicon and those lying barons can stuff their money down their gullets. I won't take a clip from them."

The blacksmith turned and left. The ranger had stopped screaming. Sim watched as Ohzem lifted her face with a bony finger. He whispered in her ear, and the woman snarled. Content, Ohzem calmly stepped away and left her lying in the dirt. Zicon motioned for Jank and Mags to drag her away.

Sim returned to his tasks. His mind raced as he tried to understand what was happening. Why were the Black Claws trying to kill Pomella? And who had hired them? Surely, if they were a legitimate threat, the High Mystic would have done something about it. Perhaps the virga ranger had been sent to investigate.

He frowned at the buckle. Nothing was turning out like he expected. The arrival of the prisoner had distracted him, and his thoughts lay elsewhere. He tossed the buckle aside and went to grab a towel to wipe his hands. He caught a glimpse of the heavy chest inside the wagon bed, its contents another mystery.

He shook his head. Maybe he was overthinking things. His imagination could run to strange places, ignoring reality. The chest didn't contain any strange or forbidden objects. Maybe the Black Claws hadn't been hired to kill Pomella. How could they have even known about her? She was only offered the opportunity a few days ago.

Yet Jank *had* mentioned her. And that chest was locked with a heavy iron lock. You didn't keep spare hammers locked up like that.

Sim wondered if the answers he sought were locked away right at his very feet.

TEN

FORGING IRON

The Black Claws broke camp and spent the day traversing the Mystwood. Sim gritted his teeth and trudged along. If only he knew where his captors were going or what their plans were. He didn't know the forest well, but as they headed south he realized they were likely going to Kelt Apar. Where else would they go? His stomach sank. How long would the Trials last? Would Pomella be protected? Surely the High Mystic would look out for her.

He missed her.

The longer he was away from Pomella, the more he regretted turning his cheek when she tried to kiss him. What kind of dunder turned down a kiss from a girl like that? He could practically feel Dane smacking the back of his head and teasing him relentlessly. But then he remembered all the reasons he'd done it. It would be simpler this way. She needed to do her thing, and he needed to do his. She would be free to move on.

Looking back over his shoulder, Sim watched the captive ranger walking in chains at the back of the caravan. Her dark hair straggled over her face, but her eyes remained hardened. Mags lumbered along behind the captive, her face like a rock. The ranger noticed Sim's attention and stared at him. He swallowed and looked away.

Something about the virga's demeanor intimidated him more than the Black Claws. But despite this, he knew he needed to find a way to speak to her.

It rained again that night. Sim huddled beneath the wagon and his rough blankets. His worries kept him awake. He adjusted his canvas travel sack behind his head. He felt the hard lump of *The Book of Songs* within, and, after a moment of hesitation, pulled it out. The cover featured a tree woven like a Mothic knot. He frowned as he thumbed the leather. He wanted nothing to do with the Myst. While he accepted that it existed, he doubted it was anything that would ever benefit him. The Myst had been powerless to save Dane and Pomella's mhathir. It hadn't saved the others in Oakspring who'd died of the Coughing Plague that year. Sim still remembered, as fresh as a clear morning, the conversation he'd eavesdropped on one night back then. Firelight flickered across his mhathir and fathir's mantel as the old Mystic murmured to them. Sim remembered having to strain to hear them from outside the window.

"It's beyond me now," the Mystic had said.

His mhathir muffled her sobs in her husband's shoulder.

"Surely, Master," Fathir said, forcing his voice steady, "surely the Myst can do something."

"My son," Mhathir moaned.

"The Myst is powerful," the Mystic said, "and wonders can be achieved. But some things are beyond even my power."

"What about the High Mystic?" Fathir asked.

"You may appeal to him, but he battles this same challenge in the cities. The plague is far worse there. Consider yourselves fortunate."

On his way out, Sim had slipped from his hiding spot to beg the Mystic to try harder. But no words had come. He'd only cried like a tyke when he tried to speak. The Mystic had put a hand on his head, and hardly spared him a glance, as if Sim were of no consequence.

Then the Mystic had left.

Sim clenched his jaw. Fortunate. The Mystic called them fortunate to lose only Dane, Goodness AnDone, and eleven others in Oakspring. Fortunate! The Mystic's words echoed in Sim's hollow chest that day, and did so again now. In failing to save Dane, the Myst had cursed him once. Now it was doing so again by taking Pomella.

He opened *The Book of Songs* and flipped through the pages. Rose-colored handwriting filled every available space, creating a mesmerizing tapestry of lines, runes, and sketches.

The most common drawings were those of animals and plants, ranging from birds and fish to maple leaves and even a highly detailed diagram of a beetle. He stopped when he came to a sketch of a fox that seemed to be on fire.

No, not fire. It was smoke, or maybe mist rolling off the fox. Sim's stomach sank. Could these animals be sketches of what Pomella had seen? He peered at the letter-runes, trying to decipher them. He wished he'd been born into the merchant-scholar caste so that he would've learned to read the noble runes used throughout the book. His common upbringing only allowed him the right to be taught to read foundational runes, not the noble ones reserved for the highest castes.

His breath misted over the book as he looked at every page, studying the sketches. He loved the beauty of the text and imagery, but wished he could puzzle out its meaning.

The next morning, when the rain gave way to a damp sunrise, Dox unlocked his manacles.

"Isn't that Jank's job?" Sim asked, stretching his ankles.

"With Mags watching the other one, Jank doesn't have time anymore. I convinced Zicon that I can keep an eye on you."

Sim snorted. "D'ya think you can talk him into giving me another ration?"

Dox snorted and smacked Sim on the back. "You're a hearty country lad. You'll be fine. But I'll see what I can do. Now, come on. I need you to craft something for me."

They readied the field-forge, which Dox described as a common utility used by armies throughout the Baronies. "Weapons get broken, armor gets torn, and horses lose shoes. Every army needs blacksmiths."

"And small mercenary bands?" Sim ventured. It was a calculated risk to say this to Dox, but he suspected he could push it with the older man's growing sympathy.

Dox muttered something Sim couldn't hear. He pointed to the bellows. "Get pumping."

"What do you need?"

"You're not repairing anything," said Dox. "You're crafting something new. Zicon needs thirty iron spikes made, each about the length of your forearm. Nothing fancy, but they need to be solid. Can you handle that?"

"Yah."

"Good. We're nearing our destination. We'll divide the work. Should have extra time today to finish."

Sim watched Dox prep and hammer the first spike. Dark ideas crossed his mind as he wondered what they would be used for. He pushed away his misgivings, though. Refusal wouldn't help his situation.

When Dox finished, Sim worked on his own, taking his time to ensure it matched the blacksmith's. They used one of the tent spikes as a starting point, although Dox wanted them longer and thicker. The old man approved of Sim's first attempt, correcting him only in that the tip needed to be sharper.

They worked in camp all day. Nobody but Dox spoke to Sim, but he had the impression that the whole company waited for them. In the late afternoon, as he hammered out the twenty-second spike, Sim caught a glimpse of movement at the edge of the camp.

He paused and stared as a glowing silver mountain lion prowled the perimeter. A fine mist rolled off its back, wafting away like smoke caught in the wind. The lion seemed only half-present, and Sim could see through it as if staring through melted glass.

"Dox," he said, "can you see that?"

Dox followed his gaze. "See what?"

Before Sim could reply, Ohzem emerged from the large tent, iron staff in hand. He swept his gaze slowly around the camp until it fixed on the place where the mountain lion stood. The Mystic pulled back his hood, revealing the sharp metal plates sunk into his head. The lion crouched and its eyes narrowed. Ohzem stared straight at the silvery creature, and the lion prowled forward.

"He does this sometimes," Dox said.

The lion leaped at Ohzem, who swung his staff and caught it in midair. The staff burst with light. Flecks of black dust stormed across the Mystic and lion. Ohzem snarled and slammed the lion to the ground. His movements seemed stiff to Sim, but he threw the lion as if it weighed nothing. Lifting the staff again, Ohzem drove its end down hard onto the lion's head. He repeated the action until the lion lay still. The Mystic stepped back, and the lion melted away, its silver light spreading out and vanishing.

"Did you see the lion?" Sim asked Dox, thinking of Pomella and the silvery creatures she'd claimed to see.

Dox shook his head. "Stay away from the Myst, lad. It'll be better for you that way."

As if to punctuate those words, a low rumble sounded in the distance. He and Dox looked in that direction. An explosion. Sim shivered. He didn't like being in the forest anymore.

That night, after completing the spikes, while the rest of the

Black Claw camp slept Sim eased himself out of his blankets. Dox had convinced Zicon to provide him with a second large helping for their evening meal. Sim rubbed his wrists, grateful that he'd also managed to convince Dox that he didn't need to be chained to the wagon anymore.

Glancing at the snoring blacksmith, Sim eased himself up and crossed the camp. No fires burned after dark, no whispers allowed, nothing to reveal the Black Claws trespassed in the Mystwood. Sim crept as quietly as he could, heel to toe, knees bent. He made his way to the tent where he'd seen Jank and Mags take the ranger. He eased a portion of the tent flap open and peered inside. Darkness filled every corner. Sim managed to spy a single lump in the same place they'd initially chained him up.

Checking once more to ensure nobody was watching, Sim slipped into the tent and hurried over to the ranger. She lifted her head and lurched to a crouching stance before he could get to her side.

"Shh! I'm here to help," Sim breathed.

The ranger remained motionless. The black stripes across her face mingled with the shadows. "Who are you?" she asked in a low whisper.

"My name's Sim. I think the Black Claws plan to hurt my friend. Are you really a ranger?"

The woman nodded and eased into a slightly more relaxed crouch. "Yes. My name is Rochella. Tell me why you are here and what you know."

Sim recounted his story as quickly as he could. Already he worried that somebody might have seen him sneak into the tent.

The ranger listened, showing no reaction. When he finished,

she asked, "Have you learned anything about who these people are?"

"Not much so far. They're from the Baronies of Rardaria. Dox, the blacksmith, told me most of the Black Claws are mercenaries, and that Zicon is paying them triple for this job."

"It's not the mercenaries who worry me," Rochella said.

Sim nodded, thinking of the cowled Mystic. He leaned in. "I overheard Jank say they're after my friend, Pomella, the commoner who was invited to Kelt Apar by the High Mystic. They didn't mention her by name, but I think they plan to hurt her."

Rochella nodded. "Do you have proof?"

Sim shrugged. "Not really."

Rochella sighed. "Can you get me out?"

Sim looked at her manacles and shook his head. "I can't break iron."

"Then find a key."

Sim clenched his jaw, then relaxed it. Getting upset with her wouldn't help either one of them. "I'll try. What else can I do?"

"Find something that tells us their plans," the ranger said. "If they really want your friend dead, it's for political reasons. These bandits work for hire. Find out who hired them."

"What about Pomella? Can we at least warn her and the High Mystic?"

"Kelt Apar is guarded by the ceon'hur. I'm not worried about a band of mercenaries lumbering in with swords and bows."

Sim glanced back over his shoulder at the tent entrance. "I need to go. I'll try to learn more, but everyone's keeping their mouths shut about what's going on."

Rochella caught his arm. "If they were hired by somebody with enough resources to fund a mercenary group this large so far from their base of operations, there's likely to be a contract or other clues to their plan."

Sim's pulse quickened. The heavy chest. Only something of real value would be kept in a thing like that.

Sim nodded. "I'll come back when I can."

The ranger slunk back into her corner, her chains not making a sound. Sim checked to make sure nobody was nearby before slipping out of the tent. He made his way back to the wagon and blanket, but couldn't get back to sleep.

They continued their slow crawl south at first light. Sim learned from Dox as they trudged behind the other wagon that they were only a day, two at most, from arriving at their destination, though the blacksmith couldn't say where that was. But he did say they would pass Kelt Apar later that day.

Sim frowned. "Oh, yah? We're not going to Kelt Apar? I was hoping to see the tower."

Dox shrugged. "Kelt Apar is a place of Mystics. If they don't want their tower seen, it won't be. But if you really want to see it, you'd be better off asking that one."

He nodded ahead toward Ohzem, who rode in his usual place atop the front wagon, head bowed within his robe. He was probably asleep again, or concentrating. Meditating, perhaps?

The attack on the mountain lion still lingered in Sim's mind.

It still staggered him to know Pomella had been right about the existence of the strange creatures. What were they? He hadn't seen another of the silver animals since Ohzem killed the lion.

The morning passed quickly, and Sim never saw the tower. They continued to follow the road south, but began to veer eastward. MagDoon, the great mountain Sim had grown up hearing legends about, loomed above them.

Jank walked beside Rochella, one hand on a long chain bound to a collar around her throat and the other on Sim's sword. Ahead of them, the forge wagon trundled along.

"Dox, what's in there?" Sim asked, pointing toward the large, iron-strapped chest.

Dox stiffened. "I told you, it ain't nothing that concerns you."

Sim frowned. "I just wanted—"

"You just wanted to put your nose where it don't belong!" Dox snapped. "Leave it alone. Not tell'n' you again."

When late afternoon arrived and they began setting the camp for the night, Zicon gathered everyone. "Starting tomorrow, there won't be any more lazing about. We'll arrive at the designated place and do our jobs. Then we'll get the hells off this island."

Jank and Hormin scouted ahead, while Mags went to find a place to secure Rochella. Zicon muttered something to Ohzem, then mounted his stallion and rode off into the forest.

Sim began to unpack the forge wagon, but Dox stopped him. "Not tonight. That work is done."

Sim opened his mouth to ask why, but a hissing voice stopped him. "That remains to be seen," Ohzem said. "I would speak with you, Master Engrav."

Dox swallowed. "Go set up the main tent, lad. Be quick about it, and don't disturb us."

Sim squirmed as Ohzem watched him. The sharp lines of iron sticking out of Ohzem's body sent shivers down Sim's spine. The Mystic's eyes searched his, as if they could see past his feeble cover story and stare into his heart. Sim hustled away but tried to convince himself his urgency had nothing to do with fear.

He went to the main wagon and began to unbundle the rolled canvas that would form the large tent. He paused as he realized he was alone. Dox and Ohzem were back by the forge wagon. Jank and Hormin were scouting. Mags was with Rochella, and Zicon had ridden off.

This was his chance.

Under the guise of unpacking the tent, Sim rummaged through the wagon, looking for the key to the chest. Or a key to Rochella's thick manacles.

He tore through the supplies, shaking down rolled bundles and setting aside other gear. He glanced over his shoulder, but nobody came. He shoved the main tent canvas onto the ground and searched the wooden crates beneath it.

Nothing.

"Bugger and shite!" he cursed to himself.

He emptied another crate of its contents, but found only iron spikes and rope for the tent. He threw it all onto the ground and rummaged more, hoping for anything at this point.

His hand found a bundle of rolled-up clothing. He lifted it, making sure nobody was watching. It contained a few spare shirts wrapped in a belt. Tucked in the middle of the roll was a smooth wooden cylinder.

His heart thundering, Sim pulled it out. It was painted black, with delicate white birds in flight across it. He'd never seen such fine woodwork before. He unfastened the latched end cap, and pulled out a tightly rolled sheet of paper.

Across the smooth surface, written in a neat hand, were foundational letter-runes he could read.

My Dearest Zicon,

Forgive me for not coming to port today to see you off. You know how my parents, Papa in particular, feel about us seeing each other. I know you detest the task you've agreed to, but please apply your greatest skill and dedication to its success. I spoke to Papa last night and he swore by the Lost Kings of Rardaria that he will ensure the documents allowing us to marry are secured if you return successful.

Besides Papa, I know of no braver man than you. Please, my Beloved, fulfill this task and put this nonsense of a commoner Mystic behind us. Once that is settled, all will be right in our world and I will be yours.

Be careful of the man who calls himself Ohzem. I do not like him and fear his intentions differ from ours. Do not cross him. Keep this promise for me?

If you can, please ensure my brother is not harmed. Saijar fancies himself to be iron, but even with his

*training, I doubt his blood is as cold as he believes it to
be. My parents put such pressure upon him to succeed.
Indeed they do for all of us. "A house without Mystics is
not noble" is the saying.*

*With the Wind
Across the Sky
Beyond the Moon
Until I die,
Charliss*

"Did you find something, boy?" came a cold voice from behind Sim.

He jumped and spun. Ohzem stood there, watching him without emotion, seemingly undisturbed by even the faintest breeze.

"Mystic Ohzem," Sim managed, bowing low. "I-I was trying
to unpack the tent. I didn't know what it was until—"

Ohzem silenced him by holding out his gnarled hand. Sim
placed the paper in it, carefully avoiding contact.

Sim shifted his feet as Ohzem read the letter. Despite the
Mystic's presence, Sim's gut twisted over worry for Pomella.
The letter proved . . . what? That Zicon and the Black Claws
were here to hurt her? Or that they were here to ensure she
didn't become the apprentice? How could they have known at all
about her coming? Pomella herself received the invitation just a
few days past. This letter had to have been written weeks ago.

Ohzem rolled the paper around in his fingers. "Zicon is just
another animal," he said. "Driven by base desires. Tell me, boy,
do you love that commoner girl?" He tapped the paper with a
pointed fingernail.

Sim swallowed. "I-I don't know."

Ohzem made a strange choking noise. It took a moment for Sim to realize that the Mystic was laughing.

"You're a young fool. Of course you love her." He stepped closer, and Sim found he couldn't pull his gaze from the man's ruined face. The bars of iron ripped through his skin, their edges bleeding and infected. "Is she pretty? Does her scent still linger? Do you see her at night, while you lone in darkness, with her hair loose and back arched as she—"

"No," Sim fired back. "I don't. Not like that."

Ohzem's eyes grew distant, as if he were looking back in memory. "You'll need to learn to stop lying to yourself, boy. And after you do, you'll need to let her go." He returned to the present and glared at Sim. "Otherwise, you're as doomed as Zicon."

He held up the note, pinched between his thumb and forefinger. A thin line of orange heat spread from his fingers and burned a charred circle into the parchment before fading.

Ohzem handed Sim the letter. "Put this back and tell nobody what you found. If you do anything to sabotage our work here, I will kill your friend slowly."

Sim took the letter back. Where Ohzem's name had been written, there was now only a small burned hole. He looked at the Mystic, who turned and walked away.

Sim slipped the letter back into the wooden case and placed it back in the wagon. He forced himself to steady his hands before unpacking the tent. There had been a moment as Ohzem spoke when Sim had realized that the Mystic wasn't speaking about his or Zicon's romantic interests. Ohzem had been speaking of his own. The thought of the iron Mystic being driven by those emotions made him seem even more dangerous.

He needed to help Pomella, but how? Time was running out. He needed to act.

Tonight.

ELEVEN

THE HIGH MYSTIC

Pomella hummed to herself as she left her cottage, carrying a folded bundle. Patchy sunshine greeted her with light slanting through storm clouds that had abated somewhat from the past few days.

Her Common Cord circled her wrist. After the events of yesterday afternoon by the pond, it felt good to wear the little bracelet woven by the women back home.

She'd taken no more than five or six steps when her hummingbirds flew overhead and spun around her, trailing silvery mist. She shooed them away. "Go on; you can buzz about me later. I don't think she'll appreciate you being around."

The smaller of the two, whom Pomella had named Ena, zipped

toward her face, wings stuttering in irritation, then zoomed off toward the moat of flowers surrounding the central tower. Her brother, Hector, followed.

Pomella shook her head. She still didn't understand how she was able to feel their emotions and communicate with them. It was strange how she hadn't really done anything to tame the silver birds. Nothing about her had changed, and she certainly didn't feel like a Mystic. And yet the little birds followed her everywhere, and she could somehow sense their emotions. It was as if each were a little fire—sometimes hot, sometimes blazing— whose emotional temperature she could discern by putting her hands up and measuring what they radiated.

She skipped up the steps to Vivianna's cottage and knocked. Still humming, she rocked back and forth from her heels to her toes.

The door opened and Vivianna glared out. Her tangled hair fell across her makeup-less face. She rubbed her eyes. "What do you want? You aren't coming to sing another song, are you?"

Pomella pinched her lips shut and stopped humming. Without thinking, she dropped a hurried curtsy. Vivianna's face hardened, and Pomella realized the other woman probably thought she was mocking her.

"I'm returning your dress," Pomella said, holding the folded garment out to her. She expected Vivianna to snatch the dress away and slam the door.

But the noblewoman didn't do that. She pursed her lips and studied Pomella. Vivianna's eyes flicked in the direction of the hummingbirds, and for a moment Pomella thought she saw a touch of jealous interest.

"I'm sorry it became muddy," Pomella added, trying to break the awkward silence. "I washed it for you and let it dry overnight."

Finally, Vivianna reached out and took the dress. "Let me tell you something. I may have been able to get past you being a commoner. But you *lied* to me. Being noble isn't just about your family heritage; it's also about acting the part. You may have impressed the High Mystic, and who knows, maybe she'll choose you. But nothing you've done so far has been noble. You can learn to use the Myst all you want, but the people will always see you for what you are. A fraud."

Pomella stared at her, eyes wide. Her hands began to shake, but she forced them steady.

"I'll see you tomorrow for the next Trial," Vivianna said, and closed the door.

Pomella stood there, picking her fingernail, her confidence draining like a bucket full of holes, leaving her empty and cold.

She left the cottage, forcing herself to relax. Why did Vivianna bother her so much? She should just ignore the noblewoman and her jealous, spiteful words. But as much as Pomella might try to convince herself otherwise, she knew a part of what Vivianna said was true. She hadn't been honest.

Just as Pomella began to eye the nearby cottages in the hope of finding Quentin, she heard his voice coming from within the nearest one. ". . . Don't be absurd."

"I can't believe you're helping her!" said another voice.

Pomella's eyes narrowed. Saijar.

Glancing around to ensure nobody was watching, Pomella hurried toward the cabin and tiptoed through its garden. She crouched beneath the window, and listened.

"Yarina invited her," Quentin said in his nonchalant voice. "I know it's unusual, but—"

"It's not unusual; it's disgusting!" Saijar snapped. "Commoners exist to support the nobility. It's for their own good."

"Perhaps," Quentin mused. "But she *is* talented."

"Yeah. And what happens when that talent wins her the apprenticeship?"

"Then I guess the rest of us go home," said Quentin. Pomella could practically hear the shrug in his voice.

"Maybe you can," Saijar said, "but I cannot. If I'm not selected as the apprentice—" His voice cracked. There was a pause, followed by a heavy thump, like a table being kicked. "Not all of us can coast through these Trials like you. Some of us actually *want* to win. If that commoner had any decency, she'd remove herself from the competition. The Myst is only for those of noble blood."

A chair inside the cabin scraped against the floor as it was pushed back. "I have no doubt you'll do anything to win," Quentin said.

Pomella slipped away from the window and hurried toward her own. She hoped the noblemen hadn't noticed her snooping. She could tell Quentin later that she overheard him, but she didn't want him to—

The ground rumbled. Pomella jumped back as patches of dirt tore out of the ground and formed into the Green Man.

"Sweet Brigid, Ox! I'll never get used to that!"

The Green Man smiled, the grass and dirt bending to show his amusement. "I'm sorry. I am told I take time to get used to, like all things. Here. An apology."

He opened his massive palm to reveal a golden lotus flower,

just like the ones that had bloomed the night before. "Its root became severed and I thought you might like to wear it while it lasts."

Pomella reached for it. "Thank you."

"Allow me." He tucked it into her hair with surprising gentleness. Bits of dirt trickled from his fingertips.

Pomella touched the flower and brushed the soil away. "It's lovely."

Oxillian straightened, still smiling. "Mistress Yarina summons you to the tower."

Pomella gaped. "Now? What for? I'm only wearing work clothes." Not that she had anything else to wear after returning the dress to Vivianna.

"Your attire is not important," the Green Man said. "The High Mystic understands this is short notice. Please come with me. We should not keep her waiting."

He turned and strode toward the stone tower. Pomella steadied her nerves by smoothing the long skirt of her work dress. She followed Oxillian but glanced toward Quentin's cottage. She smiled a little remembering her clumsy attempts to hide her nervousness after last night's Trial. She'd been hoping to go see him after returning Vivianna's dress, but that would apparently have to wait.

The Green Man led her down a thin dirt path. Two goats grazed, chewing without care. When she crossed the little wooden bridge, she heard a bark. The brown dog she'd seen yesterday ran up to her, his tongue hanging out of his grinning face. Remembering how poorly Saijar treated the dog, she reached to pat his head, but he hopped up to lick her face.

"Down!" She laughed.

"Broon!" called a voice.

The dog raced away. Pomella looked up to see the gardener standing near the base of the tower. His elderly face stood out beneath a wide-brimmed straw hat. He clutched several weeds in his gloved hands, and stretched his back. When he saw Pomella looking his way, his wrinkled brown face broke into a smile revealing several missing teeth. Pomella turned away, shivering. Vivianna had probably been right about him being Unclaimed. She prayed to the Saints she'd never become one of *them*.

Oxillian stood beside the wooden door to the stone tower. "Mistress Yarina will meet you in the foyer. Please go inside to await her."

Pomella curtsied as he merged into the ground, hardly disturbing a single flower. She took a deep breath and opened the tower door.

It swung easily on stone hinges. Warm air gusted around her as if the tower had sighed. She crossed the threshold, and her skin pebbled. An overwhelming sense of familiarity arose within her, giving her that distinct feeling that she'd been here before, crossed this same threshold, worn this same dress, and appeared just as nervous.

She stepped in all the way, and the door shut behind her.

The foyer was little more than a rounded room with a great spiral staircase ascending the far wall. Small, rectangular windows lined the stairwell at uneven intervals. It surprised Pomella how small the tower seemed from within. She'd never seen a structure this big before, but once she was inside, it was more . . . humble.

"H-hello?" Pomella ventured, pinching her fingers. "Mistress Yarina?"

No answer came, so she took another echoing step. Looking up, she caught her breath as a rainfall of glowing lights circled above her. They drifted like lantern bugs, casting a soft light around the foyer. She gaped at them. *This* was real, tangible evidence of the Myst. Why were these not present in every home across Moth? Why didn't every Goodness and her husband have lights like this so that they didn't need to buy lantern oil? Could she learn to conjure such a thing?

"Ah, Pomella," said a warm voice. Again, that sense of repeated action surged through her. So powerful was the feeling that Pomella wondered if her next words were preordained.

"Um, t-that's me. Yes?"

The High Mystic glided down the staircase, flanked by Vlenar, the laghart ranger. Pomella cringed. If she was repeating this experience, she hoped that wasn't how she'd always responded! She curtsied deeply. "I mean, yes, Mistress, I am here. How may I serve?"

High Mystic Yarina stepped off the stairs and nodded a dismissal to the ranger. "Keep looking, Vlenar. You'll find her."

Vlenar barely spared Pomella a glance before slipping out the door. Yarina stepped up to Pomella and took her hands. Maybe it was her nerves, but Pomella had to force herself to not pull away. Yarina's smooth hands were chilly and colored several shades darker than Pomella's own. Her hair hung long and loose, unlike yesterday when it had been woven up. She wore a simple light-blue robe belted with a gold sash. Pomella noted that even when dressed casually, the High Mystic was radiant. Up close, she really did seem young. Young for an old person, anyway. Pomella estimated she was about forty.

"You have the look of your grandmhathir," Yarina said. "She shines through you."

A sudden lump welled up in Pomella's throat. "You knew her?"

"Lorraina Savarti was a true friend. Come," Yarina said, releasing Pomella's hands. "Let's speak in the library." She led her up the staircase.

Stifling a thrill of excitement, Pomella followed, paying careful mind not to slip on the steep steps. They passed two landings, neither of which Pomella had time to examine. She looked at them as she and Yarina ascended the stairs, longing to explore their secrets. Finally, they came to a third landing. Yarina said, "Here," and exited the staircase.

The pungent scent of incense drifted around Pomella as she stepped into a dazzling library. Rough wooden shelves, loaded with more books than she'd ever seen, reached from floor to ceiling and circled the room, breaking only where a small window or a framed painting hung. Like in the foyer, drifting lights lit the room, but these cast a warmer glow that reminded Pomella of candles. Flat, rounded cushions lay scattered across the carpeted floor. A vase of marigolds sat atop a wooden table beside some cups and a pitcher.

Pomella studied the nearest framed portrait, a painting depicting a handsome woman with long, blond hair. She leaned in close, admiring the fine strokes of paint that created the wreath of wildflowers encircling the woman's head, and the pink touches that formed her faint smile.

"Saint Serrabeth," Yarina said, opening a small tea box. "She was the High Mystic of Moth three masters before mine."

"She was beautiful," Pomella said.

"She's even more so now," said Yarina. "Like most of our predecessors, she's awakened to the realization that she is inseparable from the Myst. She's everywhere now. *Is* everything."

Pomella didn't understand, but nodded anyway. She walked through the room, shifting her gaze to the other portraits. "Do all the High Mystics do that? 'Realize' themselves, I mean?" Too late, she wondered if what she'd said was inappropriate.

Yarina either didn't mind the comment or decided to let it pass. She poured steaming water into two teacups and joined Pomella in front of a painting with a sharp, clean frame. "It's hard to say," the High Mystic said. "I like to believe they do. I certainly feel their active presence. People and their deeds are bound to certain places and times, and here in Kelt Apar, within the Mystwood, I especially feel the light of the past masters guiding me in all my actions."

She handed Pomella one of the cups.

"Thank you, Mistress," Pomella said. She tested the unfamiliar brew and gazed at the portrait in front of her. This one showed a man with a long, braided gray beard. His hair was tied into a long tail. Like so many other things in the tower, Pomella found him to be familiar somehow. "Who is this one?"

"That is Grandmaster Faywong," said Yarina. "My teacher." She lifted her teacup in a gentle salute to the painting. Not sure of the etiquette, Pomella mimicked the gesture.

"He retired, as you know, just recently."

"Yes, I heard," Pomella said. A sudden question rose in her mind. She bit her lip but rushed ahead before she could stop herself. "Was it difficult for you, Mistress? To inherit his duties? Were you ready?"

Yarina shifted toward another painting that rested on a bookshelf, propped up from behind by some old tomes. The painting was rendered in a strange style, with long lines of various thicknesses used to represent trees. But the lower portions of the trees faded out, as if the brush had run out of paint. The effect, it seemed to Pomellá, was that the collective forest was shrouded in a misty fog that lapped at the bases of the trees. A parade of figures emerged from that mix of fog and wood, silvery and bright, and at its head walked an old man with a tall staff in one hand and a flower in the other.

Yarina stared at the painting for a long time before speaking. "Grandmaster Faywong painted this, during the time of his Anointment. He told me he did it because the effort kept him grounded. The experience that he had to go through—that indeed I went through during my own Anointment—takes a great toll. No matter how much you prepare for it, you are never ready."

Pomella thought she understood. At least a little anyway. She could barely imagine what it would be like to become an apprentice, let alone a High Mystic, but in a strange way, she wondered if the experiences weren't so dissimilar. Yarina was still just a woman, subject like anybody else to being afraid. Perhaps Pomella wasn't that much different from what Yarina had once been when she was an apprentice candidate.

Turning away from the painting, Yarina looked at her. "What is it? Tell me."

Pomella paused a moment, gathering her words. "Why did you invite me, Mistress? You had so many people to choose from. Nobles like Lady Elona. I don't understand why you . . ."

"Why I invited you despite an old tradition?"

"Y-yes."

Yarina gestured to the cushions. "Sit down, Pomella. We have much to discuss."

Pomella took her seat, but not until the High Mystic settled onto her own first. Yarina sipped her tea. "I met Lorraina when she was, like you, a candidate to become a Mystic's apprentice. I was—"

"Grandmhathir was a *Mystic*?" Pomella blurted before she could help herself.

Yarina quirked an eyebrow at her.

"Sorry, Mistress," Pomella murmured.

"I met Lorraina when she was a *candidate* to become an apprentice," Yarina repeated. "She was no more a Mystic then than you are now. I was a little girl when she arrived at my home, having traveled from a bordering province in Keffra to call upon my fathir, the Sadan. Our families had been close for generations, but this was the first time I'd met her."

Pomella was certain her heart would beat out of her chest. A thousand questions clamored in her mind, each demanding to be spoken first. But the High Mystic was speaking, so she held her tongue, squeezing her jaw to ensure nothing slipped out.

"I remember her kindness," Yarina continued. "She spoke to me openly and honestly, even though I was not yet ten years old. She shared her nervous concerns, and explained to me how special it was to take the apprentice Trials. She told me stories of Mystics I'd never heard before, and I became enthralled with their tellings. Your grandmhathir had a talent for telling stories. In years since, I've wondered if it was her natural way of Unveiling.

"Her visit sparked something in me. When she departed, I began learning everything I could about the Myst. My teachers had difficulty keeping up with my hunger to learn. The Myst courses through all of us, and I have no doubt that her inspiration led me directly to where I am today."

Pomella frowned. "I never knew she became a Mystic. Fathir said she was a fraud."

Yarina shook her head. "She was not a fraud. Some people can sense and manipulate the Myst easier than others. There is no visible pattern or reason for one person having an affinity for it over another. Your grandmhathir possessed it strongly. But she never became a Mystic, nor an apprentice."

Pomella blinked in surprise. "But . . . if she was so powerful . . . ?"

" 'Powerful' is the wrong word," Yarina corrected. "The Myst manifests in countless ways, and it is rarely about immediate spectacle. The wise understand that ritual, meditation, and acts of courage and kindness will always have the longest-lasting effects and influence on the world. You may live for years in the home of a Mystic, and never see the swirling lights glimmer. From the letters she wrote me later in life, I understood that your grandmhathir forsook her caste in order to marry your grandfathir, and, because of the political fallout, came to Moth and settled in Oakspring. She *chose* that life instead. A rare and beautiful choice."

"But why?"

"Who can guess the mysteries of a person's heart? The path of a Mystic is not an easy one, and the call of a quiet life is hard to ignore."

"Did you ever think of giving it up, Mistress?"

"No," the High Mystic said immediately, her voice strong and steady. "Since the day your grandmhathir awoke the Myst within me, I've dedicated myself entirely to its study and practice. Even when I received the affections of a young man—a boy from here on Moth—I never wavered from the path. The question now is, are *you* ready to dedicate yourself in the same way? Mystics live quiet lives, removed from the attachments of families and worldly gain."

Pomella swallowed and nodded. "There's so much I don't understand. I still don't even know what the Myst actually is, and why I can see those silver animals, and why the hummingbirds follow me. By the Saints, I don't even know how to read Grandmhathir's old *Book of Songs!*"

"You know more than you realize," Yarina said. "The book was likely an old tome, often given to noble children in preparation for Mystic studies. Your grandmhathir probably filled it with notes and basic lessons given to her from her tutors. The Myst is not described easily. It's not tangible, or something you can see. Rather, it's a force that both is natural to our world and exists beyond it. The fact that you can Unveil creatures from Fayün tells me you've been exposed to the Myst a long time, or at least been near somebody who could. Your garden back home also surely bloomed through the unconscious use of the Myst."

A rush of excitement and fear ran through Pomella. Mantepis, the snake, had mentioned Fayün.

"I've only recently learned what the fay are, Mistress, but may I ask, what is Fayün?"

Yarina nodded. "The realm of Myst. It mirrors our own, like the opposite side of a coin, and is the source of both wisdom and confusion. If you become an apprentice, you will learn more of it in time."

Pomella frowned. *If* she became the apprentice.

Yarina sipped her tea. "My comment upsets you? You are, of course, prepared for the consequences if I do not choose you to become my apprentice?"

Pomella choked on her tea, and had to catch her cough with her elbow. Yarina's matter-of-fact tone scared her.

"Mistress?"

"Oh, come now, Pomella. You know exactly what I speak of. If another is chosen, you may become Unclaimed."

Pomella gaped, her mouth wide open. "I— How did you know—?"

"I am well aware of Lady Elona AnBroke's jealous threat. Unfortunately, it is a very real one."

Mantepis' assurance that Yarina would choose one of the noble candidates flickered in Pomella's mind. "But, as High Mystic, couldn't you overrule the baron's declaration?"

"No. Traditionally, a Mystic's focus is given to protecting our land, learning the Myst, and seeking harmony with all things. We freely leave the rest to the nobility."

Pomella gaped at her. "You'd let me become Unclaimed!"

"I do not control your fate. You do."

Anger flared in Pomella. She barreled ahead, heedless of respect. "Then why invite me at all?"

"Your grandmhathir wrote about you on several occasions. It was obvious from her letters and from your gardening reputation around the north part of the island that the Myst flows strongly through you."

Pomella tried to say something, but couldn't find the words. Her hands shook. She didn't bother to hide the dismay that must've been clear on her face. In the days since she'd received the invitation to the Trials, she'd daydreamed of what the real reason could've been to convince the High Mystic of Moth to have a special interest in her. Perhaps it'd been her love of nature, or her ability to sing so beautifully. Or perhaps the High Mystic had looked upon her from afar, gazing through the veil of the Myst, to see the way she'd cared for her grandmhathir and Gabor when her fathir wouldn't. Many reasons, each more elaborate than the last, had occurred to Pomella, teasing her with their possibility.

She was such a blathering fool.

"You are disappointed," Yarina said, sipping her tea.

"I-I just thought the reason you invited me would've been less . . . simple."

"You are not special, Pomella," Yarina said. "None of us are. Renounce that misconception now. Too many would-be apprentices bring that to the Trials."

Pomella's anxiety flared, feeding the inferno of anger building within her. "Of course I'm not *special*. Commoners don't need that reminder. Every day, nobles like Saijar and Elona ensure that we don't forget. As do the Mystics, when they spit on us and force us to grovel because we crossed their path." She jammed her teacup down, slopping dregs across her hand. "Even my fathir takes the time to remind me of the inequity we live in."

"I did not say we live equally," Yarina replied, eyes narrowing. "I meant that, in the eyes of the Myst, we all have the same potential. The ocean does not distinguish between the multitude of drops within it."

"Yet you judge us and handpick only one person to be your apprentice."

"Why do you think we do that?"

Pomella set her jaw. "Why you judge us?"

"No," Yarina said. "Do you know why we take apprentices at all?"

"To pass on your wisdom?" Pomella said, trying to keep the bite from her tone.

"Partially, yes. But mostly, we choose an apprentice to complete ourselves. Most people see the Trials as a political game in which candidates need to make themselves stand out in a positive light. But what the Trials are truly about is finding the right match, on a deeper level, between Mystic and pupil. Often, it is the apprentice that defines the master. And so we choose our successors carefully, and only after we have spent time with them."

Pomella churned those ideas over in her mind. Perhaps there was something she could demonstrate to prove she would be a fine match for the High Mystic. She closed her eyes, gathered her resolve, and tried to remember the soaring feeling from yesterday, when the flower had blossomed above the water, and where everything had felt *right*.

She hummed quietly, trying to unlock her ability to Unveil.

Yarina waited, but Pomella dared not open her eyes to look at her reaction.

Nothing seemed different. Pomella wondered if she sang, rather than hummed, maybe it would—

Yarina's hand touched hers. Pomella opened her eyes.

"It cannot be forced," the High Mystic said in an infuriatingly condescending tone.

Embarrassed by her failure, Pomella pulled her hand away. "I don't know why you're putting me through this."

Yarina rose from her cushion. Pomella moved to stand, but the High Mystic gestured curtly for her to remain sitting. Yarina extended her hand, and Pomella realized she was beckoning for the teacup. Pomella placed it into Yarina's palm, and watched as she took both of their cups to the table near Grandmaster Faywong's painting.

A long moment of silence filled the room. The heavy gaze of the past masters bore down on Pomella. She stared at Yarina's back as the High Mystic tidied the teacups.

"In the end," Yarina said, "all actions I take, indeed all actions *anybody* takes, whether they know it or not, are done by the grace of the Myst."

Pomella bit back a sarcastic retort. Yarina was shifting responsibility. Mantepis hissed in Pomella's ear, whispering about true masters who could simply glance at a person and instantly measure them.

Yarina looked up at the painting of her predecessor. "You are dismissed," she said. "Your second Trial is complete."

Pomella's heart nearly erupted from her chest. "My . . . second Trial? What do you mean?"

"You have the rest of the day free. We will meet tomorrow morning for the final Trial. Upon its completion, I will choose an apprentice."

"Mistress, I—"

"I trust you can see yourself out."

Pomella stood and bowed. "Yes, Mistress." By all the Saints, had she just ruined her chances? She walked to the door, trying to appear as regal as she could.

"Pomella," said Yarina as Pomella reached the exit.

Pomella paused in the doorframe, her back still to the High Mystic.

"We don't walk this life alone," Yarina said. "We all need help at some point. There is no shame in walking a path that was blazed for you. Don't run from it. Walk it with confidence and honor the memory of those who made it possible."

Pomella didn't trust herself to speak. She nodded and fled the tower, unable to respond further without getting angry.

TWELVE

SAD SONGS

Outside the stone tower, cold wind and damp air raked past Pomella. She gritted her teeth, wanting to scream. A draft of chill air caught her hair, scattering it back. Irrationally, she swatted at the wind as if it were a biterbug.

What a complete dunder she'd been. She couldn't keep her jagged tongue between her teeth long enough to keep it from spitting nonsense. She'd just ruined her second Trial, and possibly lost the entire apprenticeship. Her rash actions might have cost her her freedom. She would be branded Unclaimed for this, just like Fathir had said. Bitterness swam in her stomach like mudshite stew.

Pomella twisted toward the tower and considered going back in. Perhaps she could apologize to Yarina and try again.

No. She needed to walk.

She walked back toward her cabin, a storm cloud of anger and fear surrounding her. Maybe she didn't even *want* to be Yarina's apprentice.

Looking around, Pomella saw nobody else nearby, not even the gardener. Heavy clouds gathered, threatening more rain. Despite the disastrous meeting, Pomella's mind swirled with questions about the Myst. Somehow, she'd left with more questions than when she arrived.

Unveilings. Fayün. Attachment. Grandmasters.

Lorraina.

She'd rarely heard her grandmhathir's name used before. Pomella's anger at herself faded, leaving only a lingering fear. Sadness crawled into the place her anger had been. She rubbed her arms to stay warm.

Grandmhathir had always just been a kindly old woman, quick with a hug or melody. But today Yarina conjured images of her as a young woman, maybe no older than Pomella was now. She tried to imagine what Grandmhathir had looked like back then. Likely beautiful, with the same strong features she'd had in old age. Raven hair rather than gnarled gray. What could it have been like to be her? A young noblewoman who traded a lifetime with the Myst for a quiet one with a man.

Why, then, had Grandmhathir encouraged Pomella to learn of the Myst? Did she regret the choice she'd made?

Unbeckoned, Sim's gentle face came to her. She wondered

what he was doing. He'd be home by now, wouldn't he? How long before he didn't even think about her anymore?

She sighed. But why should he? It didn't matter. He was part of her old life now. Her current life needed to be here in Kelt Apar, doing everything it could to survive.

The hummingbirds waited for her on the edge of her cabin's roof. Hector buzzed his wings and Ena flew off, taking him with her.

As Pomella watched them race away, her attention drifted to Quentin's cabin. She walked over to it and knocked. Nobody answered, and she couldn't hear anything inside. She glanced at Vivianna's and Saijar's cabins, but decided against checking for him there. Maybe he was out walking the grounds, perhaps even looking for her.

Thunder rumbled the air. Sweet Saints, she hoped it wouldn't start raining now! Hector and Ena caught up to her right away, flying around and ahead of her. She enjoyed their presence.

Quentin wasn't at the round clearing where the strange monument stood, so she followed the river's flow and crossed the small bridge beside the loch. Tall trees swayed in the wind. In the distance beyond the eastern treetops, MagDoon slept beneath its blanket of snow. She shivered, and wished she'd brought her cloak.

A smattering of sheep roamed an open field. She hadn't been over this way yet, where the grass was taller and more wild than the well-trimmed lawn around the central tower. On the far side, right up against the edge of the forest, a small cabin rested peacefully. Despite the hour, warm light spilled from its single window, and gray smoke wafted from a river rock chimney. Cool shades of blue and gray clouds mixed with the slanting sunlight.

Approaching the cabin, she passed sheep that were thick and ready for their spring shearing. They grazed, hardly sparing her a lazy glance. The cabin's window yawned open, its wooden shutters thrown wide. She peered in to find a sparsely furnished room with a lantern hanging from a peg on the wall. Besides the light, the only indication of an occupant was a small stone cup sitting on a crooked table.

A cold nose touched her hand.

Pomella jumped as the brown dog licked her fingers. A short distance behind him, the gardener leaned on a wooden hoe and nibbled a reed. His wide-brimmed straw hat, tied with a cord below his chin, shaded most of his face.

She took a step back. "H-hello."

The gardener bowed.

She squirmed in discomfort. You weren't supposed to talk to the Unclaimed. But with his attention focused on her so directly, she felt as though she had no choice. "Have you . . . seen my friend? He's one of the candidates. The one with dark skin?"

The old man shook his head.

"Oh, all right. Thank you."

An awkward silence rose between them. Pomella turned and began to walk back to her cabin. She felt the man's eyes on her, and shivered. He was Unclaimed. She shouldn't be around him. It wasn't right.

Pomella stopped. In a day or two, she was likely to become Unclaimed herself. "Oh, buggerish," she mumbled to herself, and made up her mind. She turned to face him. "I'm Pomella." She hated that her stomach fluttered with a small bite of fear.

"Lal," he replied in a thick accent she couldn't identify.

"Lal," she said, testing the surprisingly awkward name.

The gardener grinned and doffed his hat. "I once called that, anyway."

Pomella bit her lip. So it was true. He'd lost his name. "I'm sorry to snoop around your house. I was just looking for my friend."

"Not mine," he said, and pointed the tip of his hoe toward the distant central tower. "House belong to High Mystic Yarina." Each word he spoke was clipped, as if it were its own sentence. Pomella assumed this wasn't his native language.

She followed his gesture. Of course. Unclaimed were not allowed to own property. The dog nuzzled her hand again, clearly seeking attention.

Hector and Ena swooped down, buzzing past the dog. The dog lurched and leaped at them.

"Broon!" Lal scolded.

"It's OK," Pomella said, scratching the dog's ears before addressing the hummingbirds. "Stop it. He's being nice. You should, too."

The gardener laughed. "Your pets?"

"They're my friends," Pomella said. "They follow me around, and—hey! You can see them?"

He shrugged. "Live in woods long enough, be near Mystics and fay. Not unusual."

"Sorry they bothered your dog," Pomella said.

"Not mine," Lal said.

"Oh. Right. The High Mystic."

"No."

She looked at him, confused. "I thought you said . . ."

"Broon free. Wild dog."

The dog barked at the hummingbirds again. Suddenly Lal lifted his hoe high above his head and let out a warlike scream. Pomella gasped and backed away, bumping into the cabin wall.

The gardener charged the dog, screaming and shaking his hoe. "Wild dog! Leave hummingbirds alone! Pomella my friend!"

She watched, wide-eyed, as the dog crouched playfully and barked. Lal swung the hoe, but the dog dodged and ran. They chased each other, fur and legs tumbling and rolling through the field. Suddenly she burst out laughing.

What a strange man.

When Broon was done assaulting him, Lal invited Pomella into the cabin. He stood well clear of the doorway, smiling and gesturing inside. Bits of grass clung to his clothes. There were no chairs, so she sat on the floor. Lal brought her tea, but she took it only to be polite. She'd had enough for one morning. He carefully avoided touching her, and always remained as far from her as he could, head lowered. That comforted her a little.

After he removed his wide hat, Pomella could better see his lined face. He was old, likely older than Grandmhathir had been. Gray hair streaked his head, hacked short in an awkward fashion. His scraggly chin showed a few days of patchy growth. Pomella wondered if he ever had other visitors.

"From Moth?" he asked.

"Yes," Pomella replied. "From Oakspring."

"Ah, yes. I never there."

"Where are you from?"

"Qin. Motherland."

Pomella glanced around the empty cabin. "Have you been here long?"

"I come. I go."

"Do you have any family?"

He bowed to her again. "Thank you. No. All gone."

She thought of her own family, and wondered when or if she would see them again. Not likely. Even if she was chosen as the apprentice, she had no idea if she'd be allowed to return home. She'd miss Bethy and Sim more than anybody else, and Gabor, too. Looking at Lal, she wondered what it would be like to be entirely alone. Nobody to talk to. Nobody to call family.

"You become a Mystic?" he asked her.

She sighed and let out a little laugh at the same time. "Probably not. Mistress Yarina invited me to the apprentice Trials, but I haven't exactly done well so far."

"Can you Unveil Myst?"

"I don't know. I think so. But I don't know how I did it. I'm very confused."

"Hmm," Lal mused, scratching his chin. "You not apprentice yet. So no need to know about Myst yet, hmm?"

"Yes, I suppose. But the others already have training. They know so much about being Mystics! They've been preparing for this their whole life, I think."

"But they not Mystics yet, either. How can they know Myst if they never had real teacher?"

"Well, they know more than me. I wish I had their knowledge and skill."

"I heard you sing," Lal said. "Very good. Better to be best *you* instead of second-best *them*, hmm? Better to have quiet courage that says, 'I will try again tomorrow.'"

Pomella smiled. "Thank you. You're . . . sweet."

He stood up. "I know what you need. Be right back. Stay!"

He shuffled out of the cabin, and Pomella noticed it had begun to rain again. Broon quirked an eye from where he lay on the floor beside the fire, head on his paws. Pomella remained sitting, legs crossed on the plain floor, wondering what Lal was doing. She wondered, too, whether she should go find Quentin.

Lal came back in, holding a large clay pitcher. He gestured for Pomella to slide the little cup toward him. "I make myself. We toast you good luck!"

A nagging fear wiggled in Pomella's stomach. She couldn't believe she was sharing with an Unclaimed. She forced herself to relax and pushed the cup over to him. Lal waited until she'd retrieved her hand before tossing its old contents out the window.

"Tea no good anyway. Mistress Yarina always better at making it."

Pomella winced as if he had just ripped a fresh scab off her skin. She would need as much luck as she could get if she was to have a chance at becoming the apprentice.

He filled the cup with an amber liquid and returned it the same way, saying in a loud, almost comical voice, "For *Pomella*! She get *good luck*!" He gestured for her to drink.

Pomella sniffed the contents.

"Go!" he said, patting his round belly. "Fill basket!"

She hesitated. "Oh, buggerish," she said, and drained the cup. She exploded with coughs.

Lal burst out laughing and collapsed onto the floor, rolling almost onto his back. "Pomella! You have *very good* luck!"

Pomella kept coughing. Whatever it had been, it burned the skivers out of her throat. She could feel it swimming in her belly, like a furnace glowing bright. She'd drunk alcohol before as part of Summeryarn festivals. Oakspring-brewed beer was an important part of the holiday, so Fathir had let her try it as young as fourteen. But *this* was something else.

Lal continued to hoot, rocking back and forth on the ground. "Chi-uy burn your basket!"

Pomella glared at him. "Let's see you do it!" she snapped. She grabbed the pitcher and poured a cupful for him.

Lal waited for her to slide the cup over, bowed to her in thanks, and drank it down. He coughed once, then started laughing again through his teeth, shoulders shaking.

Pomella couldn't help but get caught up in the laughter, too. "Let me try again!" She reached out to snatch the cup from him, but his upheld hand stopped her cold.

"No, no. Too much chi-uy in young basket make you sick."

Pomella nodded. Whatever this stuff was, it acted quickly. "You make good chi-uy!" she said.

Lal bowed. "Thank you. You good, too!"

She pushed the cup over to him. "No. I'm terrible at most things."

Lal poured himself another. "Surely you good at some things. Tell Lal."

"Well," Pomella began, "I like to sing. And back home I had a really beautiful garden filled with five different kinds of roses, sunflowers that were taller than my head, and the most amazing crop of vegetables around. Last spring, people came from other villages to see it."

"Ah, very good. And you just like Lal," said Lal. "Both gardeners. Maybe gardening is your Unveiling." He raised the cup in toast and drank it.

Pomella grinned. "Maybe drinking chi-uy is yours?"

Lal exploded with laughter. *"Good one, Pomella!"*

They joked back and forth some more as the storm outside picked up intensity. Soon the laughter drifted away to silence and they listened to the rain. Pomella closed her eyes, enjoying the moment. The air from the open window smelled so fresh. The drowsy atmosphere dragged her eyelids down. She drifted in and out of sleep. Her eyes longed to remain shut.

Lal's gentle voice woke her. "Pomellaaa," he sang. "Will you sing song?"

She blinked herself to wakefulness. "Sing? Sure, I suppose. What would you like?"

"What you feel."

She yawned. "I feel sleepy."

Lal smiled, but his humor had faded. "If you feel happy, sing happy songs. If you feel content, sing content."

Pomella forced herself to think clearly. She watched the rain outside the window and thought of the songs she knew. "I only know sad songs," she said, realizing it was true.

"Why?" Lal asked.

Pomella slowly circled her finger in patterns on the floor. "I sing when I'm sad, or when I'm thinking about sad things. There haven't been a lot of happy things for me to sing about lately."

Lal just smiled at her, and Pomella was struck by his humility. She suddenly regretted what she'd just said. Surely an Unclaimed man had more to be sad about than her, but there was no sadness around him. Only . . . contentment.

"In Qin, where I come from," he began, "old village is in mountains. Maybe like Oakspring. Looks different, but same. Understand? They have tradition where full moon night everyone gathers outside and sings. Reminds me of you. Highborn welcome, too. Leader of song called *huzzo*. *Huzzos* always chosen for mighty voice. Stands middle of village and chants, '*Huzzzz-oh!*'"

Pomella started at the sudden deep resonance in his voice, like an earthquake within the small cabin.

"After few times, more people join. '*Huzzzz-oh!*' Soon whole village is chanting. In thin mountain air, it can be heard all way down to Yin-Aab. '*Huzzzz-oh*' becomes voice of mountain. A song of people and mountain together."

"I don't know any songs like that," Pomella said.

The old gardener leaned back against the cabin wall and shut his eyes. "If you say so, Pomella. But I think you are song like that, waiting to be sung." Within moments, his breathing evened and a faint snore rumbled out.

Pomella sighed, puffing out a strand of hair that trailed across her face. The little stone cup still rested in Lal's hand, and the clay pitcher sat beside him. Next to the fireplace, Broon snoozed, occasionally snoring like the gardener.

Pomella eyed the cup. Biting her lip, she eased forward and pinched the rim, lifting it away. Lal snored again, and Pomella froze. She didn't think he would mind if she had another sip of his chi-uy. She just didn't want to wake him.

As she pulled the cup free, Lal shifted, rubbing his nose. His arm bumped hers.

Pomella gasped and dropped the cup. It clunked on the floor. She yanked her hand away and instantly wiped it on her other sleeve. Glancing to make sure Lal was still asleep, she grabbed the cup and pitcher and slid to the opposite wall across from him.

She'd *touched* an Unclaimed. He was just a harmless old man, she knew, and very kind, but still, it was hard to shake the feeling that she shouldn't touch him. "Don't be such a blatherhead," she muttered to herself.

She poured some chi-uy and gagged it down. It burned again, but not as badly this time.

Lal's story of the mountain singers lingered in her mind. She closed her eyes and tried to imagine what it would be like to live in the remote village of Yin-Aab. Probably a lot like Oakspring, like Lal had said, only with more sheep. In her mind, she envisioned a clear night where a thousand stars clearly shone through towering evergreens, dimmed only by the light and smoke roaring off a central village bonfire. She saw herself standing in a ring around the fire, holding hands with the person next to her, a boy. He was handsome, like Sim, but with darker skin, like Lal or Quentin. This imaginary boy smiled at her, and squeezed her hand before lifting his deep voice in song.

Everyone in the ring sang that strange "*huzzo*" chant. "*Huzzzz-oh.*" Even now it resonated in Pomella's chest, rumbling with power, like an echo of a drum vibrating across a wide valley. It was as if she could actually hear it, right here, alive in this moment as she sat in the little cabin and drank more chi-uy.

Lifting her voice, Pomella tested the song.

She started with a quiet note—"*hhuuu*"—and slid into the next—"*zzzohh*." The word filled the room with a quiet whisper but seemed to linger, drawing strength from the air. Maybe it was just her imagination, but she could almost hear the rain, and smell the fresh scent of stormy air more clearly now.

Pomella repeated the "*huzzo*" notes again, this time a little higher, and adding a touch of musicality. They definitely echoed, dancing with the first instance of her chant.

She opened her eyes, and gasped.

The entire cabin was alight with silvery mist. Tendrils of wavy lace drifted through the air, pulsing with faint luminance. Pomella's heart swelled. She was using the Myst!

"*Huuuz-oh*," she sang again softly, and as she did, the twisting lines pulsed in rhythmic time to her notes.

Pomella wanted to rush over to Lal and wake him, and show him what she'd created, but she worried that the effect would be ruined if she did. She wished Yarina could see this. Why had the Myst awoken around her this time? Why couldn't it have worked during her second Trial, when it counted? Maybe the chi-uy was involved. It was clearly stronger than Yarina's tea.

There was nothing she could do about that now. Relaxing again, Pomella sang another gentle "*huzzo*" and smiled as the silky threads pulsed with light.

This called for a little celebration. She poured herself another splash of chi-uy.

Pomella stumbled back across the open field. The rain had slowed to a drizzle, so she'd thought it would be a good time to return to her cabin. The afternoon had long ago faded, and full dark seemed just a hair's breadth away.

As she walked, she tried unsuccessfully to keep herself from splattering through mud. She didn't *mean* to be so unsteady. In fact, with her head so full of chi-uy, she was *trying* to walk as normally as possible. But no matter how much she concentrated on putting her foot down in exactly the right spot, the muddy ground proved to be less stable than she'd initially judged. If Sim or Bethy were here, they would have called her a dunder.

The idea of it made her giggle.

She trudged through the wet grass, feeling like a soaked towel by the time she arrived at her door. She smiled and waved good night to her hummingbirds, who seemed perplexed by her condition, and stumbled into her cabin. It was dark, so she fumbled around until she lit the oil lantern with a striker. She stared into the smooth, steady flame and felt her head swirl. She began to hum, and was just about to strip off her soaking work dress when a soft knock sounded at the door.

She hopped to the door, missed the door handle, and caught it on the second try. The door opened and she managed to focus on Quentin.

"Hi," she said, surprising herself at how sober she sounded. *Very* sober.

He gave her a strange look. "Where were you today?" he asked. "I was looking for you."

"Were you?" she crooned. "That's the sweetest."

"May I come in?"

She took his hand and pulled him in, stumbling and nearly rolling her ankle. He caught her. "Are you all right?"

She steadied herself and stepped closer to him. A flash of surprise crossed his face.

"I'm fine," she murmured.

"I brought you something," he said.

Her eyes widened. "A gift?"

"Yes." He handed her a scroll case made of dark, lacquered wood. An unfamiliar coat of arms was painted on it.

Trying to be as deliberate as possible, Pomella slowly opened the capped end and slid out a roll of fine paper. Her fingers explored its smooth surface.

"This paper is so nice!" she said.

Quentin grinned. "Open it."

She rolled it open and gasped.

Musical notation, written in a fine, steady hand between perfectly straight lines, filled the entire scroll. It wasn't a complex tune, but she broke out into a wide grin and laughed when she recognized it.

"Is this 'Boom-bung Dog-ding'?"

"It is. I figured you had to be properly educated in the classics."

"Quentin, this is the kindest gift, *ever*." She wished the last word hadn't sound so slurred.

"I asked Oxillian to deliver my request to my manservant waiting in the woods, and return when it was ready. It arrived earlier today. I've also asked him to send a rider to the nearest city and hire a bard to prepare other songs for you."

She gaped at him. "Thank you. For everything. And for, you know . . ."

He looked at her, waiting. "For . . . ?"

She set the scroll down and closed the door behind him. Her hand trembled as she lifted it to touch his cheek. "For being you."

His closeness, and the chi-uy, warmed her skin. She eased closer to him. "And thank you," she said, "for being so handsome and for having these *arms*." She traced a finger along his muscular shoulder. A tiny part of her realized she was finding bravery in her unstable condition, but blither-blather, she didn't care. Her fingers found the back of his head and the coarse hair growing there.

"You've been drinking," he said quietly.

"I want to kiss you," she whispered, amazed and proud of her boldness.

"Pomella . . ."

"Quentin-my," she whispered, holding his gaze. She took a steadying breath and spoke as rationally and steady as she could manage. "I. Want. To kiss. You. Now."

She felt his shoulders tremble as she lifted up to her tiptoes and closed her eyes. Her mouth met his. She moved her hands slowly up his back, and melted when he leaned into her.

She kissed him again, more urgently this time, and he went with her, matching her intensity. Between more kissing and quick gasps for breath, their hands explored each other's bodies. Pomella didn't care, even welcomed, his hands caressing her hair, neck, and down the front of her chest. After a long minute, Quentin pulled away.

"Maybe we shouldn't," he said. "I don't want to take advantage."

"Take advantage of what?" Pomella said, kissing his neck. "I want to take advantage of right now, before we have the last Trial. I ruined my meeting with Yarina."

He gently pushed her away to half an arm's length. "Not like this. It's not right."

"Do I taste like dog?" she blurted.

His face scrunched into a confused grimace. "No, not at all."

She closed her eyes and sighed. The whole room spun around her. She gripped his arm to steady herself. "Maybe you're right," she said. "Slowing down might be a good idea right now."

He moved to the table, which was filled with fresh food and a wooden pitcher. "Let me get you some water."

"No," she replied, holding on to his arm. "Come here. Please."

He obliged and she put her head against his chest. "You're so kind," she said.

"You're worthy of kindness, Pomella-my."

A lump formed in her throat. She reached for him again, and kissed him slowly, meaning every bit of it.

"Pomella?" came a surprised voice from the window.

She and Quentin whipped their heads toward the voice at the same time. Before she could cry out, Quentin pulled a knife.

Her heart thundered. She barely managed to speak.

"Sim?"

THIRTEEN

THE ROAD TO MAGDOON

"Blessed Saints, what are you doing here?" Pomella exclaimed. She stared, dumbfounded, as a soaking-wet Sim stood outside the half-shuttered window of her cabin.

She sidestepped away from Quentin. The room refused to stop spinning no matter how hard she squeezed her eyes. For a brief moment she wondered if Sim was really there, staring at her with that hurt look on his face.

Quentin pointed at him with his dagger. "You know this man?"

Somewhere in her muddled mind, Pomella wondered where Quentin had kept that dagger. She recalled groping him thoroughly just a moment before. She shook off the thought. Now wasn't the time to be mooning over Quentin. But bugger Sim for having the worst timing!

"Yah," she said.

Sim raised his hands to show he was unarmed. "Can I come in?" Pomella wondered where his sword was.

He slipped around the corner of the cabin and pushed the door open. Water rolled off him as though he'd brought the storm inside. He set a small travel sack onto the floor.

Shaking water off his hands, Sim bent his back in just the barest hint of a bow to Quentin. Pomella could practically feel every muscle in Quentin's body tense.

"She and I are longtime friends," Sim said. "I escorted her through the forest five days ago."

"So you've left your barony without permission. Why are you here?" Quentin jabbed his blade in the air. "Answer me!"

Pomella touched his shoulder. "Quentin . . ."

The hard look didn't leave Quentin's face, but he lowered the dagger.

"I need to talk to you in private," Sim said to Pomella. "Please."

"Sim," she began, "I don't . . ." She wilted as she saw the look on his face. By all the buggered Saints in the underworld, what was he doing here?

"Oh, shite and blather. Quentin, I think he and I should talk alone."

"I don't think that's a good idea, Pomella," said Quentin.

Pomella softened her tone. "I know him. I'll be fine. Let's complete tomorrow's Trial, and then we can . . . continue."

His jaw clenched, but he nodded. He squeezed her hand before lowering the dagger. He walked to the door and bumped Sim's shoulder as he passed.

Strangely, Pomella didn't have to fight the urge to roll her eyes at them. She couldn't help the small part of herself that found it a little flattering.

Sim waited until the door closed behind Quentin. "Pomella, I—"

"What in the Dying Hells are you *doing* here, Sim?" she snapped. "I'm sorry if you saw me doing something that makes you uncomfortable, but I thought we'd decided that it would be best if we just—"

Sim stepped up to her and grabbed her shoulders. "You're in danger," he said. "There's a plot to kill you."

Pomella shoved Sim away. The room seemed very small. She looked out the window, suddenly concerned about being watched. Sim followed her gaze and shuttered the window.

"W-what do you mean? How do you know?" she asked.

"I don't have a lot of time," he said. "I snuck away from the camp to find you. I need to get back quickly before they notice I'm gone. There's—"

"What camp? What do you mean? You didn't go home?"

"I started to go home, but I stumbled upon mercenaries from the Baronies of Rardaria. They call themselves the Black Claws. They plan to kill you."

She blinked. Saijar was from Rardaria. "Why would they want to harm me?"

Sim sighed, exasperated. "Think about it, Pomella! You're a

commoner doing something you're not supposed to. You shat in their business and now they're fixing to eliminate you. There's a Mystic leading them! He's . . . he's terrifying, Pomella."

Pomella touched her temple. The only thing buzzing was her head. "What . . . what are they planning to do?" she asked.

Sim ran his hand though his wet hair. "I don't know. But I think they plan to strike soon. Tomorrow, even. We need to make you safe and warn the High Mystic."

"No!" Pomella said immediately. By the Saints, if her head didn't stop spinning, she'd retch on his boots. "I'm perfectly safe here. Nobody gets into Kelt Apar without the High Mystic's consent. And there's some sort of guardian force protecting us here. I can't remember what it's—"

"The ceon'hur," Sim said. "I met a ranger who mentioned it. Do you know what it is?"

She shook her head. "No. But it won't let anybody in."

"I got in."

She glared at him. "That's because . . ."

Sim raised an eyebrow, waiting.

"Oh, buggerish, I don't know *how* you got in, but that's not the point. The point is that I need to do this alone, Sim. I'm in the middle of these Trials! I can't jump at shadows I can't even see."

Sim threw his hands up in exasperation.

Pomella's temper flared through her drunken fog. A thousand thoughts crashed around in her skull. "Don't do that again."

"What?"

"That! Rolling your blazing eyes at me."

"You're being foolish, Pomella. You know this. I don't know what you were doing tonight, but you've obviously got a badger running your mind and mouth right now. Don't be stupid!"

She reeled as if slapped. His face blanched when he realized what he'd said. He sighed and lifted a hand toward her. "I'm sorry."

She stared at him with cold iron eyes. "You told me that you understood me," she said with controlled fury.

"Pomella," he said, easing toward her, "I didn't mean to hurt you. I want to protect you. I—"

"I don't need you to save me, Sim!" she yelled. "I'm here, doing what you and Bethy and Grandmhathir and all the others in Oakspring wanted me to do! I'm rising above my station. I'm following my heart and all that other blather and shite! Yet you won't let me succeed or fail on my own!"

"Your life is in *danger!*" he pleaded.

"And if I beg for help, if I go crying to Mistress Yarina to protect me, it will only prove those mercenaries right! That I'm just a commoner who needs special protection from a Mystic."

Sim scratched the back of his head and dropped his hand. "I don't understand why you'd endanger your life like this."

Pomella forced herself to take a steadying breath. "Fine. I'll handle this on my own. I need to think."

Sim gave her a flat stare. "I really hope you do. What would that other man say?" He pointed in the direction Quentin had gone.

Pomella scoffed and plunked down onto a chair. Why did he have to bring Quentin into this? She felt sick to her stomach. "Maybe we had a chance once, Sim. But it can't happen anymore."

He swallowed and nodded. "Yah. I suppose it can't," he whispered. "But no matter what you think, you're being foolish."

He walked to the door and opened it. Hesitating on the threshold, he turned back and said, "The Black Claws captured a ranger named Rochella. She's a virga. While you fret over whether to tell the High Mystic, at least know she's in danger, too. They're camped east of here, just north of the road."

He retrieved his sack from beside the door and removed a square bundle from it. She gasped.

The Book of Songs.

He set it on the nearby table, then stepped out into the rain. She heard him slosh through the mud and away from the cabin. The rain grew heavier, thick drops storming on the roof. Pomella stared at the book as confusion and guilt mixed with the chi-uy in her stomach. She scrambled for her night pot and vomited.

Sim stormed away from Pomella's cabin, not caring that the rain poured down onto him. Foolish girl! Why did she have to be so stubborn? She was just going to get herself hurt. She put her trust in the High Mystic when it was a *Mystic* who wanted to harm her.

He stopped and considered whether he should go back and talk sense into her. Whether she knew it or not, she needed him. He could help her. If she got hurt, or worse, he'd never forgive himself.

Sim frowned. Maybe she didn't need him. Maybe he just needed her. Perhaps they needed each other?

Dim light shone from Pomella's cabin, pushing back the night. Sim slumped his shoulders and sighed. No. He couldn't go back. He'd told her what she needed to know, the essentials anyway, and she'd dismissed him.

Again.

A lump rose in his throat. He had to accept that she didn't want him in her life. Their childhood together, their shared grief after the plague, their tenuous trust that night in the pit . . . he thought it special, but she didn't.

If only he'd stayed with her after the laghart ranger found them. If only he'd let her kiss him.

Faced with the reality that she was gone for good, that he'd truly pushed her away forever, Sim felt a hollow echo in his heart where before only she had existed.

And, of course, there was the other man. Sim had no idea who the tall, dark-skinned nobleman was but could only assume he was another candidate for the apprenticeship. He'd been wearing fine clothes, things that Sim would never in his life be able to afford. Why *wouldn't* Pomella choose a man like that over him?

He had to let her walk her own path now.

His fist clenched. Just because she wouldn't accept his help didn't mean he couldn't try to protect her. He couldn't stop the plague from taking Dane. But he could put himself between Pomella and the people who meant her harm. He could still make a difference, even if Pomella didn't know it. Even if she couldn't see him, or feel his presence, he'd be ready.

Ducking through the rain, Sim hurried to the nearest edge of the forest and slipped into the trees. He headed north, always keeping Kelt Apar in sight. Better to edge the long way around the compound than walk directly across the open lawn in plain sight.

Also, the Green Man had insisted on it.

The Green Man. Sim still found it hard to believe that he'd seen the legendary figure twice in his lifetime, let alone spoken to him. Earlier in the evening, Sim had followed Rochella's directions to locate Kelt Apar and had taken no more than a few steps onto the open grass, his eyes fixed on the strange stone tower in the center, when the ground ripped open, knocking him backward.

He'd scrambled away, watching the huge figure form out of grass and dirt and stone. He had looked down at Sim, his pebbled eyes looking straight into his heart.

"I am surprised to see you here, child of Oakspring," the Green Man had rumbled. "State your business."

Pushing himself up from the grass, Sim had faced the strange creature directly. "I'm here to warn my friend Pomella about a threat to her life."

"You are not permitted to enter Kelt Apar at this time. You may give me the message."

Lightning flashed across the sky, momentarily illuminating the forest, bringing Sim back to the present. He found a massive boulder sitting in the swollen river, the same one that flowed into Kelt Apar. He climbed it and used it to leap the water, landing on the far side. Flinging mud off his pants, he continued his way around the large clearing, lost in thought.

He'd explained everything about the Black Claws to the Green Man. He told him of Zicon's letter and Ohzem's threats. When the Green Man heard of Rochella's capture, his face contorted in anger.

"You did well to tell me this," the Green Man said. "I will inform the High Mystic. Go warn your friend, but leave immediately after. Find shelter and return to your home in Oakspring."

Sim shook his head. "I can't. I've left the barony. Baron AnBroke will declare me Unclaimed."

"Then find shelter and a ranger will come to you in a few days. The High Mystic will assist you when this storm has passed."

Sim knew he wasn't referring to the weather. He'd agreed to the Green Man's terms, but had no intention of finding shelter and hiding. He still didn't fully trust the High Mystic, or any Mystic for that matter.

Trudging through mud, he tried not to think about what he'd seen in Pomella's cabin. What he'd found still churned his stomach. For years he'd dreamed of someday holding Pomella, of kissing her, and having her love him in return. Seeing her with another man tore his heart.

Pushing those memories away, he reached the northeastern edge of Kelt Apar and found the mark he'd made on an oak tree. There would be another one farther into the forest, and another every twenty steps after that, to ensure he could find his way back in the dark.

With one last look at the tower silhouetted in the clearing, Sim pushed into the forest, hurrying back to the Black Claw camp. The rain continued to pour. The thick trees around him did little to ease his discomfort. He yawned repeatedly as he walked, realizing just how little sleep he'd had. His stomach rumbled, and each step became harder than the last.

Finally, after the rain stopped and just as morning light began to blossom in the forest, Sim tiptoed back into the camp. He glimpsed Dox's hulking form sleeping under the wagon, as expected. Nothing but silence came from Zicon's tent. Stepping uneasily, Sim made his way to the place he normally slept.

"Where you been, scrit?" came a ratlike voice.

The blood drained from Sim's face. He turned to see Jank stepping out from behind a tree. The short man scratched his scraggly chin. As always, Sim's sword hung at his belt.

"Huh? Where ya been?" Jank said.

"I was doing my morning necessary," Sim said, continuing to where he was headed. He hoped he appeared casual.

Jank followed. "That's strange, because I don't smell any piss. At least, no more than usual round you."

"Get spiked, Jank."

"Oh, you want to spike me now! Look who the tough pup is! So tell me, if you were squatting in the woods just now, where've you been all night?"

Sim's heart pounded and his mind raced. What were the chances Jank had stayed awake all night waiting for him? "I was here, where else?"

"I looked for you last night, culk!" Jank snapped, spittle flying as he jabbed his finger in the air. "You left the camp!"

Dox stirred, and sat up. "What's happening?"

"Jank's blathering on about—"

Jank's shoulder rammed into Sim's chest, knocking him down and crushing the air from his lungs.

"Liar!" Jank screamed, his hands scrabbling for Sim's throat.

Dox ran over and wrapped his meaty arms around Jank,

trying to pull him off. Jank landed a punch against Sim's head, rattling him.

Sim surged to his feet and sprang back at Jank. He crashed into the smaller man before Dox could let go.

"Leave off!" Dox roared, but Sim raised a fist, planning to break Jank's remaining teeth.

Another hand gripped Sim's wrist from behind and hurled him backward. Sim staggered, trying not to lose his balance. Zicon stood between them, fuming with rage.

"You jagged scrits," Zicon said, breathing heavily. "Do you have any idea what you could have done? Stand up, Jank."

Jank snatched himself off of Dox and stood. "He's a jagged liar, Zicon! He went to warn his girlfriend!"

Zicon loomed over Jank. "By all the dead Graces, if you draw that boy's blood during our mission, I will—!"

"Hold," came a cracking voice, and all eyes turned to the familiar hunched figure of Ohzem. The Mystic walked past them, slowly eyeing each in turn. Zicon clenched his jaw and gathered himself, bowing slightly. Jank gritted his teeth and bobbed his head forward.

Ohzem stopped in front of Sim. He reached a bony hand toward Sim's face and clutched his jaw, sending a spike of pain shivering through him. The Mystic examined Sim's face, turning it back and forth slowly.

Ohzem turned to Jank and Dox. "Is either of you bleeding?"

Each looked at his arms and torsos. Dox rubbed his bald head with a hand and checked it for blood.

Jank spit to the side. "Why does it matter? You're obsessed with blood."

"Shut your mouth, Jank!" Zicon hissed. "This is a Mystic you're talking to."

"He's right," said Ohzem. "I *am* obsessed with blood. And you should be, too, if you want to survive more than a heartbeat longer on this island."

"What do you mean?" snapped Jank.

"I mean we are on Moth with ill intent," Ohzem said. "We are in the heart of the Mystwood, in the shadow of MagDoon, where the Myst is naturally strong, where the High Mystic's power holds the greatest sway. Have you not wondered, *Jank*—" Ohzem sneered as he spoke the name, "—why we have not been destroyed by the ceon'hur?"

"Because it's a myth," Jank said.

"No! The ceon'hur watches the Mystwood every moment. He knows what happens and destroys all threats. But we are safe, because of me. Because of *my* power, you live another day. Through my sacrifice, through my power, you are hidden from the all-seeing eyes of the ceon'hur."

Jank shuffled his feet. "I don't see what this has to do with blood."

"Blood is everything," Ohzem said in his quiet, raspy voice. "Through it, we are immortal. It carries the history of our ancestors. The promise of our divinity. Because of this, even iron, the embodiment of the ancient world, must yield before it. If you shed the innocent blood of a person under the High Mystic's protection onto the ground, you destroy the iron cloak I have woven around us."

Silence swallowed them all. After a moment, Zicon stepped forward. "Mags, tie this one up," he said, gesturing at Sim. "Jank, you're helping Dox. Get the ranger ready. I want us moving in the next ten minutes."

Zicon dragged Sim away by the arm. "What's your story, boy?" he snarled. "Where did you go, and why? Did you go to the tower? Lie to me and I'll suffocate you with my own hands, the Mystic be damned."

Sim met his gaze. "Fine," he said. "I went to Kelt Apar to find Pomella, my friend."

Zicon's face hardened. "Why?"

A stream of reasons flowed into Sim's mind. Because he needed to warn her. Because he needed to stop the very man breathing into his face at this moment.

He settled on a version of the most honest answer. "Because I overheard Jank say we were near the tower. I didn't know if she'd made it there safely or not. I-I wanted to see her."

Zicon narrowed his eyes. "There's more. Tell me."

"No, there's not," Sim said, holding his ground. "I miss her, OK? I figured this would be my only chance. I won't see her ever again, and the thought of her not being in my life is hard. Surely you understand that? You ever had a woman snare you into thinking about her and doing dunder things for her?"

He knew he'd struck the metal right. Zicon's jaw tightened. Mags arrived with iron cuffs for Sim. "You're under lock until this is done," Zicon said.

Sim didn't argue. Mags bolted the metal cuffs onto his wrists. Rochella waited on her knees a short distance away. Her lank hair spilled across her striped face.

Perhaps sensing him, she looked up and held his gaze.

Zicon led them south to a crossroad. The company took the east road, heading toward MagDoon. Exhausted, Sim straggled along as best he could. They allowed him to eat some dry meat and wilted vegetables. It tasted terrible, but he wolfed down every bite.

MagDoon loomed before them, even larger than the stories implied. It cast hard shadows across their path as it blocked the sun at this early hour.

"As soon as our business is done, I'm gunna enjoy skinning you up," Jank said from behind him as they walked. "You know, to make this trip worth it. Even with triple pay, I was beginning to think it wasn't. But you're making things look brighter. Maybe I'll use your old sword to do it."

Sim ignored the taunts. He kept his eyes down and concentrated on walking. They arrived at the base of the mountain, where at least four winding paths led up. Sim's heart sank at the sight of the steep slopes. "Are we climbing that?"

Zicon reined to a stop, his muscular stallion dancing with energy. "Hormin, you and Jank unpack what we need from the wagon. You'll come up with us. Mags, remain here with the ranger and the horses. Dox, get the chest ready. You'll stay here, too."

Confused, Sim watched as Dox and Mags lifted the heavy wooden chest from the back of the wagon.

"You," Zicon said, kicking Sim's shoulder with the toe of his boot, "you'll be carrying that up."

Sim looked at the heavy chest and glowered back. "Yah? And how am I supposed to to do that?"

"Figure it out, boy," Zicon said, and trotted his horse to the trailhead.

Jank stuffed a tangle of ropes and leather strips in Sim's face. "Get going, scrit."

Mumbling curses to himself, Sim set about securing the chest. He examined the jumbled lines, trying to figure out where to start. Why were they climbing MagDoon? Pomella was in Kelt Apar.

Dox helped him unwind the straps and loop them around the chest. "Wrap it around your shoulders and waist like this," he said. "Don't use your arms."

"What's in there?" Sim asked.

"You don't want to know. I don't understand it myself, anyway."

At Zicon's command, Sim began dragging the chest uphill through mud. The leather and rope dug into his shoulder, and by the time he'd taken four steps he knew it was going to be a miserable haul. Within ten minutes, he thought he would die. He lagged behind, but Jank walked behind him, murderously taunting him.

"You're filth," Jank said. "After we reach the top and Zicon does his task, I'm going to kill you. Or maybe I'll maim you and let you starve as Unclaimed."

Gritting his teeth, Sim poured his hatred of Jank into pulling the chest. Somehow he survived an hour, and found himself looking back across the forest from a short way up the side of the mountain. Ohzem led the way up the path, using his iron staff as a walking stick. Sim eyed it enviously.

The rain held off, thank the Saints, but the muddy trail seemed endless. Zicon ordered a rest when they came to the base of the switchbacks. Hormin passed out food, as quiet as ever.

Sim welcomed the food, but the time spent resting only reminded him how tired he was. As they packed up, he stepped off the path and found a heavy oak branch that had fallen. He checked its height and thickness, and judged it to be good enough for a walking stick. Between dragging the chest and having his wrists cuffed, he thought he could manage if he used both hands. He snapped off a few extra branches and hitched the straps over his shoulder.

"Put the stick down, scrit," Jank said, hands resting on Sim's sword hilt.

Sim held his hands up to show how they were bound. "It's just to help me walk."

"I said drop it, or I'll crack you with it."

"For a little man you sure have a big mouth," Sim retorted. "Does it make you feel brave to threaten me when I'm tied up and hauling a stone weight of wood and iron?"

Jank's face contorted with rage but Zicon's yell prevented him from snapping back. "Shut it, both of you!"

Sim grinned and began dragging the chest, using his new walking stick for support. He was glad for its help, because the path steepened. With every step he became convinced that his next would be his last. At first he swore he wouldn't stumble in front of Jank, but later Sim settled for just hoping the rat-faced man didn't trample him.

As the afternoon wore on, Sim struggled to put one foot in front of the other. The angle of the sun indicated they had swung around to the north side of the mountain. Had it not been for the staff, Sim knew he would have stumbled face-first into the ground. He tripped several times, his legs barely strong enough to move. He lagged behind, and soon he and Jank fell behind the others.

"Jank!" Zicon called from up the slope. "Help him carry it!"

"Ah, dead Graces, Zicon! I didn't sign up for—"

A glance from Ohzem silenced him. The mercenary swallowed and looked at Sim. He spit to the side and lifted the opposite end of the chest.

"Walk," Jank said. "If you fall, I'll break your ribs."

Night fell, and Zicon insisted they keep walking. Ohzem conjured four tiny, floating lights, similar to the guiding stone the Green Man had given Pomella. They floated in the air, drifting lazily, giving off just enough light to walk by.

Sim found himself nodding off as he walked. Twice he fell, and each time Jank cursed and kicked dirt into his face.

They arrived near the summit after sunrise. Sim couldn't remember the last time he'd slept. Zicon motioned for them to set the chest down, and Sim collapsed, glad to be done with it. Part of him registered the stunning view to the west, but mostly he didn't care and just wanted to shut his eyes.

"Bring it into the cave," Ohzem told Zicon.

Grunting, Sim managed to stand and drag the chest with Jank's and Hormin's help, leaving the oak branch where it lay. He looked around, trying to get a sense of what the Black Claws intended. Slabs of ruined buildings lay scattered across the clearing. A cave entrance loomed against a hillside. From what Sim could tell, the path led just a little farther around the hill toward what must be the mountain's summit. What did this place have to do with Pomella?

Ohzem led them into the cave.

Dim light revealed a wide, hollowed-out cavern, about fifty feet across. The chamber was roughly circular and appeared to be natural, although Sim wondered if it had just been crafted to appear so. Drawings on the wall caught his attention, similar to the ones he'd seen with Pomella in the other cave. The style seemed the same, but time had faded the images into obscurity.

Zicon looked around, his hand resting uneasily on the hilt of his sword. Ohzem walked to the center of the cavern and swept his staff around in a slow arc. The glowing lights he'd summoned earlier followed his movement, illuminating the cave's dim recesses.

"Prepare the circle," Ohzem said.

Hormin and Jank set the chest in a deep part of the cave. As they did so, Zicon opened the large sack he'd carried up and dumped out the spikes Sim and Dox had forged.

"What are the spikes for?" Sim asked.

"To shove in your cavity," Jank said.

"Enough," Ohzem said. He looked at Sim. "Attend me."

Zicon gestured for Hormin to hand Sim one of the spikes and a heavy mallet. Ohzem tapped his staff on the ground, and a thin crack appeared. "Here," he said.

"What is—?"

"Just do it!" Zicon snapped.

Sim knelt down and balanced the spike in place. He didn't like what was happening, but as long as Pomella was safe in Kelt Apar, he'd continue to go along with this.

He lifted the mallet, and hammered the spike into the crack.

Ohzem tapped another spot on the cave floor, about a stride away, and Sim hammered in another spike. They continued in a wide circle until all of the spikes were buried half their length into the floor.

"Now we wait," Ohzem said.

Sim wiped his brow. "Wait for what?"

"For a new dawn," the Mystic said.

FOURTEEN

DREAMS OF THE MOUNTAIN

The next morning, the rain fell in slanting torrents across Pomella and the other three candidates, souring their moods even further. They stood by the lake's edge under Ox's patient gaze. Pomella shifted her feet, feeling plenty of aches. Vivianna, who stood beside her, glanced at her and rolled her eyes. None of them moved or said anything to one another as they waited for the High Mystic to arrive and reveal their next Trial.

Pomella shivered inside her cloak. She'd been up all night, sicking into the night pot. She'd slept for maybe an hour on the floor beside the bed. Her stomach lurched again as she thought of her bitter argument with Sim. It still boiled her guts how he was always trying to *save* her, but now she regretted some of her words. She'd been embarrassed when he saw her with Quentin, and drunk as well. Perhaps she could have listened better. She tried not to dwell on their argument, but not even the more pleasant memory of kissing Quentin could settle her.

Her head throbbed like it'd been kicked by a bear, and the constant pelting of rain atop her hood didn't help. Some sunshine would be nice for once. She wore her Springrise dress beneath the cloak because it was the nicest outfit she had.

Pomella dared a glance at Vivianna, and wilted anew at the noblewoman's splendor. Vivianna carried a wide umbrella to keep the rain off, so her perfectly made-up face remained a cool mask of dignity. The woman dressed far more practically than she had for the first Trial, though no less beautifully. Snug, tan breeches tucked into knee-high travel boots tightened with gleaming silver buckles. A burgundy leather vest covered a pale, lime-green silk shirt, both snug enough to emphasize Vivianna's narrow waist. To Pomella's surprise, the noblewoman's long hair was pulled back into a simple tail.

Pomella wiped a drip of wet snot from her nose and hoped Vivianna fell into a muddy puddle.

The door of the tower opened, spilling light. Mistress Yarina emerged and strode toward them. Pomella stared in wonder as the rain somehow missed Yarina, leaving her perfectly dry as she moved across the lawn.

As before, the ground rolled with the High Mystic's steps, rising to form a small hill crowned with an earthen throne. Yarina wore a tasteful dress of burgundy and pale green. Pomella stared at it, and then at Vivianna's perfectly matching outfit. How did they keep doing that?

Saijar and Quentin bowed, and Pomella hurried to curtsy. Vivianna, wearing breeches, bowed as well.

"Good morning," Yarina said. "Today dawns the beginning of your third and final Trial. I shall choose my apprentice from among you when you return."

A pang of fear shivered over Pomella. This was it.

"Your final task," Yarina said, "is to travel to the summit of MagDoon, the great mountain that looms east of here. Follow the road out of Kelt Apar until you come to the marker at its base. From there, a path will lead you to its summit. This is a road walked many times, by all apprentices before you, including myself.

"Once atop the summit, you will find an old shrine, built by Mystics from a time before record. Return with the wisdom of their lesson, and with your Mystic staff. The mountain shall provide." She lifted her own staff high and, at that very moment, the sun peeked above the treetops, breaking through the clouds to warm them with brightening light.

Without another word, she descended the rounded hill. It rolled flat as she passed over it. To Pomella, it was as if Yarina had placed the sun in the sky by raising her staff. Pomella curtsied again, and the other candidates bowed. A calm silence crossed over Kelt Apar as the door to the central tower closed.

"Green Man!" Saijar demanded at once. So much for silence, Pomella thought to herself, rubbing her temples. "We need food and travel supplies! See to it that mine are brought immediately."

"Provisions were placed in your cabins while Mistress Yarina spoke with you," Oxillian said. "You will find them waiting for you there."

"He's not your blathering servant," Pomella said, still rubbing her temples. She was exhausted. Not just from the lack of sleep, but from putting up with these arrogant people.

Saijar stepped closer and loomed above her. "You haven't the slightest understanding of how this world works, do you? I don't care who invited you, or how many flowers you can sing to life. You're a commoner. You exist only to serve your betters. While my ancestors summoned the Myst and ruled nations, yours hoed vegetables. Get out of my sight, and get out of my way."

Quentin stepped forward, but Pomella barred his path with her arm. She was also tired of people thinking she needed their help.

"What are you going to do?" she demanded, cocking her head sideways. "Assassinate me? Send your Black Claw mercenaries to do your work?"

A look of genuine surprise appeared on Saijar's face. Pomella's heart raced as she looked for any signs that he recognized the name. It was a stretch to accuse Saijar of something so terrible without evidence, but she hoped she could shock him into giving himself away. If Sim was telling the truth, Saijar had to be involved. Who else would want her to fail, and who else had the means to hire mercenaries? They were also both from Rardaria.

Quentin eased Pomella away from Saijar. "Come on. Let's go."

"And you," Saijar said to him. "You're just as pathetic as her. What would your family think?"

Before she could register the comment, Quentin surged at

Saijar, driving his fist toward his jaw. The blow would have landed, but in an instant quicker than thought a tangle of vines and grass erupted from the Green Man and caught Quentin's hand. The angle and force of the grab made him cry out in pain. His arm twisted behind his head. He fell to a knee.

Enraged, Saijar swung a kick at Quentin's face, but that, too, was caught by another tendril emerging from Oxillian. The Green Man lifted Saijar up by the ankle, his arms dangling as he cursed and swore.

"There shall be no violence in Kelt Apar," Oxillian rumbled.

"You're all fools," Vivianna murmured. She turned and hurried toward the cabins.

"Put them down, Ox," Pomella said. "Please."

Oxillian complied, releasing them onto the ground. Both men stared at the Green Man, anger flashing in their eyes. Then their glances snapped to each other. Saijar spit at Quentin's feet and gave a final, spiteful glance at Pomella before stalking after Vivianna.

Without another word, Oxillian merged back into the ground. Pomella helped Quentin to his feet and dusted some dirt off him. "Are you all right?"

"Fine," he replied. "Let's get our supplies and get going."

Pomella bit her lip. "Perhaps we should travel separately this time."

Quentin paused as he adjusted his wrinkled shirtsleeve. "You don't want to go together?"

"This is the final Trial," Pomella said, not meeting his eyes. "We should try to distinguish ourselves individually."

Quentin looked toward MagDoon in the east. "I don't want

to become the apprentice," he said. He returned his gaze to Pomella. "I want you to earn it. Let me help you."

"No, you can't. You deserve to—"

"Deserve?" Quentin scoffed. "If anyone deserves it, it's you. I would make a terrible Mystic. But you wouldn't. You not only want it more than anybody else, but you have a natural affinity for the Myst. You said you did poorly on your second Trial. I can help you with this last one. It would sadden me very much to see you disappointed."

Pomella knew she would be a lot worse than disappointed if she failed to become the apprentice. But Quentin was right; she needed help, desperately. She nodded to him reluctantly. "Very well. I'm not sure I even have a chance anymore. I could use whatever help you're offering."

A few minutes later they approached the eastern path leading into the forest. Pomella adjusted the bulging backpack that had been left on her doorstep. A quick examination had revealed two days' worth of food, a full waterskin, and a thick blanket. Without letting herself second-guess her decision, she packed the glass vial of Mantepis' venom into the bag. She'd also tucked away *The Book of Songs* Sim had left her.

Sim.

What was she going to do about him? Couldn't he just fade into her past without kicking up her old feelings for him?

She shook her head. No matter how much she wanted Sim to stop muddling up her life, she couldn't deny that a part of her had been glad to see him. She felt safe around him. He was a warm fire of familiar comfort. He'd always been there for her, and had only the best of intentions. Maybe she was too hard on him, despite his terrible timing.

She hitched her hood tighter against the rain and looked up to see MagDoon towering over them. The summit of the snow-capped mountain was lost in the clouds. A ripple of worry swam up her neck as she imagined its unfathomable height.

As they approached the edge of the clearing, she caught a glimpse of Lal's cabin, far across the overgrown field, sitting against the towering backdrop of trees. Her stomach churned in memory. A sudden awareness she couldn't describe tickled her mind, and a moment later her silver hummingbirds zoomed by. She thought of telling them to go home and stay put, but she didn't have the energy.

She and Quentin passed in silence into the Mystwood, following the trail. He was silent for a long time, lost in thought.

"What happened with your friend?" he asked at last. "Why was he there last night, and how did he get into Kelt Apar?"

Pomella sighed. "Sim and I grew up together. I don't know how he got to my cabin. He left soon after you did. He came to warn me that I was in danger. Apparently there's a group of mercenaries called the Black Claws lurking in the forest planning to kill me."

"By the Graces! Why didn't you say anything?"

"We were in Kelt Apar!" she said, feeling more and more anxious about it. Now that the alcohol had mostly faded, her choice to not tell anyone seemed foolish. "There's no safer place on all of Moth, right? Even now, we're on a wide road patrolled by rangers, heading to a frequented mountain shrine. Mistress Yarina and

Ox can see anything that happens in the forest, so if there really is a threat, they'd know about it."

"You think Saijar has something to do with this?" Quentin asked.

Pomella thought of all the reasons she suspected him. "I don't know for certain," she admitted. "But Sim insisted they were from Rardaria. And who else could know about me? You saw the large entourage he came with."

"We'll need to be extra careful," Quentin said. "And we should tell Yarina as soon as we return."

They walked in silence for a while before Quentin spoke again. "Where did you go after your meeting with Yarina? I went looking for you."

"I ended up visiting with the gardener," Pomella replied. "He's a very funny—what?"

She cut off as Quentin whipped his head to stare at her. "Pomella, he's Unclaimed! What were you thinking?"

"So?" she replied, her eyes narrowing. "He's a nice old man. He's harmless!"

"He's *Unclaimed*. You don't know how he became that. He could be a killer."

"Blessed Saints, Quentin!" she burst out. "He's just an old man! He didn't try to kill me! Well, other than leaving all that chi-uy out for me."

"You're on the verge of becoming a Mystic," Quentin said. "There's no higher status in the world. Every baron on the Continent might bow to you someday. Why would you be seen consorting with somebody like that?"

She gaped at him. "Who are you? What happened to the nobleman who was friendly to the commoner girl? There's nothing wrong with an old Unclaimed man. Do you think Mistress Yarina would let him stay at Kelt Apar if he was dangerous? He was just lonely and wanted some company. You would be, too, if all you did was trim bushes and raise sheep all day long." Pomella refrained from mentioning that she'd also been judgmental of the gardener—something she felt guilty about now.

"You're right," Quentin said at last after walking quietly for a handful of minutes. "I'm sorry. Some old habits are hard to shake. Please forgive me, Pomella-my."

She answered by taking his hand and kissing the back of it. "There you are," she said.

He smiled back. "I will admit that I didn't mind how chi-uy affected you."

Pomella smiled at him. "No, I suppose you didn't. Although I regretted it later. Drinking, I mean. Not the other stuff."

The morning stretched thin and, thank the Saints, the rain finally let up, bringing some sunshine. Pomella dared not hope that it would last. She lowered her hood, welcoming the cool breeze. The land sloped upward, and MagDoon loomed in front of them. They ate a highsun meal from the provisions in their packs. Pomella found the little stone cup from Lal's cabin in her pack. A smile crossed her face. The gardener had obviously packed their rations.

She and Quentin continued on, and the fresh air helped diminish Pomella's headache. Just as she began to feel better, her feet started aching. MagDoon was still distressingly distant, let alone its summit. She groaned and wondered if Saint Brigid ever grumbled about sore feet. Probably not, as she rode immortal steeds and traveled by blathering rainbows.

As Pomella and Quentin approached the mountain, the road thinned until it turned into little more than a footpath sloping upward. She imagined herself an ant, crawling up the leg of the mighty MagDoon. She wondered where Saijar and Vivianna were. Surely they came by the same road? Were they ahead or behind? Were they together?

Quentin walked ahead of Pomella, his long strides chewing up land. The idea that they'd be camping together alone tonight suddenly occurred to Pomella. Her heart beat faster as she wondered what that would mean, and whether there would be certain expectations.

Late in the afternoon, they came to a crossing where the trail split into four separate paths. A tall stone standing on its edge loomed above them. Faded runes crossed its flattened surface, but neither she nor Quentin could make them out. He and Pomella moved on quickly, choosing a path at random, suspecting the stone was a marker that indicated the beginning of MagDoon's summit trails.

Walking for another hour, they followed long switchbacks under the cover of spring-budded aspens standing amid towering evergreens. Soon they topped a low rise. Quentin stopped and pointed back the way they came. "Look," he said.

Tucking a loose strand of hair behind her ear and ignoring her throbbing feet, Pomella gazed across the top of the Mystwood. The sun set into the tree-lined horizon, painting the sky and clouds with dazzling brushstrokes of pink and lavender.

Pomella thought of her garden, and the flowers there that grew the same color.

A saying of her grandmhathir's sprang to mind. *Tend your garden as if it were the entire Mystwood, Pommy.*

The treetops of the forest swayed in unison under the wind howling in from the distant ocean. Hector and Ena flew by, swirling around each other.

Turning, Pomella looked up the mountain. It seemed so ominous to her, as if it were staring down at her, displeased with her presence. Her coming meant something, and the mountain knew it.

"What is it?" Quentin asked.

"It's just a long way up," she replied, unable to explain her discomfort.

Quentin shrugged. "We'll make it. It'll take a full day of hiking tomorrow, but I think we'll be fine. Assuming the weather holds."

"The stories say Saint Brigid died here," Pomella said. "After all her journeys, having lost everything, she wandered the world, but was drawn to MagDoon. She lived as a hermit, never speaking again, lest she cry out for her lost child. The Mystics knew of her presence on the mountain until one day she was just . . . gone."

"I've never heard that version of the tale," Quentin said. "I grew up hearing the stories of how her laghart followers decapitated her. But you would know better. In Keffra, we have no Saints. Beyond the Seven Graces, we only worship our ancestors. Family, you see, is all-important."

They followed more switchbacks until they found an open patch of ground beneath a large outcropping of rock jutting from the main side of the mountain. Two massive oak trees provided additional cover.

"Thank the Saints," Pomella mumbled, slipping her pack off. She yawned, no longer able to think straight.

"I'll set a fire," Quentin said.

Pomella unpacked her meager gear and slumped against her pack. She looked west and could just manage to see the dimly lit sky through shadowed branches. She watched Quentin work, admiring his tall frame, but felt her eyelids growing heavy. How many hours had she been awake for now? She tried to count them, but soon her eyelids grew heavy, and she drifted off to sleep.

Pomella awoke during the deepest part of the night. A thin crescent moon hung in the sky, creating a gentle halo of light in the black and gray clouds. A multitude of stars managed to slip through the gaps in the cloud cover.

Pomella sat up, strands of hair stuck in her mouth. She pulled them away and rubbed her eyes. Her and Quentin's campfire had burned to ash and embers. His bedroll lay empty.

She stood, wrapping her cloak around herself to ward off the cold. Silvery fog clung to the mountainside and drifted across the treetops of the forest.

"Quentin?" she called, but heard no answer. Her hummingbirds were also absent. Feeling lonely, she pulled her cloak closer.

A warm wind began to blow, scattering her supplies and

spreading ash. Fear gripped her stomach. A mournful sound echoed across the forest, as if the mountain itself had moaned.

She found herself back on the summit path, walking uphill. Her hair flew out behind her as the hot wind increased its fury and bore down onto her. She pushed ahead, not knowing why, but feeling an overpowering sense that she needed to continue.

Voices sang in the air, a chorus of deep, resonant sounds that rumbled the air and pounded her ears.

"Huzzzz-oh! Huzzzz-oh!"

Suddenly she found herself at the top of the mountain, where a massive temple of ivory and gold glittered in the moonlight. Six statues of majestic men and women, each holding a staff, stood guard before a stone archway. As she crossed beneath the arch she noticed a familiar symbol on its keystone. A tree, woven like a Mothic knot, exactly like the emblem on the cover of her *Book of Songs.*

"Huzzzz-oh!"

As she entered the temple grounds, she noticed grass beneath her bare feet. When had she lost her shoes?

The doors of the temple swung open and the song and wind blasted out. She took another step, wanting more than anything to go in.

"Don't go in there, or you'll die," a voice said to her.

Pomella twisted. A little girl, no more than ten or eleven years old, rocked on her bare heels a short distance away. The girl had a petite frame, light tan skin, and long black hair, which hung straight down her back. Her vibrant lavender eyes stared through Pomella. She wore a simple white dress, which did not move in the howling wind. Dreadful anxiety rose in the pit of Pomella's stomach.

"Why?" Pomella asked. "What's in there?"

"I saw you coming," the girl said. "I knew she would invite you."

"Who invited me?" Pomella asked, looking again into the mouth of the temple.

The girl tilted her head back and inhaled deeply. Her eyes rolled back in her head and she spoke in a strange, rasping voice that made Pomella want to run.

"The mountain shakes and the moon is wrong. Fear the iron and awake the Mystic song."

Thunder sounded, shaking the ground and nearly tumbling Pomella off her feet. The wind exploded with fiery intensity, flinging rocks and knocking over statues. A large crack formed on the face of the temple. A piece of stone blew off, hurtled through the air, and tumbled over the edge of the mountain. More pieces flew. Pomella ducked and covered her head.

"Who are you?" she shouted at the girl. "What's happening?"

The girl did not answer. She fell to her knees and screamed, then vanished.

Pomella whipped around as the temple crumbled. An avalanche of stone raced toward her. She screamed as it consumed her.

FIFTEEN

THE SUMMIT

Pomella gasped and opened her eyes.

Chill night air surrounded her, but Quentin's campfire offered some warmth. He slept on the other side of the fire with his back to her. A blanket lay gently across Pomella's body. She hadn't remembered putting it on. Quentin must have draped it over her.

Gentle rain fell across the forest. The only other sound she could hear was the quiet hiss and pop of burning firewood.

She stood up, the dream already fading from her memory. Her stomach grumbled.

Moving quietly around the camp, Pomella ate some food from the pack and stared at the black sky. What a strange dream she'd had. She remembered the little girl, the temple, and the wind with the *"huzzzz-oh"* coming from it.

This whole journey up the mountain sat strangely in her heart. She thought of the High Mystic's words to her the other day: *People and their deeds are bound to certain places and times, and here in Kelt Apar, within the Mystwood, I especially feel the light of the past masters guiding me in all my actions.*

A couple of hours later, Pomella and Quentin broke camp as daylight touched the world. They packed their gear and ate as they walked, knowing they had a full day ahead of them to reach the summit. The rain stopped early and held off throughout the morning. Hector and Ena showed themselves occasionally, buzzing from tree to tree.

Quentin spoke very little, which suited Pomella. Her dream still haunted her, as did the feeling of familiarity and connection to the mountain. She'd never been to MagDoon, so why did she feel this way? Why was she so scared? She still had no idea what they were supposed to do when they got to the summit. Like the rest of her experience at Kelt Apar, she hardly knew what she was doing.

"What do you think of this Trial?" she asked Quentin as they trudged up the steep trail along the southern slope.

Glancing back over his shoulder, Quentin shrugged. "Only that the final Trial is traditionally linked to acquiring a Mystic's staff. You try to find one that feels right to you and present it to the High Mystic afterward. She'll wiggle her fingers over it, sniff the wood, and declare it either the will of the Myst or a piece of driftwood."

Pomella smiled, but wasn't in the mood to laugh. "It's still strange to me how you agreed to do all this even though you have no interest in actually becoming a Mystic."

Quentin shrugged but kept his eyes on the trail. "I didn't have much choice. It's what I am supposed to do," he said. "Family is—"

"All-important," Pomella finished. "Yes, I know."

"And I'm not really competing anymore, anyway," said Quentin.

"Yah," Pomella said. "Well, I hope the Mystic staff will at least be helpful for climbing this jagged mountain."

He and Pomella continued on, and she enjoyed the breathtaking views of southern Moth. The Ironlow Mountains, a central feature of the island, stretched as far as she could see. She wondered if they'd be able to see the ocean from the summit.

Pomella's feet were beyond aching. Her poor cloak was filthy. She'd done nothing but drag it through mud and rain since the night Bethy had given it to her. She herself was as filthy as the cloak. She absently stroked her hair and daydreamed of bathing in a steaming tub.

Quentin stopped and held up his hand. She stopped, too. He indicated for her to follow quietly as he slipped behind a wide pine tree near the edge of the path. They peered over the edge and heard two people arguing.

". . . don't know why you need to stop. You have a walking stick now!"

Pomella's heart raced as she recognized the voice.

"My feet hurt, all right?" Vivianna snapped at Saijar. "I'm not used to walking so much."

"Hurry up," Saijar said.

"Don't complain to me about your sore feet later, then."

Pomella watched from behind her tree as Saijar and Vivianna sat by a large circle of rocks. Vivianna rubbed her feet, and Pomella was suddenly glad she'd kept her complaining to herself.

Both Vivianna and Saijar carried tall walking sticks. Mystic staves.

"Do you think they're ahead of us?" Vivianna said.

"No," Saijar said. He stood apart from her, arms crossed. "They've got to still be on their way up. It was worth pushing through the night to get ahead. By the time they get to the summit, we'll be halfway back to Kelt Apar."

"I don't think it matters who gets back first," Vivianna said.

Saijar shrugged. "Who cares? Those culks can race to the top if they want. My family has assured me that my place in history is secured. It's as good as done."

"You're such a pompous ass," Vivianna told him. "What's going to happen when you return home without becoming the apprentice?"

Saijar looked away.

Even at a distance, Pomella could see Vivianna's broad, sneering grin. "So the rumors are true. You have no Mystics in your family anymore. 'A House without Mystics is not—'"

Saijar scoffed, "You're a fool and a child!"

"You didn't think of me as those things when you propositioned me."

"Don't get sentimental. You'll start to sound like that filthy commoner."

"Well, that 'filthy commoner' might ruin your House. I hope you enjoy bowing to her."

Quentin tugged Pomella's cloak and nodded up the slope. "Let's go," he whispered.

Red-hot fury pulsed through Pomella. She wanted to scream at Saijar, run down the slope, and beat him over the head with his Mystic staff. The traitorous, hateful *culk*!

But she knew better than to act in anger. She stormed ahead, passing Quentin, and led the way up the mountain. Her anger gave her fresh legs, and every step became a defiant act of retribution against Saijar and anybody else who tried to get in her way. She would win the apprenticeship.

She would become a Mystic.

The day grew late, but at last the summit came within sight. They approached it from the southeast, hiking the final, long stretch along a saddle-shaped ridge littered with smooth rocks and snow left over from winter. Even at this altitude, large trees thrived here at the summit, as if each one strove to become the highest point on the island.

Pomella struggled to breathe the cold air. In the back of her mind she knew they needed to reach the summit before nightfall. She wanted to be there *now*. The peak called to her, summoned her with a silent song she'd been singing all her life. She didn't know what she would find, but somehow, she knew it would define her life. Nothing would keep her from it.

Within throwing distance of the summit, they came to the end of the path, which opened onto a wide, flat area upon which stood the ruins of an old structure. Snow covered the ground, refusing to yield to spring. The roof had fallen away, or perhaps had never existed to begin with. Its front entrance jutted out of the mountain and faced west, back toward Kelt Apar. Gray stone pillars, made of a type of rock unlike anything else on the mountain, stood in a circle, ringing outward in a now-broken pattern. Moss, ivy, and snow covered most of the pillars, clawing deep into the surface to crack them apart.

A heavy silence drifted in the air, giving Pomella a chill. On the far side of the ruins, the path continued a short way up to the actual summit. She traced her hand over the nearest pillar. The wet moss tickled her fingers.

"What do you think this shrine was built for?" Pomella said.

"I don't know," Quentin said. "But it's getting late. There's a cave over there. Let's take a look."

"We should go to the summit," Pomella said, still riding the surge of urgency from before.

Quentin's hand found hers. "It's fine. We'll be back in plenty of time. There's no need to be the first ones back. If anything, Yarina will admire that you took your time and didn't just rush through the Trial. Besides, the Trials will be over tomorrow. This may be our last chance to be alone."

Pomella considered his words. It was getting dark, quickly. They could visit the actual summit point and try to descend at night, but that didn't seem like a wise idea, despite what Saijar and Vivianna were doing. It had already been a long day of hiking, and Quentin was right that this might be the last chance for him and Pomella to be alone together.

Quentin grinned at her, seemingly reading her mind. He reached out his hand; his eyes dared her to come with him.

Pomella accepted his hand, and followed his lead. The setting sun touching the distant western horizon caught her attention. From their vantage, she could see the ocean sparkling. She stared in wonder, mesmerized by the endless horizon. The descriptions she'd heard didn't do it justice.

As they approached the cave and its unseen depths, the memory of her recent dream jumped unbidden to her mind. She remembered the temple, which may or may not have looked similar to the one at which they stood. She crossed the ruins and ducked her head under the threshold, entering the large natural cavern. Quentin followed.

The cave reminded Pomella of the room she and Sim had found in the Mystwood. Faded paintings with broken frames, barely visible in the dim light, ringed the cave walls at uneven intervals. Their style matched what she'd seen before, but once again, the meaning eluded her.

"It's beautiful," Quentin said behind her.

Pomella's cloak caught on something as they moved farther into the cave. She twitched the cloak free. It had snagged on a metal bar, about the length of her hand, sticking out of the ground. Glancing across the floor, she saw handfuls of them, spread out to form a wide circle.

"What are those things?" she asked.

"I don't know," Quentin said, looking from them to her. "But they aren't what I'm focused on right now."

Pomella was suddenly conscious of her travel-weary appearance. Despite that, her excitement surged. "We're staying here tonight, right?" she asked, stepping closer to him.

He nodded. "In the morning we'll go to the summit and find our staves."

"Do you think it matters that the others will return before us?"

"Doubtful," he replied, shrugging.

Pomella slipped her arms around his waist. He trembled under her touch. "Then we're alone at the top of the world," she said, and kissed him. She took it slow, savoring the feel of his mouth on hers. She'd been wanting to do this right. Her hands began to slowly move across his body. He wrapped his arms around her, pulling her tight. Pomella's hands sped up, and quick as a skittering luck'n, rational thought fled her.

She lifted off his shirt, revealing his strong, tattooed body. He tugged at her cloak, still kissing her, and soon their hands fumbled to remove every bit of clothing they could find.

Quentin reached around her back to untie her Springrise dress. She wished he would go faster.

The dress's simple string ties fell loose, and he pulled a single sleeve down, revealing her brown shoulder. Somehow maintaining her calm, Pomella ran her hands down his muscular chest and found his belt. The buckle unlatched and she prayed that her hand didn't tremble. It didn't.

"You are so beautiful," Quentin whispered in her ear. He leaned into her, kissing her again, deeply. His hands ran along the front of her neck, across her shoulders, and down her arms toward her wrists.

"Take my dress off," Pomella commanded, trying to keep the plea from her voice.

"I'm sorry," he said, and she heard the echoing sound of metal clamping together.

Panic and confusion flashed through her. Quentin stepped away from her, half-naked, his face a mask of fear and sadness.

"I'm truly sorry, Pomella-my," he whispered.

"What's going on?" she asked, looking down at her hands. Two heavy manacles bound her wrists together. She pulled at them, but they held tight.

A figure emerged from the deep shadows of the cave. He wore rust-colored robes and carried a tall Mystic's staff made of iron. Bits of metal jutted from his exposed flesh. His face was lost in the shadows of his hood.

Quentin stood still as the man approached her. "Welcome, Pomella," said the Mystic. "I hope you like this cave. You will be here awhile."

Strange dreams haunted Sim. The moment he'd arrived in the cave, he'd finally succumbed to his aching weariness and collapsed against the wall, in a distant alcove away from the spiked circle. As he drifted in unconsciousness, he saw Dane, standing outside the cave surrounded by a magnificent shrine. Behind him, a little girl with long black hair in a white dress watched with a cold expression on her face.

Dane looked up at him. Blood drained from Dane's eyes like tears.

"Wake up, Sim."

Sim jolted awake. He heard voices.

"Who are you?" said a familiar, quavering voice. Sim stood up and tried to shake the fog from his mind.

Pomella stood, her dress disheveled, in the circle of spikes in front of Ohzem. Between them stood the tall man Sim had seen with her the other night. Several tattoos wove around his bare torso and arms. Sim could see Pomella gaping at Ohzem's scarred and bloody face.

"I am the next master of Kelt Apar," said the Mystic. "I am Ohzem."

Pomella turned back to the bare-chested man. "What's happening, Quentin?" She reached toward him, and Sim saw manacles wrapped around her wrists.

"It was my family's wish," the man named Quentin said, not looking at her. "For thirty-seven generations our family has produced Mystics. The High Mystic went too far in inviting a commoner to be her apprentice."

Pomella's face filled with disbelief.

"Pomella!" Sim shouted, and lunged forward.

"Grab him!" Zicon yelled.

Jank and Hormin leaped at Sim, knocking him down. He scrambled and struggled in the dirt, but they managed to twist his arms behind his back and clamp the manacles back on. He kept his attention on Pomella even though Jank pressed his face against the dirt.

"Oh, Saints! Sim!" Pomella cried. She twisted to face Quentin. "Liar! I trusted you."

Quentin stepped closer to her. Sim barely heard his words. "I had no choice, Pomella-my. My family arranged everything. Nothing is more important than family. *Nothing.* Not even my personal feelings."

He reached out to stroke her cheek, but she pulled it away.

"Do not be so harsh on him," Ohzem said with a strange, half-mocking tone. "Lord Bartone only played the role he was given. Why, I even think he might legitimately care for you."

"He can wallow in shite!" Pomella snapped.

Hormin approached Pomella and clamped a heavy chain to the manacles around her wrists. A long chain ran from them to one of the spikes in the ground.

Quentin's face hardened. He pulled his shirt back on. "She's not to be hurt."

All mockery drained from Ohzem's voice. "I will decide who is to be hurt," he corrected. "Remember your place."

Jank hauled Sim to his feet.

Ohzem turned to him. "You're predictable. Do not fear for her, though."

He drew a long, dull-gray knife, its iron blade chipped along the edge, and stepped toward Pomella.

"No!" Sim blurted, panic welling up. He leaped again for Ohzem, but Jank punched his chest, driving the air from his lungs. He crumpled, trying hard not to lose sight of Pomella despite the blow.

"Get the chest ready," Ohzem told Zicon.

Zicon strode to the chest and snapped a leather cord from his neck. On its end, Sim saw a heavy key, which Zicon inserted into the chest. The key turned smoothly, sounding a solid thunk as the lock released.

Zicon opened the heavy chest.

It seemed as if an icy wind rushed through the cave. Sim couldn't see what the chest contained, but Zicon stepped away from it, as if to give it room. He placed himself behind Pomella, and grabbed her arms.

"Sim!" she cried.

"Pomella, I—!"

Jank ground his face into the rock.

Ohzem held the knife above his head. "Ceon'hur! By this action, I summon thee!" He struck with the knife. Pomella screamed. Sim's eyes widened in horror.

From his compromised angle, Sim couldn't see what happened. But he saw Pomella lift her arm and look down at her side. Blinking, Sim focused.

The strike had cut her dress and sliced her ribs.

Silence filled the cave. A thin red line of blood leaked out of the cut.

Ohzem lifted the knife and held the bloody blade in front of his face. With a grim expression he flicked it downward, speckling Pomella's blood across the stone floor.

"What did you do?" Pomella said, voicing Sim's thought. Why hadn't Ohzem killed her? Wasn't that what they'd come here to do?

Suddenly the floor cracked and erupted as stone shot upward. The cave shuddered and pebbles trembled down from the ceiling. Large boulders rolled upon one another, forming the huge shape of a man.

The Green Man towered over them all, except instead of being made of plants and soil, he was formed entirely of rock pulled from the mountain. Sim's heart thundered. The Green Man was here! Like a massive armored warrior, he rose over his opponents. Bits of dirt crumbled from his stone arms as he stretched them wide.

"Ox!" Pomella called.

"Who shed the innocent blood of a candidate under my protection?" the Green Man roared.

"Ceon'hur," Ohzem said, bowing slightly. "I am privileged to once again be in your presence."

Sim gasped. The Green Man was the ceon'hur?

"Why have you bound this girl in iron?" the hulking creature asked.

"It is not her who shall remain in iron," Ohzem snarled.

He lifted both his arms, staff and bloody knife stretched toward the ceiling, and made a throaty sound, somewhere between a cry and a gurgling chant. Light flared, and a large ring of iron lifted out of the nearby chest into the air. Shaped like a single massive wrist cuff, it was wider than Sim could wrap his arms around. Four thick iron chains hung off of it.

With a piercing yell Ohzem punched his arms outward, and the ring of metal flew toward the Green Man, striking him around the neck and clasping shut. White-hot light blazed from the metal, burning stone. The Green Man clawed at it with his rocky hands and stumbled backward. The chains connected to the neck band lashed out and secured themselves to the spikes trapped in the ground.

Zicon dragged Pomella outside the ring of spikes. As the Green Man flailed, Ohzem also backed away until his boots were just beyond the circle's edge.

"I have waited decades for this day," Ohzem said, maniacal glee on his face. "They said the guardian, the ceon'hur, could not be defeated. But I have learned of a greater power. The Myst exists in all things, but in iron, it is weakest. And atop this mountain, of all places, you are vulnerable."

Quentin stepped up beside Ohzem. "Is it trapped?"

The Green Man charged toward Ohzem, hurling huge shards of stone at him. Quentin leaped back, but the Mystic did not flinch. The chains around the Green Man pulled tight. The flying rock crashed harmlessly against an invisible barrier at the circle's edge.

"Yes, he is bound here," Ohzem replied. "You are free to destroy the High Mystic. We leave for Kelt Apar immediately."

The Green Man thrashed, but his chains held him fast. "Defilers!"

Sim's mind wheeled. The Black Claws had never planned to kill Pomella. It was Yarina they were after. All this was just a ploy to disable her guardian.

"What about this one?" Jank asked, shaking Sim.

"Do whatever you like with him," Ohzem said.

A vicious smile spread across Jank's face. He stepped away from Sim and drew his sword.

"Sim . . . Sim!" Pomella yelled.

Zicon crossed his arms and waited. "Make it quick, Jank."

Sim panicked. With his hands still bound, he ran for the mouth of the cave, but Jank was ready. The mercenary swung, sword biting deep into Sim's side and slicing across his abdomen. Searing pain cut into him as he went down. Blood poured across the ground and Sim marveled at how much there was. Somewhere behind him, Pomella screamed.

The Green Man roared and charged toward Jank, but the iron collar and chains burned white hot as he came to the edge of the circle. The ground rumbled as the creature merged back into the floor, but rose again and again, seeking a way out of the trap.

Sim convulsed in pain. Tears streamed from his eyes. By the Saints, this was it. He was going to die. What a blathering fool he'd been after all.

Jank wiped the blade clean with his bare hand. "Now the real question is, should I finish you here, or let you die of slow rot?"

He stepped around Sim, angling for a different line to attack. Sim forced himself to sit up and face his killer. He thought of his parents, his sister, and Dane. Maybe soon he would be with his brother and they could wander the Creekwaters as ghosts together.

"Stop!" Pomella shouted.

Jank leered at her and chuckled. "You're a pretty thing. I'll enjoy taking my time with you, too."

Quentin drew his knife. "Touch her and I'll ruin you, commoner!"

Sim coughed blood. The world spun around him. He shook his head to clear the fog. He had to focus!

"The Mystic said I could do as I wanted!" Jank yelled. He glared at Zicon. "I don't care what you're paying us. I'm sick of being held on a jagged leash this whole time! This island is a stinking pile of mud and I'm tired of trudging through—"

Pulling from his deepest reserves, Sim roared and slammed his shoulder low into Jank's body. By the Saints, it hurt! They fell together and the hard ground knocked the remaining air from Sim's chest. He rolled off of Jank, trying to pull in a breath. Jank scrambled to his feet beside him.

With a snarl, Jank lifted Sim's sword. "You're finished, scr—"

With a roar, the Green Man's stone fist erupted from Jank's chest. The guardian lifted him into the air, twitching and gurgling, as if he weighed nothing.

Sim looked down. He and Jank had landed within the ring of spikes. Zicon took another step away from the edge. Even Pomella, her eyes wide with horror, stepped back.

The Green Man, the benevolent creature Sim had daydreamed of meeting as a child, stood in the center of the circle, his rocky form covered in fresh blood. The iron collar seared with white-hot heat, smoking against his neck. He dropped his raised arm and dumped Jank's lifeless body onto the ground.

Sim sensed a rushing of feet as Pomella hobbled into the ring and knelt beside him.

"We leave now," Ohzem said, not a hint of emotion within his quiet voice. He waited for Quentin to whisper something to Pomella that Sim couldn't hear. Pomella snarled in response. Ohzem gave Sim one last look, like a cat leaving its kill, and slipped out of the cave. Hormin and Zicon followed, leaving Sim to die.

He couldn't move his body anymore. The gash across his chest burned, making it hard to breathe. His breaths came in quick gasps now. Somewhere, he thought he heard his mhathir call his name. Or perhaps it was Pomella. Bethy, maybe?

His eyelids became too heavy, and he lacked the strength to keep them open. Behind Pomella, the Green Man looked down on him, splattered blood running down his face like tears.

The last thing Sim saw before darkness took him was Pomella stroking his face. He wished she didn't look so sad.

SIXTEEN

BLOOD AND STONE

Pomella trembled as Sim's eyes closed. His head rested in her lap. The cave seemed to press down on her, making her feel small and cold and lonely.

"Is he dead?" she managed, her breath and hands shaking.

Oxillian's stony form leaned forward to peer more closely at Sim. One of his giant fingers reached down to touch Sim's face. "He is alive, but he will not last long."

"You're the Green Man! Please, do something!"

"I can do very little," Ox said, touching the collar around his neck. Black scars burned across his stone neck where the collar lay, but he gave no indication that he felt any pain.

Managing as best she could with her manacles, Pomella tore

a long strip from her dress, beginning where Ohzem had cut it open. Needing more, she tore another from the bottom of her skirt.

She placed the strips across Sim's wound as best she could. His face was pale. Fevered sweat covered his face.

Pomella's composure threatened to break. A single jagged tear betrayed her and leaked down her cheek. Just an hour ago everything seemed to be going so well. But in a single moment of betrayal, everything had fallen apart. Gone were her hopes of becoming Yarina's apprentice. Saijar and Vivianna would return to Kelt Apar in the morning, and Quentin soon after. None of them would claim to know where she was. Pomella imagined Yarina selecting Saijar as her apprentice. Or, worse, selecting that culk Quentin! A ridiculous, bitter part of Pomella hoped he was selected just because she knew he didn't want it. Or did he? How much of anything he'd told her had been true?

"Who were those people?"

Ox looked at the cave's entrance as if trying to see beyond. "I do not know, but even now, I cannot see them. They blind and bind me with their iron."

"Why did they do this?"

"There have always been those who oppose the Mystics and their ways. Kelt Apar has been contested many times."

Pomella wracked her mind for a solution. Anger rose like boiling water bubbling over the edge of a pot. Easing Sim from her lap onto the ground, she stood and yanked against the chains binding her ankles to the spikes, but they held tight. She pulled harder, biting her lip against the pain until she cried out.

There had to be a way out. There had to be a way to save Sim.

Her eyes widened as she remembered *The Book of Songs*. She looked around in the dark for her canvas pack and found it a short distance away. She leaped for it, but her chains prevented her from reaching it. "Shite and blather!" she screamed. She dropped and rolled to her back, reaching with her legs. The toe of her shoes just barely touched the bag's edge.

"Come on!" she snarled, and stretched farther. She hooked the tip of the bag onto her foot and pulled it toward herself with a triumphant yelp. Her hands yanked the bag open. Dried rations spilled out along with her bottle of chi-uy and the glass vial containing Mantepis' venom.

Pomella froze. Her hand trembled as she lifted up the vial of vemon. If all else failed, perhaps she could ease Sim's passing. It pained her to hear his shallow breathing.

She clenched her fist around the vial. No.

Setting the venom carefully aside onto the ground, she put it out of mind and drew *The Book of Songs* from her pack.

"What are you doing?" Ox asked.

"There has to be something in here to help us," said Pomella. "Do you know anything about the Myst that can help us?"

Ox shook his stone head. "I am not a Mystic. But I believe that if a Mystic were here, he or she would say there is always a way with the Myst."

"Well, I *am* a Mystic!" Pomella snapped, ignoring the fact that it was presumptuous and unlikely to ever be true.

She flipped through the familiar pages, trying to remember if there was anything in the book that could help her escape. The pages flew by, but nothing appeared to be right. She gritted her teeth, frustrated that she understood so little. The only entry that seemed relevant was the page that described the song of opening, the same one she'd tried in the other cave with Sim. It hadn't worked then, and she doubted it would now.

"This is the last time I'm getting trapped in a cave with you, Simkon AnClure," she muttered.

She paused on a page decorated with familiar lotus flowers. Other drawings beside them showed wounded animals: a dog, a horse, and a strange furry-faced creature she didn't recognize, with a long winding tail. The illustrations seemed to provide instructions for how to apply simple bandages and poultices. She couldn't understand the neatly written runes on the page, but she thought perhaps she could try to replicate the results if she managed to find the illustrated herbs. She only recognized a few of them.

Her heart sank. It didn't matter. She couldn't leave the cave to find herbs. All she could do was sit and watch Sim die.

Pomella slammed the book shut. How in Saint Brigid's holy name was she supposed to help when she was *locked up*!

She took a calming breath. She couldn't fall apart. Not now. Her all-too-familiar anxiety lurked within her, like night spirits waiting for evening shadows to arrive before coming out.

Her hand traced Sim's face, running from his hairline to his strong chin. Bruises covered his otherwise peaceful face. If she ignored them, along with the scrapes and dirt, he looked like he was asleep. She brushed his hair off his forehead and kissed him between the eyes.

"I was a blathering fool not to listen to you," she whispered. "I'm sorry. Please don't leave me."

The memory of her grandmhathir flashed in her mind. Lorraina had looked peaceful and sleepy, too, at the end.

Pomella's stomach clenched. She'd been as powerless to stop Grandmhathir's passing as she was now to stop Sim's. There was only one thing she could do. The only thing she really knew how to do.

She could sing.

It had been what she did for Grandmhathir during her last hours. Pomella still didn't understand the connection between her singing and the Myst, but she knew it existed. She'd seen what it could do, even if she couldn't explain it.

She brought to mind the last song she'd sung to Grandmhathir. It was the same one she sang at Mhathir's grave on cool summer evenings. Looking at Sim, Pomella tried not to think of how he'd soon be another person she sang to on those nights.

She cleared her throat and closed her eyes. All she could do right now was try to comfort him. Beginning with a soft hum, she eased into the song.

> *"Now as the sun sets down*
> *Arise comes the soft moon*
> *Here between our distant lands*
> *You will see me soon*
>
> *"Long like the night of winter stars*
> *Far as the Mystic sea*
> *I will hold your gentle hand*
> *Until you part from me*
>
> *"Then as a swift bird I'll follow*
> *Searching throughout the sky*

Yearning for your warm touch
Only to fade and cry"

The last echo of her song resonated throughout the cave. Pomella waited, stroking Sim's hair, hoping for something to happen, a sudden miracle from the Myst. But nothing changed. She hid her face in her arms and knees.

The last rays of the setting sun disappeared from the cave entrance. The cold iron chains made Pomella shiver.

Minutes passed, then hours. Pomella thought about her entire journey, tracing it back to when Ox interrupted her village's Springrise festival. She should never have left home. She should have listened to her fathir. This whole venture had proven to be nothing but a selfish attempt to become something she wasn't. She wasn't special, just like the High Mystic said. She wasn't good enough to succeed. All she'd managed to do was kill Sim and probably the High Mystic as well. Poor Lal would lose his life. Ox was trapped, maybe forever, and she'd waste away in a cave atop MagDoon.

She had to do something for these people. It wasn't fair that they would all bleed and die while she sat here.

A buzzing sound filled the cave as Hector and Ena flew to her, trailing silvery smoke. They hovered in front of her, and she held out her palms for them to alight on. "Can you help me?" she said. "I need something."

The hummingbirds cocked their heads, seeming not to understand. She sighed. Of course they didn't. They were just birds.

"Those little ones have taken quite a liking to you!" the

Green Man said, his voice booming despite its subdued tone. "Did you summon them with a song? Your singing is quite beautiful."

"Thank you, Ox," she said. "I'm not sure how they came to me. But it neither matters nor helps."

"Over the centuries," Oxillian said, "I have always had a fondness for the apprentices and Mystics who sang. The number of Mystics I have met is beyond my recollection, but the ones my feeble memory keeps are those who Unveil the Myst with their songs."

"Do you ever sing?" she asked.

"Sing? No. It never occurred to me."

"Maybe you should try sometime. Perhaps it is *your* Unveiling, too?"

Oxillian smiled, a strange contrast to his bloodied, stony form. "I was grown from the Myst," he said, "but cannot use it."

"We're alike then," Pomella said. "Because I can't control it, either. Any success I've had was pure luck. I feel so powerless."

"I was grown by a ritual of song," Ox told her, staring toward the horizon.

"How—how old are you, Ox?"

"Grandmaster Faywong once estimated I was sung into existence nine hundred years ago. It is hard to know. Time is a difficult concept for me to understand."

"Do you remember being . . . grown?"

"I remember the song that called me forth. The first human High Mystic of Moth pulled me from the soil and stone of Kelt Apar. I am one with this land, this forest, this mountain."

Pomella bit her lip, thinking. "Ox, how did that Mystic summon you earlier? Why did he cut me?"

"I am the guardian of this forest. When the blood of one I protect is shed by violence, I feel it in soil and stone. I came to protect."

"They lured and trapped you," Pomella said.

The Green Man's expression darkened as he touched his collar. "With accursed iron, which stands above stone in the Mystical Hierarchy. I have broken it before, but here, atop MagDoon, which has always been shrouded in mystery, my strength is somehow lessened."

The Mystical Hierarchy. Pomella's eyes widened. A sudden understanding flashed within her. She touched the cut in her ribs Ohzem had given her.

"Ox," she said. "That's it."

She rushed to *The Book of Songs* and tore through the pages. Her hands shook with excitement.

"The first Trial. Iron was poisoning animals," she mused. "That's why Mistress Yarina needed blood."

In the center of the book Pomella found the elaborate diagram depicting the Mystical Hierarchy that she'd looked at the night she and Bethy had spoken. The runes around it labeled each of the Mystic Essences: water, flesh, stone, iron, blood, and fire. There were more above that, but her attention was drawn to three in particular.

Stone, iron, blood. Iron above stone. Blood above iron.

Pomella looked at the wound on her ribs. A milky scab had already begun to grow over the shallow wound. Dry blood stained her skin and torn dress.

Her heart raced. She flipped through the pages again, searching for something else. In a perfect moment of clarity, she realized what she had to do.

Blood above iron.

Squeezing her jaw against the pain, Pomella carefully rubbed the iron manacles against the bloody cut on her side. The thin scab opened, oozing fresh blood to the metal.

Hoping it was enough, Pomella found the page she'd been looking for and cleared her throat. Beginning in a gentle hum, she sang the bars of the song of opening. It was the same song she'd tried in the other cave with Sim. Her grandmhathir's musical notes filled the page.

As Pomella sang, swirling tendrils of fog appeared in the cave. She wasn't sure if she could have explained what happened. All she knew was that this time, when she sang the notes, she put power into it. Power from her desperation to save Sim. Power from the raw pain she felt. And power from her blood.

The wordless song filled the cave, reverberating off the walls. The cut in her side burned as if on fire. It took all her effort not to cry out in pain. She sang louder, somewhere between a chant and a hymn. She drove the pain away with her song. She grasped her chains and pulled. She willed them to break.

The silvery fog circled around her, moving faster and faster. As she belted out the highest note she could, nearly a cry, but with perfect pitch, the iron in her palms burned like fire but did not hurt her. The burning blood in her side surged with the rising tide inside her. She pulled with all her strength.

With a blinding surge, the silvery fog spiral rushed into her hands. The cave exploded with light. The iron bonds shattered, and she pulled her hands free.

Ox stared at her, his stone eyes wide with surprise.

Surging to her feet, Pomella gasped and laughed. By the Saints! Ox rose to his full height. "Save the High Mystic. Hurry."

"I can free you, too! My blood—"

"No!" he said immediately. "You freed yourself with your blood. I have none to give. It will not work. You shouldn't risk using more. What you did is very dangerous."

"I can't worry about that right now," she said. But sure enough, she couldn't deny the feeling of light-headedness washing over her. The surge of emotions, her overall fatigue, and even her wound, all nearly overwhelmed her.

"Go," Ox urged.

"What about Sim?"

"There is nothing you can do. I will help however I can."

Pomella nodded, then remembered her hummingbirds. She flipped *The Book of Songs* open to the page she'd seen with the herbs and wounded animals. "Ena," she said, "I need your speed. And Hector, I need your strength. Find these herbs. Please. Bring them back here to the Green Man."

A part of her felt it was silly to be making such requests. But the better part of her now realized it was her old assumptions that were the real blather. Setting them aside, she poured confidence into her requests. "Go, my friends. Now. Bring as much as your wings will allow. Help Sim."

She wasn't surprised when the hummingbirds blazed out of the cave and down the mountain.

She bent over and gently kissed Sim's lips before leaving the circle of spikes, wobbling only slightly. Much of her side and belly was exposed now, bloody cuts standing out against her light-brown skin. Her clothing still hung together, if only barely. So much for her Springrise dress.

"Keep him alive," she told Ox. "I'll return with help as soon as I can."

The Green Man held out his hand. In his palm was a smooth pebble. "Take this. You remember how it works?"

Pomella nodded, and took the stone. "Yes. Thank you."

She picked her cloak up off the floor where Quentin had slipped it off hours before, and slung it over her shoulders. Then she ran for the cave entrance.

"Pomella!" Ox said, calling after her.

She stopped and turned.

"You were wrong," he said. "You are not powerless. What you Unveiled just now not only exceeds anything I've ever seen a would-be apprentice do, but is beyond what many full Mystics have achieved. No matter what happens today, I know you could be a great Mystic. You *are* worthy of it."

She swallowed a lump in her throat. "Thank you, Ox," she said, and ran out of the cave.

Full night enveloped her, but it seemed like a new day. The moon only shone half-bright, but it gave her hope. How in the name of the Saints would she make it back to Kelt Apar in time to make a difference? The others were hours ahead of her. She knew they wouldn't rest and would strike at Yarina as soon as they arrived.

"Well," she said to herself, "you fall faster down the hill than up." It would be hard to see in the dark, so she picked up a tall oak branch she spotted nearby. It seemed to her like a solid enough walking staff that might prevent her from breaking her neck.

She threw Oxillian's stone onto the path before her and intoned, "Lead me to Kelt Apar!" The stone burst into green light and flew down the mountain path. Taking a determined breath, she ran after it, staff in hand, her cloak and dark hair billowing behind her.

The flight down MagDoon went slower than Pomella hoped, but the guiding stone led her true. She stayed on the old trail, using her walking staff to help prevent any accidental spills.

Somewhere in her mind, a familiar voice called her a fool for running in the dark in a torn-up dress, bleeding, hungry, and exhausted. *Nothing but a dunder, girl,* muttered her father's voice. She shut the voice out and descended the final leg of the trail.

Dawn arrived as she came to the base of the mountain, its light rising reluctantly on the shadowy side of MagDoon. She pushed exhaustion and pain away. When the first hint of pinkish blue touched the sky, dimming the stars, she wolfed down the last of her rations like a bear freshly woken from her winter slumber. She needed her strength for whatever was yet to come.

She reached the trailhead and paused for a moment to stretch her back. Raw blisters ached across both feet. The thought of having to walk a full day's worth through the forest made her heart sink. Perhaps she shouldn't have eaten the last of her food.

Sighing, she retraced the steps she and Quentin had taken, following the trail west toward Kelt Apar. Before she'd taken even a few steps, a figure erupted from the side of the road, armor and scales gleaming in the early sunlight. Vlenar stood before her, hand on sword.

Pomella stumbled backward, her heart racing. Sweet Brigid, had he betrayed her, too?

"W-what do you want?" she said.

"I am looking for a misssing ranger," Vlenar said, dropping his clawed hand from his sword. "Whatttt happened ttto you?"

Pomella pulled her cloak tighter to hide her torn dress. "Mistress Yarina is in danger. A Mystic and a band of mercenaries trapped the Green Man at the summit of MagDoon. With him locked up, they plan to kill the High Mystic!"

Vlenar's hand flexed on the hilt of his sword. He looked over his shoulder toward Kelt Apar, then up the slope of the mountain.

Pomella rushed on. "My friend, Sim, is dying up there. Quickly, please, can you help him?"

"We need ttto ffffind Rochhhhhella," Vlenar said. "Ssshhhe isss clossse."

"But that will take too much time!" Pomella protested. "I'm going back to Kelt Apar right now."

Vlenar grabbed her shoulder. "Myy ffffriend needsss help, ttoo," he said. "Ssshe can help greattttly. Come."

He cut into the forest, moving with alarming speed and agility. Pomella stared after him. Shite and blather, this better be worth the time! Gritting her teeth, Pomella followed. She was taking an awful risk, and likely further endangering both Yarina and Sim. But she needed help, and right now Vlenar and this other ranger were her only chance.

She trudged through dense forest, walking across soggy underbrush left over from last autumn and winter, or even earlier. Her guiding stone trailed behind her, waiting for her to return her attention to it. After a few minutes, Vlenar slowed to a tiptoe, hand ready on his sword.

Pomella crouched and followed in the same way. "Do you think there's a way we can free Ox?" she whispered.

Vlenar cut her off with a sharp gesture. Pomella obeyed and waited. The laghart paused beside a tree and became as still as a stone. For several long minutes he waited. Pomella grew uncomfortable with his stillness. She forced herself to stop fidgeting.

Just as she was about to risk another low whisper to ask what the skivers they were waiting for, she heard something. It sounded like a person muttering to himself. The voice sounded male.

A horse snorted and jangled his reins. Pomella tried to peer ahead, but couldn't see anything.

Suddenly Vlenar moved, flowing like water out of his stance. He ran from behind the tree with his sword drawn. Pomella blinked, then hitched up her torn skirt and ran to keep up.

She passed gnarled trees she suspected hadn't seen a live person in decades, then burst into a clearing and stopped short. A horse and a wagon rested beside a smoldering campfire. Vlenar stood in a wide stance, his reptilian legs squared as he held his sword against a captive man.

The man had pale skin and a bald head. A black beard grew on his square chin, but his cheeks were shaved clean. He was on his knees, with his hands behind his head.

"Don't hurt me, please," he begged. "The ranger is unharmed. She's over in the wagon."

Vlenar caught Pomella's eye. He nodded toward the wagon.

Catching his meaning, Pomella hustled over to where he had indicated. Quiet shadows lurked everywhere. The wagon looked normal enough, but for some reason, its heavy iron structure repelled her. She pulled her cloak close again, making sure not to touch anything.

On the far side, chained to the wheel spoke, was a woman with skin as brown as her own, slashed with black stripes. Pomella caught her breath. She'd heard of the virga people, but finding one chained up as a prisoner was a shock.

"Wh-who are you?" she asked.

The virga woman scrambled to her feet. "Look out!"

Pomella whirled around. A large woman with braided blond hair, her raised arm holding a cudgel, screamed and charged Pomella.

Without thinking, Pomella spun out of the way just as the blow ripped past her. She stumbled, but caught herself against the wagon just as the woman recovered from her initial swing. Pomella's heart thundered. Who was this beast of a woman?

The attacker grunted and stormed toward her. Pomella scrambled away, but tripped and landed in the dirt.

A blur of brown and green flashed, and Vlenar was there, his sword knocking the cudgel away. He punched the woman in the chest and side of the head, then spun away as she doubled over. He locked into a guard stance, and flicked a forked tongue.

"Shite and blather!" Pomella said, staring wide-eyed at Vlenar. "That was amazing!"

"Took you long enough," the virga woman sneered, grinning at Vlenar.

The laghart ranger turned his slitted eyes toward her. "Your captorsss hid themssselvvvves by iron, Rochhhhella."

She rolled her eyes. "Obviously."

The bald man who had been working the camp appeared from around the wagon. He ran over to the large woman crumpled on the ground. "Mags!"

"She'll be fine, Dox," said Rochella. "Now get me out of these chains before I tell my humorless friend here to punch you up as well."

Dox fumbled with a set of thick iron keys before unlocking her bindings. "I want to help," he said, holding up both hands. "In Rardaria, I'm well known for my work as a blacksmith. Ohzem and the Black Claws took my family and forced me to forge all these strange manacles. I didn't know what they had planned, and I tried to help the boy, Sim. He looks . . . a lot like my Aden."

Vlenar stared at him with slitted eyes. "Thennn why did you atttttack ussss?"

Dox grunted and looked at the unconscious woman in the dirt. "Mags doesn't talk much. I think she just did what Zicon told her."

"Havvve you sssseen Zzzicon?" Vlenar asked.

Dox nodded. "I spied them coming off the mountain in the middle of the night. I'd hidden the wagons and horses while they were away 'cause I'd figured enough was enough. When I saw Sim wasn't with 'em, I snuck away. I know they wanted to look for me, but Ohzem said not to waste the time."

"We don't have time to talk about this. The High Mystic

Yarina is in danger," said Pomella. In a rush, she explained what had occurred at the summit of MagDoon.

Rochella nodded, looking grim. "I wondered what all the iron forging was for, and I knew it couldn't be good."

"Sim's hurt," Pomella said. "He's still up in the cave, and he's dying. I know we need to warn Mistress Yarina, but please, we need to help him, too."

Dox shook his head. "I should'a let that fool boy escape. Just had a feeling he'd get himself in trouble."

"We'll split up," Rochella said. "Vlenar, you can move faster through the forest. Go to the tower. I'll go to Sim. Perhaps I can figure out a way to free Oxillian."

Vlenar nodded and streaked away, his powerful hind legs carrying him smoothly between the trees.

"What about me?" Pomella asked. "I want to return to Kelt Apar, too."

"You won't get there very quickly on foot," Rochella said.

"I can help," Pomella insisted, although she had no idea *how* she could.

"Maybe so. But you won't get there in time to make a difference."

"She can take Zicon's horse," Dox said. "He's a fine Rardarian stallion and I think he'd love to stretch his legs."

Pomella's face paled. The black horse nearby stamped his hoof. "Couldn't I ride one of those other brown ones? They look gentler."

"If you need speed and power, you'll want the Rardarian," Dox said.

"You've never ridden a horse before, have you?" Rochella asked.

"Fathir let me ride one once. In a circle. When I was ten." Pomella winced.

"Well, it's time to learn. Just hold on."

Dox unhooked the stallion from the tree he was tied to. "Up you go, girl," Dox said, boosting Pomella up.

Sitting atop the horse, Pomella felt . . . well, tall.

"Keep to the western path," Rochella said. "I'll return to the tower as soon as I can. If Yarina falls, take this horse south to Port Morrush. I'll look for you there."

"Thank you," Pomella said. She glanced at Dox and the large woman still lying unconscious in the dirt. "What about them?"

"Don't worry about me," Dox said. "I won't cause trouble. Neither will Mags. I'll make sure of that."

Dox rubbed his head and added, "If . . . I mean, when . . . you see Sim again, give him my best. Tell him I'm sorry I contributed to this mess."

Pomella smiled as Dox draped her cloak across the back of the horse. He lifted her staff up to her. "I won't need that walking stick," she told him.

"Oh, pardon then. I assumed it was your Mystic staff," he said. Pomella's heart swelled. He'd assumed she was a Mystic! She could have kissed him.

"On second thought," she said, "I'll keep it."

Just as she took the staff, Rochella slapped the horse's rump and yelled, "To Kelt Apar! *Hi-yee!*"

The guiding stone shot down the trail, and Pomella's horse bolted after it.

SEVENTEEN

THE GUARDIAN

Pomella clutched the horse's reins so hard her knuckles whitened. The stallion galloped after the guiding stone that zoomed ahead of them like an arrow flying toward its mark, trailing silvery-green light. Pomella had no idea what else to do, so she leaned into the wind, nearly pressing her chin against the horse's mane.

The forest surged past her in blurring streaks of green and brown. The sun finally lifted above MagDoon, shining light across her back and onto the path ahead.

After only a handful of miles, her legs and thighs ached like never before. She clenched her jaw and buckled down for the long ride ahead. She *had* to make it back before it was too late. She wondered how long the horse could sustain his gallop.

"Don't blow your wind out, friend," she said.

Whether the horse appreciated her words or not she'd never know, but they didn't seem to help. The poor thing slowed to a canter, then to a light trot. Before long, they moved at an exhausted limp.

"Come on, *please*," Pomella pleaded, flicking the reins. "*Hi-yee!*"

But the horse just shook his mane and continued at his slow pace. Pomella growled in frustration. "Shite!" So much for her heroic return on her mighty galloping steed.

A voice called to her from the nearby trees. "Pomella?"

Pomella whirled in the saddle, her heart thundering. "Vivianna?"

The noblewoman stumbled onto the road. Pomella had never seen her so disheveled. Dirt caked her normally perfect dress and hair. She carried a long oak branch, presumably the one she'd found at the summit of MagDoon as part of her Trial. The other candidate's voice trembled. "Where'd you get the horse? Who gave it to you?"

"It's a long story," Pomella said. "I need to get back to Kelt Apar. The High Mystic is—"

"No!" said Vivianna. "We have to get help. There's another Mystic and he has Mistress Yarina trapped in the central tower. He's trying to knock it down!"

Pomella's gut churned. She couldn't be too late. There had to be something she could still do.

"I know about the Mystic," Pomella said. "He's trapped Ox

up on top of MagDoon. I don't know what can be done, but I have to try. I'm returning to Kelt Apar with or without you."

"We should find my entourage," Vivianna said. "Or one belonging to the other candidates. They can help."

"Do you know where they are?"

Vivianna bit her lip. "Not exactly."

"Then there's no time. I'm going to the tower." She flicked her horse's reins again, but this time he didn't even bother to move. "Jagged horse!"

"You're doing it wrong," Vivianna said.

"Of course I'm doing it wrong!" Pomella snapped. "Everything I ever do is wrong, but at least I'm doing *something*. Now if you know how to make this horse run again, I'd appreciate the lesson."

Vivianna stiffened. At first, Pomella thought she would turn her nose up and stalk into the forest. But instead the noblewoman chewed her lip and finally sighed.

"Here, let me get on behind you."

With unexpected tenderness, Vivianna held her hand out to the Rardarian and approached. She murmured comforting words. Pomella gasped as she saw silvery vapors of Myst swirl from Vivianna's hands. A sprinkling of silver butterflies misted into view, fluttering their wings.

"You aren't very good with animals, are you?" Vivianna said. She used a soothing tone for the horse, but meant the words for Pomella. "It's a wonder you bonded with those hummingbirds."

Within moments, Pomella felt the horse relax. Vivianna stroked his neck, and slid her way toward his rear. "What do you know about them?" Pomella said. She recalled Vivianna's jealous stares from the previous days.

Vivianna shrugged. "I'm good with animals. I've had fay pets since I was very young. But never a full bond like you have." Quick as a luck'n, she swung herself onto the Rardarian's back, sitting behind Pomella.

Pomella wanted to ask more, but they had no time to waste on chatter. "Well, use your talents to make our friend take us to Kelt Apar."

Vivianna heeled the horse. "You heard her, *hi-yee!*"

The horse tore away at a dead gallop. Pomella held tight and tried not to fall off. Hadn't she tried the "*hi-yee*" call? Someday, she was going to have to learn how to do that properly.

When they finally emerged from the forest and walked onto Kelt Apar's wide lawn, it was with renewed confidence.

A cool breeze washed over Pomella as she looked across the lawn toward the tower. A dread chill ran up her spine.

They were too late.

Zicon and Quentin stood before the central tower. Between them knelt Saijar and Lal. Both prisoners had their hands bound by iron behind their backs. Each wore a black gag and blindfold. Ohzem stood behind Lal, pushing the bottom of his iron staff into the gardener's back. Broon the dog barked and pulled against a chain tying him to a nearby willow tree.

A harsh chant filled the air, sounding like thick branches snapping in a thunderstorm. Pomella couldn't recognize any words.

She shivered at the thought that this might be a language spoken by people.

The repeating chant struck the air like thunder. With each resonance, the stone tower shook, as if something large had crashed into it. The trees on the border of the clearing swayed with each hit.

Pomella's eyes widened as she reined their horse to a halt. Ohzem was trying to break the tower.

"No," she whispered.

The lanky bowman Pomella recognized from the mountain cave patrolled behind the others, for the moment looking in another direction.

Ohzem drove his staff down onto Lal's back. The gardener screamed, twisting against his bindings. Broon whimpered.

Vivianna shifted uncomfortably behind Pomella. "Mistress Yarina has to be in the tower. She's probably trying to hold it together. What do we do?"

Pomella bit her lip. "I don't know, but I hope you know how to use that new Mystic staff you found."

The bowman spied them. With a movement as quick as a sharp wind, he lifted his bow and drew back an arrow. "Zicon!"

The bandit leader whipped his head in the direction the bowman was pointing.

"Shite," Pomella said, her mind scrambling for ideas. What, by the Saints, had she planned to do when she arrived here? She was unarmed and had a trained soldier pointing an arrow at her!

Vivianna slid off the horse and ran for tree cover.

"Where are you going—ugh!" Pomella gritted her teeth and faced the bandits.

Ohzem turned his attention toward her. He no longer spoke, but the harsh chanting continued to echo across Kelt Apar, swirling like wind, and hammering into the tower. The Mystic jabbed his staff at Lal again. The old man's screams harmonized with the chant.

Zicon ran toward Pomella with one hand on his sword and the other motioning the bowman to follow. The bow never wavered.

Behind them, Quentin started to move toward her, but the Mystic barred his way with his staff. Quentin snarled and tried to push it aside, but Ohzem struck him across the chest. Quentin doubled over and staggered. He glared at Ohzem, then looked toward Pomella.

"I don't know how you escaped that cave, or how you got my horse," Zicon called, "but this game is finished, girl. Get down, or Hormin will put that arrow through your eye. Don't test his skill!"

Pomella's hands shook on the reins. She silently cursed herself for being such a coward. She doubted somebody like Mistress Yarina would panic this way.

She mustered every ounce of courage she could find. "You— you are not welcome here. Begone from Kelt Apar!"

Zicon chuckled, his broad shoulders shaking. He stopped, and the bowman paused as well. They stood only a short distance away. "Did you hear that, Hormin?" Zicon said. "The little shadow flower is telling us to leave!"

He stopped laughing and his voice grew hard. "She just told me, Zicon of the Black Claws, to abandon the most important commission of my life. You're over your head, girl. Now get off my horse and get on your knees!"

"N-no," she managed.

Zicon snarled, "Hormin, show her how serious I am!"

Before he'd finished the last two words, Hormin's arrow hissed past Pomella's head. She screamed and ducked, but felt the iron-tipped arrow tug at her hair before streaking into the forest.

She whipped her head up. The bowman nocked a replacement arrow.

Zicon's face contorted in rage. "The Green Man is bound, girl! There is no guardian to protect you! Get down, now! The next arrow won't miss!"

As she shivered with terror, Pomella's mind spun. All sense of reason fled her. Distantly, she thought of Sim and how he'd tried first to warn her, then to save her. He'd gotten himself killed for it, but at least he'd stood for something. He'd been noble of heart, and if he could do that with the last of his strength, so could she.

She ripped her oak staff from the saddle and lifted it into the air. "The guardian is not gone!" she cried. "In Oxillian's absence *I* am the guardian of Kelt Apar! Bring no violence here, or the land will take you!"

Blessed Saints protect her. Where had *that* come from? Fool or not, she held her ground.

"Hormin!" Zicon yelled.

Pomella inhaled her last breath. She thought of her grand-mhathir and that gave her enough strength to not close her eyes.

Before two heartbeats could finish thundering in her chest, she felt another whistle of air flash by. She tensed, expecting the jolt of an arrow.

But it never came.

Two blinding streaks of silver, Hector and Ena, zoomed past her, flying like Saint Brigid's arrows toward Hormin. Ena reached him first. Hormin cried out in surprise and loosed the arrow wildly. It sailed in a high arc deep into the forest.

Hector darted right behind his sister and crashed into Hormin's face, drawing a painful scream from the bowman. Both hummingbirds dove again. Flecks of blood danced in the air. He swatted them in vain, crying out each time the birds wove past his wild attacks and drew another red line. Hector jabbed his beak straight into Hormin's eye, causing him to drop his bow.

Shaking off his look of dumbfounded surprise, Zicon snarled and drew his sword. He screamed and charged Pomella. She lifted her staff to try and club him, but didn't need to.

Another streak appeared from behind her, but this time it was much larger and wore armor.

Vlenar's sword struck out and caught Zicon's, the clang of their blades echoing across the wide clearing.

Pomella's heart burst with relief. Moments ago she'd been prepared to die and now, beyond her wildest hopes, help had come.

Vlenar drove Zicon back, the laghart's every motion smooth and effortless. Zicon snarled and tried desperately to block the oncoming assault.

The ranger grabbed Zicon's forearm and twisted the sword out of his hand. He punched up hard against Zicon's elbow, cracking it loudly in a direction it wasn't meant to go. Vlenar spun, sweeping Zicon's legs out with his tail. He flipped Zicon's sword into his hand with the tip of his boot and drove it through Zicon's thigh, pinning him to the ground.

Zicon screamed. Vlenar turned to Hormin, who was still trying to fend off the hummingbirds. The bowman, his face covered with thin, bloody cuts, saw Vlenar standing over Zicon. Scrambling away, Hormin tore off running toward the edge of the forest, pursued by Hector and Ena.

From the northern tree line a herd of silver animals stalked into the clearing. A dozen fay wolves, lions, and elk all made their way toward the central tower, trailing misty smoke. Walking among them was Vivianna, looking like a true Mystic, striding with her staff in hand. Pomella gaped. The noblewoman really *was* good with fay animals.

Not wanting to linger, Pomella leaped from the stallion, her staff still in hand. She ran to Vlenar and would have hugged him, except he gave her a hard look that reminded her they were still in danger.

That, and Vlenar didn't seem like the hugging type.

Hurrying toward the central tower, Pomella saw Quentin still kneeling, clutching his chest beside Saijar, who was blindfolded and bound. Ohzem loomed above Lal, the gentle morning wind rippling his rust-colored robes. The moat of flowers spread around them, fresh and beautiful where they hadn't been trampled.

"Come no closer, ranger," Ohzem said.

Vlenar sprinted forward, his back bent low, sword ready.

The moment Vlenar crossed the threshold of flowers, Ohzem slammed his iron staff against the ground. Vlenar stumbled, but managed to catch himself. He lifted his foot for the next step, but it moved as if a heavy weight held it down.

The laghart attempted another step, but could not lift his foot at all. Twisting at the waist, Vlenar thrashed silently.

"Struggling speeds the petrification," Ohzem said without concern. He turned his gaze to the fay animals swarming toward him. He sneered and spit a word in the harsh language that matched the echoing chant crashing against the tower. He snapped a clawlike hand outward, and spikes of iron shot from his fingertips. Iron pellet after iron pellet struck the fay animals, dropping them. They misted away in a cloud of silver smoke as they crashed and slid across the ground.

Vivianna dove to the ground to avoid the iron.

Ohzem shook his head. "Pathetic."

He turned to Pomella. "I should thank you, for it is because of you that I was given this opportunity."

Pomella inched her way toward the moat of flowers, eyeing its edge.

Quentin struggled to rise. A trickle of blood leaked from his nose. "Run away, Pomella! He doesn't care about you. He just wants Yarina. Please!"

Pomella's eyes narrowed. She had to keep them engaged so they didn't hurt Lal any further. The old man lay on the ground, shivering. "Don't pretend to care about me," she said to Quentin. "I trusted you, like a blathering fool."

To her surprise, he sighed and looked at the ground. "You're wrong. I do care for you. I know that must sound hard to believe, but it's the truth."

Ohzem gave a rasping laugh. "You're both fools. Your lust and petty affection will ruin you. They make you weak."

"Like they did for you, Jollin?" said a voice behind them.

Pomella gasped. The High Mystic stood in the doorway of the tower, majestic in the morning light with her staff in hand and dark hair spilling down her back. Not a hint of anger or worry radiated from Yarina.

A smile slowly spread across Ohzem's face. He turned to her.

"That name is long dead, Mystic," Ohzem said.

Vlenar still struggled to move. His legs were locked solid in what appeared to be iron. The dull gray color rose up his leg, slowly transforming him into metal.

Yarina walked slowly toward Ohzem. "Only in your mind, Jollin. The withered man that stands before me now is the same angry boy that once professed his love to me when we were young. I should not be surprised that you chose to exact your revenge upon me using apprentice candidates, just as we were all those years ago."

Ohzem clutched his iron staff harder. "That boy is dead. I care nothing for you! I will depose you and take this tower for my own. It was I who deserved to become Master Faywong's apprentice, not you!"

"Of course you still care for me, Jollin AnFollus," Yarina said, drifting on slippered feet toward them.

Pomella looked at the line of flowers in front of her. Her heart pounded as she debated crossing them. Blessed Saints give her strength! She prayed the strange petrification wouldn't grip her like it had Vlenar. Taking a breath, she stepped across the threshold and waited. A heartbeat passed, but nothing changed. She exhaled and crept toward Ohzem.

"By raging against me," Yarina continued, "you reveal your hatred. That hate stems from the same fear and bitterness you had when we were young and you realized my life was dedicated only to the Myst. To one who looks closely enough, your emotions today are grown from that same seed. You obsessed for me to the point that it consumed you and carved a hole in your heart that you then filled with poisonous bitterness and iron."

Pomella was almost within arm's reach of Ohzem. A plan formed in her mind, though she had no idea if it would work.

Ohzem heaved angrily, now squeezing his staff with a white-knuckled grip. "Then I will purge you from my mind, just as I have everything else that holds me back."

Screaming, he lifted his staff and swung at her. Yarina closed her eyes and waited for the strike.

Without thinking, Pomella swung her own staff and caught his mid-swing. The collision sent a shock through her, rattling her bones. She held on tight with all her strength.

Ohzem turned his terrible face toward her. "Pathetic commoner!"

Quentin surged to his feet and kicked the back of Yarina's knee, knocking her to the ground. She cried out as he stood behind her and yanked her hair back. A dagger flashed into his hand and he held it against her throat.

But Pomella could spare no attention for the High Mystic. Ohzem twisted and struck his heavy staff hard against hers. She adjusted her grip and pushed back.

"Pomella!" Yarina cried, sounding concerned for the first time.

Ohzem loomed over Pomella, somehow finding considerable leverage against her despite his frail frame. "Your dedication to your master is admirable. Perhaps I should raise you up as my own apprentice. The fools who hired me in Rardaria made me agree to take their precious son as my apprentice when I conquered the tower. But you have proven to be made of stronger stock." He pushed his staff against hers even harder. "Perhaps you are iron to their oak."

Pomella struggled against his towering strength. Terror surged through her. She couldn't overcome him. Not alone. She remembered the wound on her ribs, and the blood that could empower her. Perhaps, if she could manage to reopen it, or wipe the blood against the metal in Ohzem's flesh . . .

No.

She couldn't. Ox had said it was dangerous to use blood like that. She wouldn't harm herself to empower the Myst. Ohzem bore down on her, and she saw the wretch he'd become. She would not become that, ever.

Ohzem screamed and slammed her against the ground, driving the wind from her lungs.

The Mystic straddled her belly and leaned over her, shoving their locked staffs into her chest. His staff glowed red and smoked against hers. The red flared to white, heat radiating against her skin.

"You were doomed to fail because you are driven by emotion. Those feelings are weak." The white-hot staff touched her neck and she screamed as searing heat burned through her flesh.

"A true Mystic knows that life is temporary and filled with nothing but suffering." His eyes danced wildly. Spittle flew from his mouth as he raged. Pomella thrashed, all rational thought leaving her. "Life is a prelude to death. The only honest emotion is *pain!*"

The last word tore away the last of Pomella's rational mind. Strangely, she no longer felt her skin burning. She no longer felt his weight upon her. She felt only the calm embrace of silence, as if she floated in a space beyond her body and emotions. It was like she sat beside a quiet stream, alone, in another time, in another life perhaps. A life where she'd been crying beside the Creekwaters for her lost family. Crying for Sim. For herself. Now here she was again, but this time she understood that the fear she felt was temporary. She sensed a power welling inside her that was stronger than any torture upon her body. It raged like a secret song, yearning to be sung.

The fear drained from her. She focused her gaze upon the Mystic and managed to sneer. "I am beyond you."

She inhaled deeply and felt the power peak. She pulled it in from the air, from the ground beneath her back. In that place she'd come to, devoid of distractions and thought, she saw only the light of a power, the luminance of the Myst, and heard a song she'd never sung, but knew immediately. That song, like a chant, built inside her until she could no longer bear it.

With a mighty exhale she sang out a word. A word she'd learned from an old gardener. A man who was Unclaimed yet stated she was worthy to sing it.

"*Huzz-oh!*" she sang. "*Huzz-oh!*"

A blinding light flared from her staff and burst across Ohzem, knocking him back. She scrambled to her feet. He snarled and swung his staff at her, but filled with confidence and the strength of the Myst, she blocked it and sang, "*Huzz-oh!*" at the moment their staves collided.

Ohzem's iron staff shattered like glass, its shards exploding outward. Several of them struck her and drew blood. She ignored it. Her body, hurt and scarred, was nothing. *She* was more than just dark skin and hair, bones and teeth. Labels and castes melted away. The real Pomella, she now knew, was a song, a Mystic song beyond words.

Beyond limits.

Ohzem reeled back, bloody gashes lashed across his face from the shards. One of his hands lacked all its fingers. He lunged toward her, ruined hands outstretched as if to strangle her.

Pomella summoned the Myst from all around her. She could feel the power of this place, the island of Moth, the great forest, Kelt Apar, and the central tower. The Myst sang in her heart like a symphony of nature itself.

With supreme calmness she sang another perfect note, "*Huzz-oh!*" and tapped her staff.

She could not see, but rather felt, the Myst swirl around Ohzem, delving into the smallest pores on his body and feeding on the poison there. Mid-leap, his body disintegrated into a shower of blossoms, beginning from his chest and spreading outward. His final scream made no sound, or if it did, it was consumed by the all-encompassing might of the "*huzz-oh.*"

His gnarled hand reached for her, but just as it touched her, his fingertips turned to flower petals and flew away, caught in the quiet wind.

Metal clicked, and the other candidates' manacles dropped to the ground. Pomella looked to Quentin, who stared wide-eyed, his dagger only halfheartedly held to Yarina's neck. The High Mystic beamed at her, seemingly no longer aware of Quentin's threat.

"It's over, Quentin," Pomella said.

Remembering himself, he resumed his tight grip on Yarina. "Don't move or I'll cut her throat!"

"No, you won't," Pomella said. "You're better than that. You're more than what your family expects of you."

"Family is everything," he said, his hand shaking.

"I don't think you believe that. You told me I was worthy of being here," Pomella said. "If that's true—and it is—then you are worthy of being more than what your family demands."

His face contorted as if to sob.

"Put it down, Quentin. You'll gain nothing from hurting anybody now. Please."

He dropped the dagger to the ground.

Vivianna ran up to Saijar and unbound him. Saijar blinked to clear his vision and, seeing Quentin, ran over and kicked the dagger away. He pushed Quentin to the ground.

Lal stirred, helped up by Vivianna.

At that moment, the world seemed to rush back to Pomella. Searing pain raced through her body. Dropping her staff, she gasped and fell.

Steady arms caught her before she hit the ground. "By all your Saints, I'm impressed," Yarina whispered over her. "Sleep now, Pomella. All will be well."

"I used the Myst," Pomella said through a haze of pain. "Why didn't you call upon it to save yourself?"

Yarina's gentle smile was the last thing Pomella saw before sleep took her.

"I did," Yarina soothed, stroking Pomella's hair. "I called to the Myst, and it sent us you."

EIGHTEEN

THE APPRENTICE

Pomella woke to the sound of swiftly buzzing wings. Her eyes fluttered open, and she found herself lying in bed in her little cabin. A sharp pain burned across the base of her neck, making her groan.

She sat up, realizing she was mostly naked, wearing only loose undergarments. *Silk* undergarments.

She winced at the other things she wore. Bandages covered her body, covering cuts and bruises she could only imagine. By the Saints, what had happened? Her mind raced as she recalled the struggle with Ohzem and the other events outside the tower. How long ago had that been?

The buzzing sound caught her attention again. She looked

through her half-shuttered window to see Hector and Ena hovering outside her cabin. They swirled around in the air, seeming excited.

"I'm OK." She winced. "No need to buzz like a honeyhive. I'll come out in a minute."

She stood, wobbling slightly, and looked for her clothes. There was no sign of her cloak or Springrise dress, or anything else she'd brought with her from Oakspring. A pot of tea steamed on her table beside a plain white dress and sash.

Beside the dress was a wooden vase containing a bouquet of flowers. And resting beside that was her *Book of Songs*. Her heart leaped. She'd left the book with Ox in the cave. Had he returned?

She quickly slipped the white dress over her shoulders, enjoying the feel of the material that matched her undergarments. She didn't see any shoes, which was fine. The cool grass outside would feel good.

Her oak walking staff leaned against the wall beside the door. Combing her hair with her fingers, she picked up the staff and book, and left the cabin.

The sun hung high in the sky with only a scattering of clouds. Hector and Ena zoomed over and danced around her. She giggled as she felt their giddy joy. "Yes, hello, I'm glad to see you, too!"

"Ah, you're awake!" boomed a familiar voice. "You recovered quickly."

Pomella's face lit with happiness as she turned to see the Green Man striding toward her from across the lawn.

"Ox!" she yelled, and ran to him. He laughed as she crashed into his leg and hugged him. "You're free! How did you get here? Are you all right?"

He knelt down to bring his face closer to hers. "I am well. Ranger Rochella reached the cave a short time ago and managed to break the iron binding. She tended to Sim while I rushed back here through the ground immediately."

Fear and hope twisted in Pomella's stomach. "Sim! Is—is he alive?"

Ox's smile faded. "When I left him, he sat at death's edge. But your little hummingbirds returned with a steady stream of friends, who all carried herbs. Rochella indicated it should be enough to stave off an infection. I do not know if the wound itself can be healed in time. The ranger will do everything she can."

Pomella stilled her thundering heart and held out her hand for the hummingbirds. "Thank you," she told them as they alighted on her palm. "You may have saved my friend, and you definitely saved me." She bowed to the two tiny birds in her palm, not feeling silly whatsoever. They buzzed their wings and flew toward the central tower.

"I heard what you did to save the High Mystic," Oxillian said. "I am in debt to you, Goodmiss AnDone."

"Oh, Ox," she said, "Don't be such a dunder. It's I who should thank you."

He hugged her. "I should be careful not to soil your apprentice dress."

"My . . . apprentice dress? Am I her apprentice now?"

Ox shook his head. "Not yet. It is tradition for all candidates to wear their apprentice whites on the afternoon of the selection. Lady Vinnay was the one who tended to you in your cabin. She has been worried about you. Apparently, she has skill with brewing herbs and making salves."

Pomella thought of the tea and the flowers waiting for her when she awoke. "I haven't seen her, or anybody else. Where is everyone?"

"Come, I will escort you to the point of past masters."

He led her down the dirt path to the grove of trees that jutted out from the western side of the clearing. She remembered this place from when she and Quentin had strolled into it on her first day. The towering rune-carved pillar rose from the center of a ring of stones.

"Who were they?" Pomella asked, remembering the faded names written upon the obelisk's surface. Quentin had not been able to tell her when she'd last visited.

"They list the names of the past masters of Kelt Apar," Ox said. "This monument has stood longer than I've existed. It is likely to be as old as the tower itself."

"So many are faded," she said, gently touching one side of it.

"Not all of them," Ox said. He strode back toward the tree line. "I will summon the others and tell them you are here. They will join you soon."

The ground rumbled as he sank into it. Pomella strolled around the pillar, until she came to the side with the most recent names inscribed. These, she could read: *Yarina Sineese*. Above her, *Ahlala Faywong*.

A sense of reverence floated through Pomella. "Thank you," she said, bowing deeply, "for allowing me to be here."

Ox returned soon after with Saijar and Vivianna behind him. Each wore the apprentice whites—Vivianna in a dress and Saijar in loose pants and a shirt—and carried their own staff, presumably found somewhere on the slopes or summit of MagDoon. Quentin was nowhere to be seen.

Vivianna hurried past the Green Man but stopped when she reached Pomella. The noblewoman looked at the ground and bit her lip, obviously uncomfortable.

Pomella reached out. "I heard you watched over me. Thank—"

Vivianna threw her arms around Pomella. Pomella stumbled back half a step, smiling.

"I was wrong about you," Vivianna said, squeezing. "You are *truly* noble."

Pomella pulled away. "I'm sorry I lied to you about my caste. I hope we can be friends. And I hope I can borrow another dress, sometime."

Vivianna leaned in close. "I'll have a whole wardrobe made for you!" She squeezed Pomella's hands. "Also, I asked Ox to deliver your festival dress and cloak to my seamstress. She'll patch them up before they take me home."

Pomella couldn't help but notice the disappointment in Vivianna's voice. Her gaze fell across Saijar, who glowered at her.

"It was my family that hired the Black Claws," he said, dropping his gaze. "The Bartones somehow discovered that the High Mystic would invite you. They revealed that to several Continental nobles, including my family. That culk Zicon was in love with my sister. Apparently my fathir told him that he could marry her only if he successfully—" Saijar sighed again. Pomella was sure he'd been about to say, *if he successfully killed the High Mystic.* "If he succeeded in the mission. They never told me of these plans. I swear it."

Pomella believed him. The nobleman just seemed upset that somebody of a lower caste had outperformed him in the final Trial. But it still didn't answer the question of how the Bartone family had known about a commoner being invited to begin with.

"Well," Pomella said, smiling, "at least you won't have Zicon as a brother-in-law."

Saijar shook his head. "Your efforts to save the High Mystic are commendable. But that doesn't make us friends, and I still think it's wrong for you to be here as a commoner."

"She won't be a commoner for long," Vivianna said. "She's all but guaranteed to become the apprentice. And a fine one she'll make."

Pomella bit her lip. "What happened to Quentin?"

Vivianna and Saijar exchanged looks. "Mistress Yarina declared him Unclaimed," Vivianna said. "After she freed the laghart ranger, he took . . . that man . . . away. That's all I know."

Pomella suppressed a shudder. *That man.* That man who had once been named Quentin. Despite her changed perceptions of the caste system, she hated to think of the life that awaited him.

"The High Mystic comes!" Ox intoned.

The three candidates bowed or curtsied as Yarina glided into the grove. She wore an emerald dress accented with cream-colored highlights. Her hair was raised, showing off her long neck. Her staff glowed in the sunlight.

The ground shifted, forming a gently sloped path beneath her feet. The High Mystic approached the monument, bowing when she reached it. Pomella and the other candidates copied her before watching Yarina sink onto a throne-like chair that rumbled and rose from the ground. As she sat, flowers bloomed at her feet and across the throne.

"Welcome," she said, smiling. "It has been a troubling few days, made all the darker by the events of this morning. Pomella, I trust you are feeling better?"

Her body ached all over and the burn along her neck seared constantly, but Pomella curtsied and said, "Yes, Mistress, I am. Thank you." It occurred to her that the neck wound would become a permanent scar. She suppressed a sigh.

"Despite the unusual set of circumstances surrounding these Trials," Yarina continued, "we must conclude the process and declare a new apprentice. For that reason, we are gathered here, beneath the witness of past masters, to make that declaration."

Pomella closed her eyes. She thought of her grandmhathir, who had dreamed of becoming a Mystic but had given it up for . . . for what? Love, maybe? And she thought of her fathir, a man who, despite the smaller man he'd eventually become, had once wanted to be a Mystic as well. Each of them, in their own ways, had helped bring her to this moment that she knew would forever define her, and perhaps be remembered in history. She waited, with her breath held and her eyes closed tight.

"Therefore, I, Yarina Sineese, High Mystic of Moth, do hereby select Vivianna Vinnay as my apprentice."

Silence filled the grove. For a moment, Pomella wondered if she'd misheard or if a paranoid part of her mind had filled in the name. She opened her eyes and saw Vivianna staring at her with a stunned expression. Saijar, too, looked from Pomella to Yarina, and back again with wide-eyed surprise.

"M-Mistress Yarina," Vivianna said, "did you just say my name? Didn't you mean her?" She pointed at Pomella.

"No, Vivianna," Yarina said, "I choose you."

Numb shock washed over Pomella. She had been so certain, so confident that she'd be selected the apprentice. How could she *not* become a Mystic after all she'd done?

"But Mistress Yarina," Vivianna blurted. "I don't deserve this! Pomella—"

Yarina held up a hand to forestall her. "The Trials are not just about the candidates' outward accomplishments. They are about an apprentice finding her true master, and the master finding the proper successor. The Myst weaves through lives in ways we cannot predict or understand. But it is always right, whether we can see its ends or not. You remind me of myself, and I sense profound potential within you to one day inherit the duties of nurturing this land. Now please, come forth, speak your vows, and accept your Mystic name."

In the end, she will choose one of her own.

The cold bite of Mantepis' words echoed through Pomella.

With a final, sorrowful look at Pomella, Vivianna stepped forward and knelt before Yarina. The High Mystic rose and held out her hand. "Your staff."

Vivianna offered up her staff. Yarina held it aloft.

"Do you, Vivianna Vinnay, swear your life to the Myst, and to the service of all beings in all times and places under its reach?"

"I do," Vivianna said.

"Do you swear to follow and obey me, your chosen master, along with the Grandmasters and all who have come before us?"

"I do."

"Finally, do you revoke all former title and property, oaths and obligations, and start afresh for the benefit of yourself and the Myst?"

"I do."

The High Mystic leaned over and whispered into Vivianna's ear. Her Mystic name.

Yarina straightened. "Speak the sacred oath upon this monument."

Pomella heard Vivianna's words, but her attention drifted. A terrifying realization dawned upon her.

Vivianna had just gained a new name. But after today, Pomella would lose hers. She would be Unclaimed.

Later, as sunset kissed the island, Pomella sat on a rock beside the swollen creek, sniffing back her tears. After all she'd been through, she finally allowed herself a time to let the tears come. She'd excused herself for the evening, and found a quiet place beyond the pond to sit and think. Vivianna, at least, seemed to understand.

The stone utensil knife from Pomella's cabin lay in her lap, on top of *The Book of Songs*. She'd grabbed them both on the way out here. She'd been paging through the old tome, thinking of how it would be her only connection to the Myst.

After the ceremony, Ox had told her that tomorrow one of the rangers would escort her home if she wished. Pomella had just nodded. She managed to ask about Sim, but all Ox could tell her was that he hadn't returned from MagDoon.

Saijar had stormed away as soon as he'd been able to, and in some strange way Pomella sympathized with him. But while she knew he had to travel a great distance to return to the Continent and face his terrible family, she knew she could never go home.

When word of the new apprentice reached the barony, Lady Elona would ensure the baron declared Pomella Unclaimed.

How had it come to this? Fathir had been right. Pomella thought of running away. Perhaps she could join the Unclaimed living in the old shrine she and Sim had seen. Or maybe there were other places where the Unclaimed could live quiet lives. Despite the sadness, she wondered if there was still a chance of another Mystic accepting her as an apprentice.

No, who would want to take on a commoner when the High Mystic herself had rejected her?

Unbidden, Pomella thought of her garden back home. She wondered if anybody had tended it since she left. Probably not. Like her, it would wilt away, unnoticed and uncared for.

She lifted the knife and considered its weight. Perhaps it was time to let go of this foolish notion that she'd ever be something more than a commoner. More than an Unclaimed.

Pomella stroked her fingers through her hair once, and held it out straight. She lifted the knife and poised it against the base of the tresses. She closed her eyes.

"Why sad, Pomella?" said a voice behind her.

She turned to see a short figure in a wide-brimmed hat. She sighed and relaxed the knife. "Oh, Lal. I didn't want anybody to see me like this. I think I just want to be alone."

"I leave you alone if really want," he replied in his thick accent. "But I think you could use a friend right now."

She opened her mouth to tell him no, she didn't, but then thought better of it and nodded. "Yah, maybe that'd be nice."

"Thought so," said the gardener. He walked over and sat beside her. She instinctively pulled her arm away from him, but stopped when she realized what she was doing. She was sick of the whole caste system and how rigid it made things. Besides, she was as good as Unclaimed now, anyway. Lal was a nice man and it wouldn't harm her if she had incidental contact with him. She hated how easy it was to fall back into old habits.

"Did the Mystic hurt you badly?" Pomella said.

Lal waved his hand. "Yes," he said. "Very badly. But I OK. Still breathing! Now tell me why sad. Need more chi-uy?"

Pomella sobbed a little laugh. "No, definitely not. I think that caused me more trouble than anything else."

"Tell Lal."

Pomella grasped for the words. They came slowly at first, but soon they poured out of her. "How is this fair? I know I did something special; I *know* it! And now I have to go home, but I can't just do that. The baron's daughter said I would become Unclaimed. Who'll take me in? No other Mystic will teach me! No matter what I did today, I'm always going to be worthless."

They sat for a minute while she held back tears.

"Do you really feel worthless?" Lal asked.

"Of course!" she blurted. "Have you been listening to what I said?"

"Yes, Lal listens. But prove it. If you really feel this, then sing it."

"What?"

"Sing song. You owe me from before. Remember? Sing me song that says, 'Lal, I am worthless goat shite.'"

"I-I can't. That's just blather."

"Exactly. It *blather*! You grew since you arrived here. Now let go of fears. Give yourself the gift of not attaching to your worries. Show Lal how you give thanks for this precious life. I heard you sing the mountain's song. *Huzzzz-oh!* Now sing me song about *you*. Not song about you being sad, or song about losing boys. Close eyes and sing me the song that calls the hummingbirds and breaks iron. Sing me 'Pomella's Song.'"

Pomella looked at him and scrubbed the tears from her face. She swallowed. "OK."

She closed her eyes and took a deep breath. Her mind chattered like a crazy luck'n, but she kicked those thoughts aside and did her best to quiet herself. The gently flowing stream and even Lal's patient presence helped her find the stillness she sought.

She listened for the melody that always played in her mind, day and night, that she'd learned to tap into at an early age. Sometimes she'd hear it and need to hum it. Sometimes she'd sing it to words her grandmhathir taught her. But this time, right now, she listened to her heart and pulled the words as they arose.

When she had it ready, she lifted her eyes to the flowing stream and sang just above a whisper:

> *"You kick me down*
> *You shout at me*

But now I rise
And I am free

"You draw your blade
You strike at me
But now I hold
The remedy"

Pomella recalled the experiences of the past days in which she'd found strength. Perhaps her life would be fine. No matter her caste, even though Yarina wouldn't train her, the Myst would never abandon her. Her grandmhathir had lived a happy life. If that was enough for her, then maybe it was enough for Pomella as well.

She wasn't worthless.

She rose the power in her voice:

"You crash the sun
You darken me
But now I shine
And I will see

"You lift me up
You make me see
And now I am
Completely me

"Now I am . . . completely me"

Pomella lingered on the final note. Then she leaned into him and hugged him, not caring about the labels others put upon them both. She rested her head on his shoulder, and let peace wash over her. When she pulled away, Lal seemed different somehow. But before she could dwell on it, she glimpsed a figure leaning against a tree a short distance away, watching them. A smile burst onto Pomella's face.

"Sim!" she cried, and rushed to him.

She heard him grunt as she crashed into him, squeezing him hard. "You're alive! I'm so glad you're back. I'm sorry I didn't believe you about . . . about everything."

His arms tightened around her. "You're safe," he said. "That's what matters."

Pulling away, she traced her fingertips over the angry scar peeking out from his shirt. "But how did you survive?"

Sim touched her neck scar. "I don't fully understand it myself. I was asleep, and I dreamed of silver animals coming to me. Birds and squirrels and other small creatures. And then something larger, something I didn't recognize and can't describe, sat beside me and sang. The singing was deep and resonant, like it was sung by the mountain itself. But it also . . ."

"Also what?" Pomella said.

"It was you," Sim said, his voice as soft as the drifting clouds overhead. "Your voice lifted me as I fell. I am here, without a doubt, because of you."

Pomella swallowed a lump in her throat.

"Then I woke up," Sim said, "and Rochella was there, patching my wounds."

Pomella touched his face. "Thank you for coming back."

Sim touched her *Book of Songs*. "I'm glad you have your book again. I'm sorry we didn't go back to get it when you wanted to. It comforted me, and helped me remember you while we were apart."

She placed the book in his hands. "Keep it. Please. I won't be needing it. Another apprentice was chosen."

Sim's eyes widened. Pomella told him of Vivianna's selection, despite what had happened at the tower. But she couldn't bring herself to remind him of Elona's threat about becoming Unclaimed.

Sim looked at the ground and scratched his head. "I'm leaving soon, Pomella. After I rest for a day or two, Rochella said she would take me away to train me to become a ranger."

Pomella's heart sank, but she smiled. She'd already let him go once, and so she could do it again. "Then we'll make these last few days the best ever."

Pulling his face to hers, she kissed him. It wouldn't last, she knew, but they'd been through so much and right now it was perfect.

She kissed him for what felt like the life of the stars, one perfect moment that could last forever. He pulled her close, holding her in his strong arms.

When they finally eased apart, somewhat breathless, Pomella glanced back over Sim's shoulder, and glimpsed Lal. In that moment, as the daylight lit upon the wrinkled gardener, she understood.

Gone was the whimsical set in Lal's posture. His smile had shifted from one of lighthearted fun to a serene glow that lit his whole face. She recognized him. She'd seen him before, in a painting. A trembling fear, as swift and powerful as the nearby river, washed over Pomella. Her hands began to tremble.

The name on the monument. The master who had retired.

Sim followed her stare. "Um, Pomella, are you going to introduce me?" he said, his voice sounding awkward.

Pomella crashed to her knees.

"Grandmaster Faywong," she said, her voice trembling. "How—forgive me, I never even suspected it was you."

"Sweet Brigid!" Sim said. "A Grandmaster!" He bowed.

"Oh, Pomella," Lal said. "Dear, dearest Pomella. Rise. Nothing to forgive. You honor too much. I not High Mystic anymore. Just Lal."

"You're a Grandmaster!" she said, still kneeling.

"Some see only that, and others see Unclaimed. Neither is truth. I am Lal, your friend, and I am of the Myst."

Pomella stared in wide-eyed surprise, not knowing what to say. They looked at each other for a long moment, then both burst out laughing.

Sim shook his head in dismay, but laughed along with them.

When they finally stopped, Lal said, "Pomella, the Myst teaches me every day, even as I lift beyond this world and into the Deep. You not here by accident or by any designs we can understand. If you have question for me, the *right* question, I will not deny you."

Pomella understood and lowered her head. "Grandmaster Faywong . . . Lal . . . will you have me as your apprentice?"

"Yes, Pomella. I will."

He cupped her cheeks in his wrinkled hands, and kissed her

forehead. Then he leaned to her ear and whispered her Mystic name: "Huzzo."

Huzzo. Of course. As a name it was a little ridiculous, but it was hers now, and she loved it.

The song in Pomella's heart radiated outward, and beside the creek and her lifelong friend she spoke the oath Vivianna had recited:

> *"On the wind, my breath*
> *By the light between*
> *My eyes to far-lost Fayün*
> *So shall I hold dear*
> *All that lives in harmony*
> *Within the Myst and*
> *Carry it into the Deep"*

The Myst stirred within her, resonating with the rhythm and tone of her new master. The three of them laughed again, and this time the sound rose into the air and danced with her humming-birds, spreading all across Kelt Apar, where it was heard by every-one from the young and living to the past masters long gone, who live on in the silence of the Deep.

ACKNOWLEDGMENTS

As a filmmaker I learned the valuable lesson of surrounding yourself with talented and positive individuals who help your project succeed. This wisdom proved essential throughout the process of writing this book. It would not exist like it does today had it not been for the knowledge, encouragement, and opportunity offered to me by so many people.

In particular I need to offer special thanks to Jennifer, for her encouragement and support as I set off on this new writing journey. To my boys, Aidan and Andrew. Thank you, guys, for loving your dad and being excited about what I do. Thank you for the games of dodgeball to help me unwind from the long stretches of writing.

To my writing group, whose help was invaluable in the crafting of this novel: Andrew Wilson, DJ Stipe, Cary Vandever, Heidi Craig, Johnna Rehman, George Hahn, Ruby Petargue, Kathy Leland, and Jeremy Nation. And a special, extrabig thank-you to Laura Harvey, the Editor-Among-Us, who combed through this book dozens of times, carefully helping me slay passive voice and build stronger characters. Remember these names, because they will someday be on the covers of many fine novels.

To Brad Kane, my biggest critic and best friend. Thank you for always holding me to the highest possible standards.

To my friend and mentor Brandon Sanderson, for reading an early draft of this novel and for embracing me as more than just a fan and letting me glimpse the innermost workings of his craft.

To my niece Lexy Awalt, for being one of my earliest readers and biggest fans. You can show this to your friends and prove that you weren't making it all up.

To Trisha Jones, for taking care of Irma and encouraging me always to write.

To my mom and dad, as well as Jim and D'Ann Burns. The stability you've offered me during the writing of this book has meant more to me than you know. Thank you.

To Tom Doherty for taking the time to consider this novel and for believing in it right away. To Melissa Frain, my editor, for being a wonderful collaborator, and to my agent, Eddie Schneider, who threw himself into this project and has represented it in the way it deserves.

And, of course, thank you to all my beta readers, who took the time to give me their honest feedback: Tess Burningham, Wendy Brodersen, Jonathan Khoo, Helane Darazi, Robin Allen, Addison

DeBolt, Alana Welz, Sean Adams, Charles Bryan, Jason Koelewyn, Meesha Lenee, Blue Cole, Eddie Yin, Rebecca Lovatt, Amy Romanczuk, Diana Trent, Melanie Murray, Steve Godecke, Ross Newberry, Reannon Haight, Bill Jansen, Georgene Jansen, and the amazing, always dependable Gary Singer.

Huuzz-oh!